D0379411

MARS
EVACUEES

MARS
EVACUEES

SOPHIA McDOUGALL

HARPER
An Imprint of HarperCollins Publishers

Library of Congress Cataloging-in-Publication Data
McDougall, Sophia.
    Mars evacuees / Sophia McDougall. — First U.S. edition.
        pages   cm
    "Originally published in the U.K. by Egmont UK Limited, London."
    Summary: Twelve-year-old Alice Dare is one of 300 seven- to sixteen-
year-olds evacuated to Mars to attend school and train as soldiers, safe from
the war with Earth's invading aliens, the Morrors, but when all of the adults
and robots mysteriously disappear, the youths must survive on their own.
    ISBN 978-0-06-229400-5
    [1. Life on other planets—Fiction.   2. Survival—Fiction.   3. Missing
persons—Fiction.   4. Refugees—Fiction.   5. Mars—Fiction.   6. Science
fiction.]   I. Title.
PZ7.M4784458Mar   2014   2014005867
[Fic]—dc23   CIP
                                                                                          AC

Typography by Carla Weise
17 18 19 20   OPM   10 9 8 7 6 5 4 3 2
❖
First U.S. paperback edition, 2016
Originally published in the U.K. by Egmont UK Limited, London

To Freya, who gives very good advice

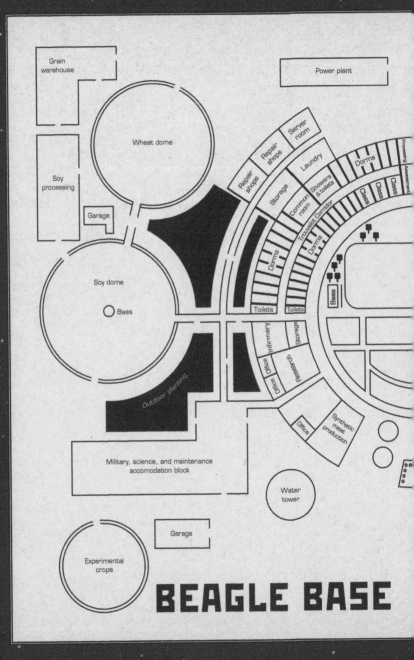

BEAGLE BASE

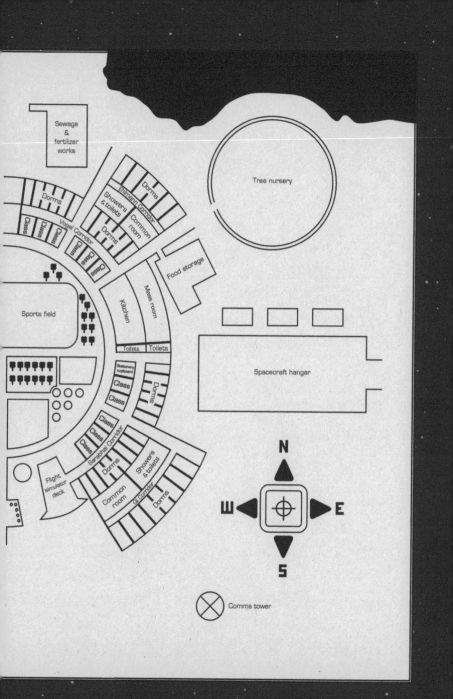

1

When the polar ice advanced as far as Nottingham, my school was closed and I was evacuated to Mars.

Miss Clatworthy called me into her office to tell me about it. I'd had in the back of my mind she might be going to say the aliens had finally shot down my mother's spacefighter, so on the whole I took the actual news fairly well. And that's even though I knew Mars wasn't really ready for normal people to live on yet. They'd been terraforming it for years and years, but even after everything they'd squirted or sprayed or puffed at it and all the money they'd spent on toasting it gently like a gigantic scone, still you could only *sort of* breathe the air and *sort of* not get sunburned to death. So you can see that the fact that someone had decided I would be safer there than, say, Surrey, was not a sign that the war with the aliens was going fantastically well.

Still, after eight months of Muckling Abbot School for Girls, I thought I could probably cope. It was one of those huge old posh schools that are practically castles, and must have been pretty drafty even before the Morrors came along in their invisible ships and said, "Oh, we're going to settle on your planet! We only need the poles, which are more suitable for our needs! Don't worry, you will hardly know we're here! And as a sweetener, we will reverse global warming!" (Because that was a bad thing back then, apparently.) And of course it turned out "the poles" meant rather more of Earth than we were entirely happy about, and that they could reverse global warming rather more thoroughly than we liked.

"Of course," Miss Clatworthy said, "it's an Emergency Earth Coalition project and an Emergency Earth Coalition school up there. So it's rather taken for granted you will enroll as a cadet in the Exo-Defense Force."

Well, that was a bit sooner than I expected, but I'd gotten the general idea of my future a long time ago, and whether I liked it or not, it was always going to involve shooting things.

"Of course," I agreed.

Now that I knew what was really going on, I thought I might as well relax, and I could even enjoy the fact that the office was warmer than most of the school. We were on the coast and about fifty miles south of the worst of the ice, but that wasn't saying much, what with the snow scouring across the playing fields in July and icicles the size of your leg dangling off everything, and there never being enough power to keep anywhere properly warm. But there have to be some perks to being the head-mistress, I suppose, and Miss Clatworthy had a tiny coal fire going. I inched toward it and hoped she'd keep talking for a while.

She did. "And they'll have those new *robots* teaching you, I daresay! No more boring old fuddy-duddy *human* teachers!" she said, all tight-lipped and fake jolly, even though she obviously didn't think it was a good thing.

I nodded. I *was* quite looking forward to seeing the robots. We only had a couple of robots for cleaning at Muckling Abbot, and they were really old and didn't even talk.

Miss Clatworthy sighed. "It's all such a different

world from when I was your age! But I'm sure you'll be a credit to Muckling Abbot, and you'll be following in dear Captain Dare's footsteps. Your mother is *such* an inspiration to us all, Alice."

"Of course," I said again. There was actually a framed poster of my mother on the wall. This wasn't as odd as it sounds. That particular photo of Mum, tossing back her hair in front of the British flag on the fin of her spacefighter, was very popular. She'd just blown up a lot of Morror ships at the Battle of Kara and that picture ended up all over the newspapers. That was when she started to become famous. Miss Clatworthy's poster was one of those ones with FOR EARTH! FOR ENGLAND! printed on them.

I didn't like looking at it very much.

"There's a letter for you—I think it must be from her," said Miss Clatworthy rather wistfully, as if she wished a small nugget of Mum's war-hero glory would fall out of the envelope and make everything a little bit better.

"Thank you," I said.

"You must be so proud of her."

"Yes," I said. And I was. But Miss Clatworthy looked at me in a vaguely discontented way. Teachers often thought being Stephanie Dare's daughter meant I ought to march around the school setting a splendid example of morale and patriotism, and sometimes took me aside to tell me so. The other girls tended to think it meant I was in constant need of being taken down a peg or two, and sometimes took me aside to tell me that.

This time Miss Clatworthy had other things on her mind, though. "And when you're old enough," she said, "I'm sure you'll give those fiendish creatures what for! Those cowardly, invisible brutes! Teach them to come and freeze over our planet as if they own the place!"

That was when I noticed it wasn't just because of the cold that she was trembling and that her eyes were watery and pink. I felt sort of awful. She really must love the school, I thought. She was always telling us in assembly how we were supposed to, but it hadn't occurred to me that anyone actually could.

Later I wished I'd thought of saying something plucky and full of School Spirit, like "Oh, Miss Clatworthy, it'll take more than a few invisible aliens to shut down Muckling Abbot School for Girls forever! We'll soon be back—and more ladylike than ever!" But I'm not very good at that sort of thing, and at the time all I could think was that I wanted to say sorry. I mean, not just "I'm sorry you're sad," but sorry as if it was partly my fault. I don't know why, unless it was because of being twelve and not being able to remember what it was like *not* to have fiendish creatures freezing our planet over as if they owned the place. Sometimes I did feel like that, when adults got upset and homesick for how things were before. It made me feel as if the aliens and kids my age were all part of the same thing. We all happened at around the same time.

Obviously I was scared of the Morrors, because you can't see them and they can kill you, and obviously I really wished they would go away. But I don't think it ever bothered me so much that they *exist*, the way it bothers adults. When we studied history, I could imagine Romans, or Vikings, or Victorians— but I can't imagine fifteen years ago and everyone running around being almost normal, but no Emergency Earth Coalition and no one even knowing what Morrors were and hardly anyone being in the army at all.

I couldn't say any of that, so I just said, "Yes, I'll try to kill lots of aliens, Miss Clatworthy." And that didn't seem to cheer her up much.

Now, you'll have noticed that Miss Clatworthy wasn't making this announcement to the whole school. I certainly had. "It's just me going, then," I said. "Just me from Muckling Abbot."

"There are only a few hundred places open for now. Maybe they'll send more later," said Miss Clatworthy. "The rest of us will just head south to wherever will take us. There are some evacuee programs on the south coast . . . and the Channel Islands . . . and closer to the Equator for those who've got the connections and money, I suppose. So you are *a very lucky girl*, Alice," she finished. "And it might be wise if you don't brag about this to the other girls."

That annoyed me. "I wasn't going to *brag*," I said, feeling less sorry for her. Honestly, didn't she realize I had enough trouble with people like Juliet Maitland and Annabel Stoker lurking around the school whispering, "Alice Dare thinks she's so *special* just because of her mum," and Finty Carmichael reminding me all the time that before my mum's exploits became so *fashionable*, she was just a bank teller and my dad was a plumber and really I was a charity case.

That was one of the reasons I did not like Muckling Abbot. The others were these:

1) Even with a desperate battle for the survival of humanity going on, we were still all supposed to be highly ladylike and virtuous and proper, which

meant that you should not run in any circumstances except after a ball or away from an alien, and that you should prefer to die rather than wear a hair band of an incorrect color, and that you should act at all times as if you had completely failed to notice that certain aspects of our situation maybe kind of *sucked*.

2) Horrifying sludge-green uniforms in which we were all slowly dying of hypothermia while the teachers could wear as many sweaters and coats as they liked.

3) We were all divided up into houses with stupid names like Windsor and Plantagenet and expected to have House Spirit on top of School Spirit and get really upset if our house didn't win trophies for punctuality or tennis. Which I thought amounted to an incredibly obvious trick being played on us, as it does not benefit you personally if your head of house is allowed temporary custody of a small silver cup with a picture of a Tudor rose on it. But no one else seemed to agree.

4) Lots of *singing*.

Finty Carmichael was perfectly right that back in the good old days which none of us could remember, I wouldn't have ended up at a posh school like

Muckling Abbot. But I had to go somewhere; Gran's health wasn't great, so she couldn't look after me very well anymore, and after the Battle of Kara, there was this Emergency Earth Coalition program about the education and care of the dependents of front-line fighters (especially the dependents of people who got made into posters, though obviously they didn't say that). So the government was already in the habit of sending me places, even before this Mars thing.

"Good luck then, Alice," said Miss Clatworthy at last.

"Good luck to you too, Miss Clatworthy," I said, and wondered if I ought to salute, since I was going to be in the army now.

2

What I was supposed to do after seeing Miss Clatworthy was go to the main hall with everyone else to sing the school song a few hundred times and listen to encouraging speeches and broadcasts from the EEC President. But I didn't feel like going, and under the circumstances, I thought there was a limit to how much trouble I could get into if I dodged it. So I went up onto the school battlements—yes, there were battlements—and read Mum's letter.

> *Darling, so exciting that you'll be exploring*
> *Mars! I wish I could go too! Maybe one day*
> *if the Morrors give us a break. I've just come*
> *back from my first run in one of the new*

spacefighters. They're called Flarehawks—had you heard about them? Wonderful machines, much faster than the old Auroras. Mine handles so beautifully, I feel as if she knows what I want to do almost before I think it. As soon as I climbed into the cockpit, I knew we were going to do some great flying together.

So out we went, and I was glad because we've had a boring few weeks sub-atmo, just blasting up invisibility generators on Morror bases near New Zealand; I couldn't wait to get out into space again. You never quite get used to seeing that net of light shields round the planet, Alice—you'll see it on your way to Mars. And I can't tell you how much I hope one day you'll get to see the world without it. But we made some nice big holes in it—before the Morrors caught up with us.

You know I've got a sort of sense about these things—I can tell when a pack of Morror ships are on to me even before the sensors pick them up. Sometimes I almost forget they're invisible. I was sweeping up the reflector disks 3000 kms somewhere over the Pacific when I got that feeling and swung round as fast as I could, and sure enough the sensors started going wild. Then I launched a spray of torpedoes into the dark and it lit up the Morror ships for a split second, horseshoe shaped and glowing in the sparks. And there were a lot of them.

So I charged straight into the midst of them, where it would be hard to get a shot at me, and we tussled and dodged and eventually I managed to soar up and pounce down on them. I took out three before my wingman came in to help me out. Then I went diving back toward Earth with the last two behind me, and I pulled out just before I hit the atmosphere. One of them went straight through; the other one hit at the wrong angle and I could see its outline again for a second in the burning air before it was ripped apart. Then I dipped through into the atmosphere to find the last ship—and we fought it out one-on-one over Antarctica.

The best woman won, I hope! The poor Flarehawk took some knocks—sad when it looked so new and shiny when I went out—but the mechanics'll soon have patched it up and I'll get back to work. And right now a few more kilowatts of sunlight are keeping Earth warm,

*and even if victory's still a long way off, I hope
we got a little closer.*

DON'T WORRY about me. I'm fine!
I miss you lots. All my love—Mum

I sighed a little bit. It's not that I wanted Mum to
be unhappy, of course, but I couldn't help wishing
she didn't *enjoy* the war quite so much. She had to
be one of the only people in the world who did.

I don't want to give you the wrong idea about
her. If, as she merrily swooped around the planet ter-
rorizing the invading aliens, some sort of genie with
time-traveling powers had whooshed up in front of
her and said, "Look, Stephanie Dare. Say the word
and the war will *never have happened* and everyone who got killed in it will still be alive and your
daughter will actually get to live with you and everything will be *fine*—but of course you will have to be
a bank teller again and never get to charge around
in a spaceship blowing things up, or be on a poster
or anything"—then of course she would have said,
"Go ahead." Because she is a good person. But some
people never find out what they want to do, or what
they're good at. And even if my mum had somehow figured out, when sitting behind her counter at
the bank, that what she really wanted to do, and

was good at, was being an alien-fighting, flying-ace space pilot, you can see how the knowledge would not have been all that useful to her.

I hoped Dad at least knew where I was going. He was an engineer on a submarine laying mines under the ice cap, so there wouldn't be a letter from him for a while. I hadn't seen him for even longer than Mum, but apart from some interest in getting to see the various odd creatures that the Morrors had released into the oceans, he had never given the impression he was having a nice time.

The sea was thick with clots of ice, a few loose bergs drifting along in the distance. I could just hear the purr of wings from a flight of heatships hovering low over the North Sea, and when I looked I could see them; the giant round lamps fixed underneath them glowing cherry red through the plumes of steam from the water. They were crawling northward, trying to slow the march of the ice, and they left curling streaks of clear dark water behind them. But the air was stinging cold on my face, and ahead of those few ships there was so much white.

It was a good time in Earth's history to be a polar bear. Unless the rumors were true about the Morrors eating them.

✧

I did have *some* friends at Muckling Abbot, though I might have given you the impression I hadn't. And it was just now hitting me that I wouldn't be seeing them again for years, if at all.

I found Dot and Lizzy in our dorm; they'd had the same idea about skipping assembly and were sitting on the beds and watching videos on their tablets.

"Are you okay?" asked Lizzy. "What did Miss Clatworthy want?"

"She wasn't ghastly, was she?" asked Dot, who said things like "ghastly" on account of being just as posh as Annabel and Finty, without ever being so snotty about it.

"It was just army stuff," I said, looking at the floor and the video of patriotic cats rather than at my friends' faces.

"Do you at least know where you're going yet?" asked Dot.

"Oh . . . ha-ha, sort of . . . ," I said. "What about you?"

Lizzy snorted glumly. "Into the government program. Staying with some random family in Cornwall."

"Cornwall's supposed to be nice!" I said rather too brightly.

"Still don't know for sure," said Dot. "But I've got cousins in the south of France."

"Oh, that's brilliant!" I said. "It's still even sunny there, isn't it?"

"Sometimes. Supposedly. But Alice, where are you being evacuated?"

So I told them. There was a pause, and then they both started being nice about it.

"Well, that's . . . cool," said Lizzy. "You'll probably see some really interesting stuff."

"And the robots," Dot said.

"Yeah, the robots," I said. "But it won't be that great being stuck on a rock with hardly any oxygen and no way home. They're using us for an experiment, really." Which was true, but I said it because I didn't want it to seem like I was getting this amazing special treatment and they weren't. But that didn't work very well, because it *was* amazing special treatment I was getting and they weren't. Although I would have preferred to go to the south of France.

Dot and Lizzy said they wouldn't tell anyone, and I don't think they did. But it didn't really make much difference, because the next morning a lot of buses turned up at the school gates and it became rather conspicuous that I was not getting onto any of them. People started looking at me in a suspicious and accusing way, and I could hardly stand it. Of course they guessed something was up and that it must have something to do with who my mum was. And I almost felt glad that Annabel Stoker and Finty Carmichael used to give me a hard time, because in the end the EEC thought my life was worth more than theirs and it wasn't fair. And so they'd kind of been right about me all along.

Finally the last bus pulled away and everyone had gone, except for the people boarding up the windows and Mrs. Skilton, who'd gotten stuck with me until someone from the EEC came. Mrs. Skilton was my favorite dinner lady, not because she was nice but because she was gloomy and dour and silent. And she didn't prance around the dining hall chirruping about how everyone who did not eat up every scrap was basically evil, because think of the starving Canadians.

Mrs. Skilton grunted with vague contempt—either for me or for the universe in general—and then stood there on the terrace smoking a cigarette and glowering balefully into the icy distance. Which was pretty much what I'd been doing the day before on the battlements, so I didn't judge and wandered off on my own.

It was sort of interesting seeing Muckling Abbot with no one in it, although lonely too, and I went into all the places I hadn't been allowed before. I went into the staff room and ate some cookies I found there. I drew a little picture of the Earth on the wall in green ballpoint pen with an arrow pointing to it, and next to it I wrote ALICE DARE WAS HERE. And I wondered if anyone would ever find it or if the school would fall down under all the snow and ice before that happened.

Then Mrs. Skilton bawled that the EEC man was here, and I went down to the drive and there was a jeep painted in whitish-gray camouflage and a young soldier waiting for me.

Mrs. Skilton dragged on her cigarette and announced fiercely, "I don't *agree* with messing about on *other planets*," which took me aback, and then she grimaced in farewell and stomped off.

I got into the jeep and we drove away and I knew I'd never see Muckling Abbot again. And I never did.

The soldier's name was Harris and amazingly he did not say a single thing about my mum and I quite liked him. He glanced back at Muckling Abbot's icy towers and grinned and said, "Wow, my school was mainly trailers" and I said my primary school in Peterborough had been much more like that too, but presumably on Mars it would be something else altogether.

"So, you'll be safe from the fighting for four years," he said when I'd finished explaining the new arrangements for my future.

"Yes. Well. In theory." I tried not to think about all the various things that could go wrong between Lincolnshire and Mars. "It's a privilege—I'm very lucky," I added dutifully.

"But, in return, you have to join the army."

"Yes."

"Even though you're *twelve*."

"Yes." It sounded awfully grim put like that, despite all of Miss Clatworthy's cooing about how brilliant it was. "They're only going to be training us," I said. "It's just that we've got to start young so we can be this new wave of special fighters or whatever. I won't actually be up against Morrors until I'm, oh, *at least* sixteen."

"Hmm," said Harris, and made a face as if something smelled bad.

"Everyone's in the army," I said. "*You're* in the army."

"I wasn't when I was twelve. And I did have a choice."

"Well, that was a long time ago, wasn't it?" I

said. Because he was grown up.

This did not cheer Harris up particularly, so I asked him what he'd been doing in the war and he sighed and said he hadn't been doing anything for a long time because he'd been hurt by Morror shock rays over Norway and had only just gotten better. "And after all that, look what they've got me doing. Ferrying little kids about."

He smiled, and I got the impression he was actually pretty pleased to be ferrying kids about, compared to some of the stuff he could have been up to.

We drove through a few little villages, some of which were completely abandoned to the cold, but some still busy and pretty with their snow-covered roofs. Except for the lines outside shops, everything looked as if there was no war with aliens going on at all.

"Still, seeing *Mars*, though," mused Harris, as if he'd been carrying on a debate about it in his head. "That's something. Are you excited?"

I said, "Yes," automatically, because life is generally easier if you answer such questions the way the person asking them obviously wants you to, but I really hadn't been excited until then. I'd been busy thinking about Lizzy and Dot and Miss Clatworthy and Mum and about having to be in the army myself and other such considerations. Still, it was a good question, because it made me wonder for the first time if I *could* be excited. After all, I was going to be one of the first children living on another planet; anyone ought to be at least mildly excited about that. So I cheered up a bit and made an effort to stay that way.

We drove for about three hours, and eventually the snow thinned out and the landscape was mostly brown and gray instead of just white, and there were hundreds and hundreds of greenhouses growing food. It was still pretty bleak, but at least it was easier to play I Spy.

Then we got to an air base in a valley somewhere in Suffolk, where there were planes and heatships and even some Auroras and Flarehawks standing around the muddy runways. And Harris said, "Well, have fun up there," and stupidly I said, "You too," and he smiled, but his face was tight. He said he would be going north again soon and it would be good to see the rest of his squadron. But he didn't look as if he expected it to be fun.

So he drove away, and a lady led me into a rec room in one of the boxy buildings where there was a television and a game screen.

Through the rest of the afternoon, other kids turned up looking dazed and lost, until by dinnertime there were fourteen of us. There were a couple of little kids and a lot of teenagers, who monopolized the game screen and the TV, so I felt a bit stuck on my own and I thought, Oh, god, is it going to be like this for the next four years? Because I didn't know how many of us were going altogether.

But there was this girl called Kayleigh who was fifteen and very excited about everything in a slightly desperate way, and she had multicolored hair and a bag full of all sorts of things she wasn't supposed to have. Most of it got taken off her later, but not before she and some of the other teenagers got fairly drunk after supper and Kayleigh had helped me dye pink streaks into my hair, which my mum probably wouldn't have let me do and Muckling Abbot definitely wouldn't. And that made me feel bold and intrepid and up for adventure. Well, relatively speaking, anyway.

So there was some unpleasantness when the soldiers found out what was going on and a corporal shouted at us for being so irresponsible and a disgrace to the Exo-Defense Force uniforms we were going to end up wearing. After various people burst into tears because of that and other reasons, and when the boys and girls were sorted back into their separate dormitories, we all went to sleep. The next morning we were all packed onto a distressingly battered-looking plane and off we went to the middle of the Atlantic.

Kayleigh had cried a lot the night before, but she seemed to change moods very quickly and now she got everyone singing. And while endless cheery sing-alongs generally annoy me, I had to admit hers were better than the songs at Muckling Abbot.

They told me pull your socks up.
They told me wash your face.
They stuck me on a rocket and shot me into
    space!

Oh, captain, bless my soul,
But your spaceship flies like a toilet bowl.
Oh, Mum, let me come home soon,
'Cause I lost my panties somewhere
    near the moon
And a shooting star flew off with my bra,
'Fore we ever even got to Mars.

They played some films on the flight, but I was feeling too nervous to concentrate on them and so mainly I looked out the window a lot. Underneath the plane, the world turned green and then blue and it was the most color I'd seen in ages. Even now I'm not exactly sure where we went, but I saw what had to be the coast of Africa rolling past, all huge and golden, and once a scattering of islands. And I remembered my little green drawing on the wall in the Muckling Abbot staff room, and my heart started pounding too hard as I thought, But that's where I'm *from*. And there's so much I don't know about it yet and what if I never come back?

At last we landed on a platform in the middle of the ocean like a small round metal island, maybe two hundred meters across. And crouching on this platform was a large spaceship shaped something like a stick insect, with the name *Mélisande* on its bow. There were soldiers stationed around to stop people from climbing on it, although nothing could stop the seagulls from perching all over it and pooing, which I thought was very amusing because it made Kayleigh's song almost prophetic.

Even with all the seagull poo, I thought it was an amazing place. There was no ice at all and the water and the sky were blue and sparkling and it was so *warm*.

Planes kept swooping down and dumping loads

of children on the platform until there were about three hundred of us rattling around. There were some international games and sandwich swapping, in the spirit of comradeship and standing united against a common foe. And there was also some international fighting, which was more in the spirit of history and tradition. But it was so sunny that after a while a lot of us just sprawled around on the painted steel, feeling completely dopey and blissful in the heat and really not wanting to go anywhere.

I was lying near the edge of the platform, gazing dreamily at the glittery water, thinking that what I really wished I could do was go for a swim, when a pair of bare feet whisked right over my head. I looked up just in time to see someone leap up onto the edge and go catapulting over it. The light was too bright for me to get a good look at this person, but I heard a yell like a kind of war cry and, a second later, an equally loud splash as he hit the water.

I jumped up, wondering if someone really objected to our looming Martian exile so much that he was prepared to drown himself over it. With several other kids and nearby alarmed crew members, I looked over the side. What I saw was a big fizzing patch of white bubbles, and in the middle of it, a pair of legs in jeans was waving idly in the air. Then the legs tipped over with another splash, and up came the head of a stubbly-haired boy about my age, who looked maybe Malaysian or Filipino or something. He bellowed:

"EVERYONE COME IN—THE WATER'S AWESOME!"

He was Australian. He had an amazingly loud voice. I don't know how there was even room for the lungs he must have had to produce that kind of noise. And all the crew had to react pretty quickly to stop about fifty of the nearest kids from doing exactly what he said and plunging into the water right then and there. And . . . well, I guess I might have been one of them. Although I did also think that kid was an idiot. I don't know. I was torn.

So the platform crew ordered us in their scariest military voices to get back from the edge, while a forlorn little boy with tously hair was hopping about, clutching what must have been the older boy's abandoned shirt and shoes and shouting, "Kuya! . . . Kuya! . . ."

And meanwhile the kid was happily turning another somersault and whooping and spitting spouts of water into the air until an extremely annoyed soldier stomped down a ladder to the ocean, jumped in after him, and fished him out.

By the time the kid was sploshing across the deck, we were all lined up in our National Groups to stop us from acting on any more clever ideas. Honestly, I think even people in orbit could have seen that here was someone who wasn't the least embarrassed at being hauled out of the ocean, soaking wet with no shirt on, in front of a couple of hundred people. On the other hand, the little boy clutching his shoes, who was now lined up with the other Australian kids, looked mortified.

The wet soldier turned the boy over to a sergeant, who roared at him, "NAME?"

Even when the boy wasn't actually yelling, his voice had a bit of a boom to it. He replied, "Carl Dalisay," which was a little confusing to me because of the Kuya thing.

"You think you're funny, do you, Dalisay?"

Carl Dalisay just gazed up at the sergeant with wide earnest eyes and said, "Come on! It's my last chance to go for a swim on my own planet!"

The EDF people were all so angry, I almost thought the sergeant might shoot Carl Dalisay right there as an example to the rest of us, and tell his family he unfortunately fell off the spaceship. But instead he just made him do push-ups, which Carl did, sploshily, while giggling the whole time.

After that he bounded over to the little kid, who was clearly his brother, and wrapped a damp arm round his head just to be annoying. The little one wriggled away and lamented, "Why d'ya have to *do* things like that, Kuya?"

"Oh, what was going to happen? There was a ladder right there! I'm not a *moron*."

"Oh, yeah?" said the little kid. "And are there hammerhead sharks? A big metal beam under the water? You don't know! And you're in massive trouble!"

"Yeah, well," Carl-or-Kuya said. "It was worth it."

The little one sighed heavily and went off to try and feed a seagull.

Before any of us had really gotten our breath back from this incident, there was a cascade of noise from overhead—sonic boom after sonic boom—and people started pointing excitedly upward, where, sure enough, a small flight of spacefighters had just punched through the atmosphere and were blazing down across the blue sky. And evidently they weren't alone up there, because as they plunged, they were wheeling and swooping and dodging and firing into what looked like a completely empty sky. Except that sometimes, just for a shaving of a second when they took a hit, you could see the outline of the Morror ships—U-shaped and transparent in the rays, flickering like ghosts. A Flarehawk looped backward from a shock-ray blast. There was a mixture of cheers and screams from the kids on the platform, depending on how often they'd seen this sort of thing before.

In my case? Often enough that I didn't make any noise. Not so often that my chest didn't get tight either. Spaceship battles would be very pretty, if you could forget you might be about to watch someone die.

The EDF seemed to agree that it was time to get us off the planet. All the doors of the *Mélisande* sprang open, and soldiers started hurrying us inside, one National Group at a time alphabetically. This meant Carl and the other Australians were soon on board, but there was a lot of hanging about for those of us from countries down at the bottom of the alphabet, like United Kingdom.

"This is ridiculous! You are going to get us all killed!" burst out a tall blond girl in expensive sunglasses in the Swedish section. None of the EDF officers took any notice, and she subsided into complaining loudly to the few other Swedish kids.

At last I got jostled down an aisle and into a seat by a window, and at first I was too busy trying to look out to take in much about the inside of the ship.

We could still *hear* the battle shrieking and booming, but no matter how uncomfortably I strained against my seat belt and pressed to the window, I couldn't *see* it, which somehow made it a lot more nerve-racking. No one was cheering at all anymore.

A trio of EDF officers assembled at the front of the cabin. "I'm Captain Mendez," said the man in the middle. "Everyone stay calm. You're perfectly safe. The walls of this ship are strong enough to withstand any stray shock rays."

He had a nice reassuring voice, but the effect was rather undermined by the crewwoman next to him, nodding vigorously and adding, "*Mostly* strong enough."

Forty or so hands went up at that, but no one seemed to be in the mood to be taking questions. Captain Mendez just scowled and said, "*Thank you*, Sergeant Kawahara," to the crewwoman and "We'll be leaving very shortly" to us, and then they strode away again.

And yet we didn't move. The windows flashed with the Morrors' shock rays, and we just sat there. I twisted around in my seat, trying to see what the holdup was. The *Mélisande* must have been some kind of luxury tourist liner before the war: it was all curved pearly surfaces, and on the wall beside my head was a faded poster of a couple with champagne glasses in their hands, gazing soppily back at the Earth with the slogan ARCHANGEL PLANETARY: TAKING YOU TO THE STARS! But the shiny walls were lined with scars where the luxurious private cabins had been ripped out and sensible military fixtures had been bolted in. Now the ship was crammed with padded benches for both sitting and sleeping on. They were arranged in pairs with a table and a little curtain that could go around the two of you, and that was all the privacy you got.

But there wasn't anyone on the bench opposite me.

The few crew members who seemed to be in charge of us kept stalking around looking tense, with their communicators beeping all the time. I heard one of them whispering to another, "We're just going to have to go without them!"

"Who's missing?" Kayleigh was saying, a few seats back from me. "What's happened to them? Have the Morrors got them?"

"Come on, we have to move," yelled the angry Swedish girl from before.

Instead of actually talking to us, the EDF people let the ship do it. And apparently the ship's idea of a useful contribution was to start playing twinkly music and waterfall noises. "Please relax and stay in your seats," crooned a soothing automated voice. "Imagine a stream of healing energy flowing through you. . . ."

Outside, *something*—one of our ships or one of theirs, we didn't know—exploded. I started digging my fingernails into the palms of my hands. I tried to remind myself that there was no particular reason the Morrors should bother with a passenger ship trying to *leave* the planet.

Then there was a roaring sound, very close, that rattled everyone, but it was just an ordinary plane landing on the platform. All the crew's communicators started beeping even more furiously, and finally a door opened and twenty kids ran up into the cabin, looking rather agitated, to say the least.

Before they'd even sat down, the door had slammed itself shut and there was a whirr and a lurch as the spaceship's legs retracted. And then we were moving, skimming low over the Atlantic; I looked out and saw it melt into a dark-blue blur. Already the artificial gravity was working against the drag of the natural stuff, which meant you didn't fall about as much as you would have otherwise, but felt very odd. None of us were used to it, and some people started throwing up into the bags provided. Luckily

I don't throw up very easily, but it made me feel as if I was being hit lightly but persistently all over with tablespoons.

And then we began to climb. One of the new arrivals came staggering down the aisle and toppled into the seat opposite me, panting. "Hello," she said. To my surprise, she was English too.

"Nice to meet you," I said as we shot upward into the flashing blue sky.

3

Earth fought to hold on to us—we could feel its pull in our bones, and in the way the ship shivered. But we dragged stubbornly on, and the planet dropped away. And then there was that moment when the surface you're leaving curves in on itself and the horizon bends into a circle and you see the world really is round after all. Even though you know it's going to happen, it's still like the biggest, most shocking conjuring trick ever.

Now we could see the bands of white at the poles, pressing in on the bright stripe of color in the middle. Here and there, the world glittered with little sparks of explosions and shock-ray fights.

The girl opposite me whispered, "Beautiful,"

with a sort of break in her voice.

She was pressed as close to the window as she could get. The ship, mercifully, had stopped advising us all to imagine we were relaxing in a sunlit glade, and everything felt strangely quiet and still. I just stared back as the Earth got smaller and smaller behind us.

Then she added thoughtfully, "I've forgotten my suitcase."

I was appalled. "What?" I cried. "Oh my god!" And I actually moved up a bit out of my seat, as if I could run back to Earth and get it for her.

She seemed much less worried than I was. "Oh, well. It only had clothes in it."

"But—what, you've got nothing?"

She looked reproachful. "There was a lot going on," she said. "And no, I didn't forget anything important." Now I saw there was a large shoulder bag slumped open on the seat beside her, the stuff inside it on the point of spilling out. So she began to take things out of it and set them on the table between us.

"This is all you've got in the entire world?"

She shrugged, vastly. The shrug went all the way to the tips of her fingers and up into her hair. "We're not in the world anymore."

She had: a battered tablet, which was almost the only thing that had an obvious point. A tangle of string. A magnifying glass. A gold wire star that looked as if it had come from a Christmas tree. A harmonica. A square silk scarf. A thick roll of duct tape. A little round silver bottle. A small patchwork cushion, which might have started out as dark red but was now mainly gray and holey. A tiny wooden sculpture of a cat. And lots of stones, some with holes in them.

"You have rocks," I pointed out. "In your bag. Which you're taking into outer space. Rocks. And no clothes or a toothbrush."

She stared at me blankly, as if this was what everyone should be doing.

I did some minor flailing and said, "You can borrow things of mine."

She seemed surprised, and sort of amused. "That's nice of you. You don't even know my name yet."

"Oh," I said, flustered by this point. "Well."

"It's Josephine Jerome. Have a cookie."

She shook a packet of them at me. Well, that was one more thing I could see the point of. "Alice," I said.

Any of my clothes would be too big on her,

though, I thought, looking at her. She was small and black and spindly with a pointy chin and a wide bulgy forehead. She had an explosive cloud of hair, held tightly back from her face with clips, and her large, starey eyes gave her the look of being in a mild state of shock the whole time. Though just then, it occurred to me, she actually might have been.

"What happened?" I asked her. "How come you were all so late? And you're English—why weren't you on the same flight with us?"

Josephine slotted her thumb through the hole in one of the stones. "We should have been. But, uh, there were some shock-ray hits in London yesterday. Everything shut down."

"In *London*?" I said, shocked, and angry no one had told us. Despite everything the Morrors had done, direct attacks on major cities were pretty rare. They were more about freezing everything over and zapping the hell out of anyone who tried to stop them.

Josephine nodded grimly and gripped the stone more tightly. "They could flatten the whole city if they wanted; they must just want people to *leave*. And now we are."

I was quiet. It hadn't quite struck me before that at this rate the whole of Britain would probably be *gone* by the time I came back to Earth, if I ever did.

"So the flight out from Belgium got diverted to pick us up. Anyway, we made it in the end. And they'll *have* toothbrushes," she added reassuringly. "They couldn't expect us to use the same ones for years and years, could they?"

At this point we were interrupted by a demonstration of what to do if the spaceship came under attack or got into an accident (though clearly the real answer was: die). And then a man came by with a register to make sure they'd got all the right people, although it was a bit late to do anything about it if they hadn't.

"Alice Dare," I said, after Josephine had given her name.

The crewman's eyes lifted slowly from his tablet, and he looked at me. He said doubtfully, "Alistair . . . ?"

"*ALICE*. DARE!" I said, possibly rather loudly. Now, I did once know a boy called Lauren, so anything is possible, but I do *not* look as if my name should be Alistair. I was wearing a skirt, and as well as the pink streaks in my hair, I also had some glitter.

I always speak very clearly too, so the reason this keeps happening is that people do not listen.

A few people looked around at us, and the

crewman grimaced and moved on quickly.

"I think you scared him," said Josephine, grinning. She leaned forward to study me quite blatantly in a way that some people might think a little rude. "Dare, huh," she said. "No relation . . . ?"

I thought, I've got one second to say no and come up with a whole new identity and maybe not have to deal with any of that she-thinks-she's-so-special-because-of-her-mum stuff. And then I realized I didn't have that long at all, because immediately Josephine said, "*Ohhh* . . ." and sat back in her seat with her eyes even wider than usual. In a lower voice, she asked, "What's *that* like?"

I sighed. "It's like nothing at all," I said. "I haven't seen her in over a year."

"But that's why you're here," she went on, relentlessly. "Too demoralizing if people heard the Morrors got you. They'd never look at that poster the same way again."

"Yes, well," I said, rather irritably. "What are you in for?"

"Oh . . . ," said Josephine, biting her lip. "I sort of . . . well, there was this exam, and . . . not that they told us why, but . . ."

We looked at each other and both grinned sort of shiftily. And I knew we were both thinking that there just wasn't a reason to be chosen for this ship that wasn't kind of dodgy and unfair, whether it was doing well on an exam or having a famous mum or even being chosen at random (because that was the other way they did it). But there wasn't a lot we could do about it. We were twelve.

"Is it true your mum's *seen* a Morror?" asked Josephine, because except for some singed tentacles that had been picked out of some wreckage in Minnesota, and bits of what might have been a head found floating in the Pacific, no one *had* seen a Morror. They were really good at staying invisible, even when they were dead.

"No. She's got this . . . *sense* about them—you know, it's been on the news. Sometimes she says it's *as if* she can see their ships, like she forgets they're invisible. But she doesn't know what they *look* like or anything."

"I thought so," Josephine said. She put down her stone and looked at her collection of objects on the table for a moment, wriggling her fingers absently in the air. She picked up the bottle. "This is a Morror ship, right? The invisibility shield guides light all the way round it." She slid her forefinger over the silver surface. "But maybe some does scatter off. Maybe your mum is sensitive to some wavelength of light most people can't pick up consciously."

I thought about this. Most people—Mum included, actually—seemed to think her special Morror-finding sense was practically magic. I never said so, but secretly I'd always assumed it was just good luck. I liked the idea of it being something sci-encey like that instead. It made it seem more likely it would go on working.

"What's in the bottle?" I asked.

She squirreled the bottle away back into the bag and answered, "Perfume."

I wondered why someone who evidently didn't care about clothes at all cared about perfume, but I didn't press it. Maybe it was her mum's or something.

She had another look at me and grinned again. "You like pink, huh?"

"*Yes,*" I said, a little menacingly, because I thought she might be laughing at me.

She held up her hands to show she didn't mean any harm. "What do you want to do when you grow up?"

I stared at her. From what she'd said about light wavelengths and passing exams, I had the impres-sion that she must be pretty clever. So this was just a bizarre thing to say. "I'm going to be in the army," I said flatly.

"I'm going to be an archaeologist," said Josephine dreamily, assembling her stones into another pattern. "And a composer. And a mum."

"Why are you saying this?" I asked, baffled.

"Why not?"

I folded my arms. "Well. I expect you could write some music, if you wanted. In your spare time. And you could possibly have a baby. In your spare time. But you're *not* going to be an archaeologist. You're going to be in the EDF, like everyone else on this ship. Didn't they tell you that part?"

Josephine's hands went still, and for a few seconds she didn't look at me. Then she threw back her head and smiled again, but in a more complicated sort of way. She remarked, "You're a fairly gloomy person, aren't you?"

"I am not gloomy," I said. "I'm *realistic*."

"The war can't go on forever."

"But look," I said. "I'm twelve. We're going out to Mars, where we're going to have *military training*. We won't be able to use it until we're sixteen or so. So the EEC plainly thinks the war's going to go on for at least four years and then some! Because otherwise it wouldn't be worth it! And it's already been going on forever with no end in sight—certainly no sign that we're *winning*—"

"Fifteen years."

"A *lifetime*."

"But still. It has to end sometime. Wars always do. Everything has to end," said Josephine, eating another cookie and getting unexpectedly philosophical.

"Yeah. Things like *human civilization*," I said.

She went still again. She bowed her face over her objects and asked, "Is that really what you think will happen?"

She said it in a very calm, neutral voice, as if she were just curious. But it was at this point, rather late, I suppose, that I realized I was actually upsetting her. "No," I said, trying to sound less . . . harsh. I felt suddenly very tired. I looked out of the window again. "I just think things are going to go on the way they are for a really, really long time."

"Hmm," said Josephine, loading a book on her tablet and slumping down on the seat-bed thing with the patchwork cushion under her cheek.

Mum had been right. We could see the net of light shields around the Earth now. From the outside of it, the reflectors shone brightly, beaming all that warmth back toward the sun. So many of them, it looked as if Earth was wrapped in a glittery spider's web. But there were wide, raggedy holes here and there, and I smiled and wondered if the gap in the net we were passing through was one Mum had made.

"About your mum," murmured Josephine from across the table. "I wouldn't worry about getting any hassle out here."

"I never said I was worried!"

"Well, if you *were*," said Josephine patiently, "you're not going to be the only VIP on board. If you're here, then everyone in the Coalition cabinet must have sent their kids out."

"Oh," I said, feeling at once very relieved and kind of stupid. "I guess so." I thought about it a bit more. "Thanks."

4

We were on the *Mélisande* for about a week. By the end of the first day, Earth was just a little blue-and-green bead in the far distance. By the end of the second, Mars was an orange spot on the blackness ahead. Like a red lentil, then a copper penny, then like the amber light of a traffic signal. And now you could see how the terraforming was changing it from the bare red rock it had once been. The bruise-purple seas. The silvery clouds. The dark-green smudges of arctic grasslands. The red-and-turquoise blazes of algae lakes.

The view was not enough to satisfy Christa Trommler, the Swedish girl I'd noticed before. "There's been a mistake. I need a cabin to myself," she told Sergeant

Kawahara on the first day. "My father's contributed a *lot* to the war effort."

"There aren't any cabins, miss," said Sergeant Kawahara.

Christa put her hands on her hips and stuck out her jaw. She could only have been fifteen or sixteen, but she was tall and square shouldered in an impossibly crisp white blazer and looked easily twenty. "There are cabins for the crew; some of them will have to move out for me."

Kawahara stared at her blankly.

"My father would never have allowed me to come if he'd known I would be treated like this. This ship is practically mine, anyway."

"Well, your father isn't here, now is he?" snapped Kawahara at last. Christa's eyes bulged and her face got red and wobbly.

"Who *is* her father?" I asked Josephine. I was beginning to assume she knew everything.

"Rasmus Trommler. He owns Archangel Planetary," Josephine said. "But they mostly do robotics now."

"But I can't possibly sleep with all these people around," cried Christa. And for a moment she didn't look grown-up at all. In fact, she looked about to burst into tears.

As it turned out, getting to sleep wasn't a problem for anyone—or at least not in the way Christa expected. At the end of each day, the ship would try to soothe us gently with the sound of wind chimes or waves lapping at a shore. But just to make completely sure, they also used sleeping gas to knock us out. I mean, I could see their point, I guess, because there were only five crew members to manage three hundred kids, and those five were looking pretty rough and ragged by the end of day two. By then there were not only romances but tearful shouty breakups going on, tribal allegiances forming, and fights. And then there were also things like the fort some of the younger ones built out of suitcases in the exercise room, and the game where you tried to get around as much of the spaceship as possible without touching the floor. So I suppose the crew did value being able to blast us with Somnolum X and get nine hours or so when they could be sure no one was up to anything.

Still, we were all outraged after we woke up the first morning and remembered the crew putting on oxygen masks and the captain pressing a button on the wall, and then a sort of whooshing noise and a funny smell in the air and then . . .

"This is completely unethical," said Josephine, the moment she opened her eyes.

"What about our human rights?" demanded Carl, who'd gathered a small deputation of kids within minutes.

"There's a *war* on," said Crewman Devlin shortly.

I wondered if this meant grown-ups actually listened to you when there *wasn't* a war on, because somehow I was skeptical.

✫

The best thing about being on the ship was that sometimes they'd turn off the artificial gravity in the exercise chamber and let you float and glide and bounce off the walls. But it did tend to make some people sick, which is definitely not a good thing to happen during weightlessness.

Sorry, there is rather a lot of throwing up in this part of the story.

Josephine mostly liked to read in there, drifting through slow somersaults, past windows full of stars, her tablet in her hands. But then, she liked to read everywhere, lying with the curtain drawn round our beds, tablet held above her face and a heap of stones with holes in them piled on her chest like some weird prehistoric ritual for the dead. When she was not reading, she was the most fidgety person I had ever met. I think someone else must have clipped her hair back so neatly that first day, because after that she lost nearly all of her hair clips. She made wild and wavy hand gestures when she was speaking and sometimes even when she wasn't. She even twisted small screws out of their holes in the paneling on the walls (using one of her few remaining hair clips). At that point I said, "Don't do that—you'll get in trouble," and she gazed at me in that blank way of hers and said, "Oh, I didn't know I was doing it."

I thought it was just as well she hadn't been at Muckling Abbot, which was very down on that sort of thing. And then I thought that the army was probably down on that sort of thing too, and became worried about her. Or even more worried about her, because I never completely got over that suitcase business.

She often held her harmonica to her lips and pretended to play it, but didn't—"Even though I'm very good at it," she told me candidly—because she thought it might not be the best way to make friends on a cramped spaceship.

Not that she seemed very interested in making friends. Except with me, and she didn't exactly *make* friends with me; she just seemed to accept that it had somehow happened.

She was getting a reputation for being weird. One day I came back from the exercise chamber and found six kids gathered around our beds, where Josephine was sprawling as usual, this time with her legs propped against the wall so that she was half upside down.

"Oh my god, don't you ever change your clothes?" asked Christa Trommler, who seemed to be the leader of the outfit.

"No," Josephine said regally, without lifting her eyes from her book. "I like these."

"Ew," chimed in an American girl called Lilly. "Gross."

"Yeah," said Gavin, another British kid. "You're really starting to stink."

Josephine sighed. "If you're going to do this," she said, "try to take account of modern technology. Obviously I don't stink. *No one* stinks anymore."

I was impressed at how good she was at seeming not to care, but I could see that her hands held tight to the tablet.

And of course she didn't smell. For one thing, no one who is taking reasonable care of themselves in other ways starts to smell after only a few days of wearing the same outfit—even if that outfit *doesn't* have nanotech in it, and practically all clothes do now. For another, there were not only ordinary showers on the ship, there were these sonic baths that could blast the dirt right off you, and you could use one of them in your clothes.

"You might as well say I've got bubonic plague," concluded Josephine. "Or demonic possession."

"Well, I bet you *have*," said Gavin, who clearly wasn't very quick on the uptake.

"She's one of those exam kids, Christa," said Lilly, stealing one of Josephine's stones and tossing it gleefully to Gavin. "They all think they're something special."

I was already stomping up in a state of indignation, but that last bit didn't improve my mood at all. "Get out of our cubicle," I said.

"Or what?" said Lilly, rolling her eyes.

"Or I go and tell Sergeant Kawahara how you are *harassing* us, obviously. It's not very complicated."

"Oh, like she would even care about your whining," said Christa.

I shrugged. "Well, I'll give it a try and find out."

"You're a snitching little cow," said Gavin.

"Yes," I said grimly. "That's exactly what I am." I sat myself down next to Josephine and glared at them until they wandered off, huffing and shrugging and generally making a great show. I do have a good glare.

Josephine didn't say anything at first, but then

she reached up and patted me on the arm.

"Yeah, well," I said. "I'm used to it."

✰

On the third day, Captain Mendez told us we would be slowing down to pick up a new passenger. This gave me an amusing mental image of an isolated bus stop hanging in the void of space, but it turns out there was a research ship on its way back to Earth from the asteroid belt. A scientist was going to shuttle over from it and join the *Mélisande* on its way to Mars.

We were all quite pleased to see someone new. We felt a silent *clunk* as the shuttle attached to the port bow, and a small group of nosy kids gathered around the doors. But nothing happened; the scientist did not come out. Captain Mendez went in and presumably said hello and checked that there really was a scientist in there and not an attack squad of Morrors. But then he came out by himself and said, "Everyone back to your seats. Dr. Muldoon is *very busy*."

Josephine sat up in a clatter of falling pebbles. "Dr. *Valerie* Muldoon?" she asked in an uncharacteristically high-pitched squeal. "*Oh my god*. She's on *our* spaceship! She's going to be on *our* planet!"

I watched her jump up and down a little. "And . . .

we like her because . . . ?" I asked.

"She's a *biochemist*," said Josephine, in the tone in which other people would say, "She's a *rock star.*" "You *must* have read the profile on her in *Nature.* . . ." She saw my expression. "Okay, no. But she's one of the minds responsible for accelerated terraforming! She's why Mars is supporting animal life as much as it is!"

She bounced again and then abruptly sat down and hugged her knees, looking agonized.

"Do you want to go and see her?" I said, trying (or at least mostly trying) not to sound amused.

"I can't *bother* her," whispered Josephine. She sounded almost crushed.

"Why don't you write her a fan letter?" I suggested.

"Huh," said Josephine, rolling her eyes and trying to look like she was above such things, which didn't work very well considering everything I'd just witnessed.

She managed to hold herself together for about fifteen minutes, lying on her bed and pretending to read a book, and then she cracked and started scribbling on a piece of paper. It took about five tries before she produced something that didn't send her into fits of self-loathing, which I took to Crewman

Devlin and asked if he could give it to the scientist when convenient. Crewman Devlin looked skeptical for a moment but then glanced at Josephine, whose eyes were now enormous wells of pleading. He smiled a bit and did something on his tablet, and a few minutes later the doors of the shuttle slid open to let him inside.

We waited, and Josephine tried not to have a nervous breakdown. Then eventually Crewman Devlin came out and said, "Okay, she doesn't mind chatting to you, but keep it quick, all right?"

I came along with Josephine out of nosiness and for moral support. Dr. Muldoon's shuttle was a dimly lit, confusing place, like a small laboratory that was also a cozy bedroom and a rather alarming museum, and, of course, a small spaceship. There was a bed with a patchwork quilt beside a window looking out onto the stars. There was a tank full of swimming things that I assumed were fish until they turned out to be *gerbils* with fins and furry fishtails, swimming around underwater and nibbling seaweed as if that was perfectly normal. Another tank held several gallons of violet goop, sloshing quietly under its own power and emitting a gentle hum (B flat, Josephine told me authoritatively). And in a plastic case was what looked like a pink football hanging in a tangle of red wires, but which unfortunately seemed more likely to be a living ball of *skin* in a tangle of *blood vessels*. The room was lit by the amber glow of virtual screens hanging above a bank of whirring devices. Dr. Valerie Muldoon was rapidly adjusting figures on one and flicking the results over to another. She had a lot of long, red wavy hair and a pointy nose. I could see at a glance she was another one like my mum— one of the few who were having a really good war. Dr. Muldoon's eyes were almost *too* sharp and awake and bright as she turned and looked at us. You only noticed the tired look around the eyes of most grown-ups when you met someone who didn't have it.

"I'msorryI'msureyougetthisallthetime," said Josephine in a rush.

"Actually, *no*," said Dr. Muldoon drily.

"Could you . . . uh . . . autograph . . . ," Josephine stammered. She'd called up a book on her tablet and handed Dr. Muldoon her stylus so she could scribble her signature on the screen.

"So are you both into biochemistry, then?" she asked.

I said, "I haven't read your book yet, Dr. Muldoon, but I am sure it's very good and I am interested in biology." I didn't add ". . . but I like it to be more *normal*," because that wouldn't have been polite.

Josephine said, "I'm a little more interested in physics, and, well, archaeology, but—"

"Then we can't be friends!" cried Dr. Muldoon.

Josephine smiled at the joke, but she'd become still and solemn instead of twitchy and excited. I started to see that although all that fangirling was perfectly genuine, it wasn't her only reason for being there. "But do you think . . . I could be like you? I mean, doing *science* for the war effort. Any kind of science. Anything, really . . . rather than being in the army."

So she'd still been brooding over that first conversation we'd had.

Some of the Good War spark went out of Dr. Muldoon's eyes.

"Even I'm an EDF officer, technically," she said gently. "I've yet to fire a shot at a Morror, but it *could* happen. I had to go through the training, and that was . . . oh, probably around the time you were born. And I can't do much about the rules . . . but I'm afraid they're tougher now."

Josephine nodded but said nothing, and her face had gone very blank.

"Come round to the lab on Beagle sometime, if

you like," Dr. Muldoon said kindly, looking back to her screens.

Hugging her tablet to her chest, Josephine turned quietly back to the door. But I couldn't help asking, "What's living on Mars really *like*?"

"Make sure you're careful," said Dr. Muldoon. "It'll kill you if you give it the chance." She looked at us again, and her face softened a bit. "It's beautiful, though. It's home."

✧

Obviously the issue of what Mars was going to be like was on everyone's minds, and there were some orientation sessions to give us an idea of what to expect. They were not very reassuring.

"You must *never leave Beagle Base* unless you're accompanied by an EDF officer or one of the civilian robots," said Crewman Devlin. "There are still flash floods and dust storms, and you'll need extra oxygen if you're out on the surface for any length of time."

The Exo-Defense Force school at Beagle Base would be run in English, Mandarin, Hindi, and Spanish. If you already spoke one of those as a first language, then you had to learn another one to make it a bit fairer for everyone else. This left a lot of people thoroughly fed up, but at least there were enough people who spoke French, say, or Arabic, that they could talk to each other. The worst off were the twenty poor kids, like Obsiye from Somalia and Taimi from Finland, who were all stuck being the only ones speaking their particular languages and were going to be that way for a long time. There would be messages beamed out to us from Earth sometimes, but we were trying to hide our channels from the Morrors so we couldn't just bat emails back and forth whenever we wanted. And it could take as much as forty minutes for a signal from Mars to get to Earth, so you couldn't have any kind of phone conversation anyway.

We were going to have to get used to each other.

The one person everyone was already having to get used to was Carl Dalisay. He was hard to miss, partly because he was one of the reigning champions of the Getting Around as Much of the Spaceship as Possible Without Touching the Floor game (indeed, he was rumored to have invented it), but mainly as an activist and Leader of the Resistance—that is, because of his ongoing campaign to stop the crew from gassing us unconscious every night.

"OKAY, PHASE ONE," he boomed the afternoon after his first delegation failed. While some of us were minding our own business and trying to do useful things like learn Hindi, he and other kids started marching purposefully down the aisles as the crew exchanged oh-god-not-again looks.

Carl's tously little brother came past our cubicle with a tablet and said, "Er, hi. We're doing a petition? About the sleeping stuff? Could you, um . . . ?"

The text of the petition wasn't exactly elaborate. It just read:

GASSING US. YOU SHOULD STOP.

"They already know we don't like it," I said. But I signed it anyway, partly because I didn't want to give anyone the impression I *did* like it, and partly because I felt sorry for the kid. He was only about eight, with gappy teeth and a pinched, homesick little face. He did not strike me as cut out for a life of protest politics in space. I said, "What's your name?"

"Noel. Um, Dalisay, obviously . . ."

"And he's called Carl? Not Kuya?"

"Kuya just means older brother," said Noel, shrugging.

Josephine's arm emerged suddenly from under the table, and Noel jumped. She'd been sitting cross-legged under there, which was the kind of thing she did sometimes.

"Give it here," Josephine said, reaching for the petition. She took quite some time with it, and when she passed it back, she'd written a whole paragraph:

> **We deserve a better answer than that**
> **there is a war on. War does not justify**
> **something just because you want it to.**
> **Therefore I wish to protest in the strongest**
> **possible terms your indiscriminate and**
> **punitive use of a substance whose safety**
> **record has never been shared with us.**
> **Sincerely, Josephine Jerome**

As I was reading it, Josephine poked her head out from under the table and peered at Noel with narrowed eyes. She asked, "Is that a *snail*?"

Noel blushed, clapped a cupped hand protectively over *something* that was crawling up his sleeve, and squeaked "No!" before he scurried away.

Anyhow, obviously the petition didn't work, even though I think every kid on the ship signed it. Except that Captain Mendez made an announcement informing us that Somnolum X's safety record was *excellent*, thank you very much. But still, Carl did not give up.

Phase two started with about ten Australian

voices, an hour before Somnolum X time. *"Don't push the button,"* they all chanted in unison. *"Don't push the button."* At once, other voices joined in. By the time the chant rang out in every language on the ship at once, it sounded fairly hellish. But even though it was so clearly a losing battle, I did sort of admire Carl's persistence. I told Josephine so.

"Oh, this doesn't count as persistence anymore," she muttered crossly. "This is just *showing off.*"

I joined in anyway, and Josephine, who was trying to read, shot me a look of annoyance. The only result of the chanting was that Crewman Devlin pressed the button half an hour earlier than normal, and Josephine woke up the next morning with a very dim view of Carl Dalisay indeed. This didn't get any better the next day, when they started chanting again, and even earlier this time—two hours before the usual Somnolum X time. Josephine snapped after five minutes of it and shouted, "SHUT UP!" to the spaceship in general. And then Lilly and Gavin teased her for being a suck-up in the exercise room the next day, and I had to enlist Kayleigh to help make them leave her alone.

But we still didn't actually *know* Carl—until he embarked on phase three.

On the fifth day we were just finishing lunch

when I saw Josephine raise her eyes suspiciously toward the ceiling. I didn't see anything, but I could hear a scuffling, scrambling noise, as if there was a *rat* up there. You never want there to be a rat in the ceiling, but particularly not on a spaceship. We both got up and stood staring as the noise came closer, and then suddenly a bit of paneling gave way, and Carl tumbled through and knocked us over. This is how we met him properly.

Not that the conversation got very far. Josephine got up, rubbing her shoulder, and said, "*What*," and Carl said distractedly, "Oh, hi, I'm Carl. Listen, I think I've kind of—"

And then there was a hiss and a whiff of Somnolum X in the air. And Josephine said, "Oh, you are *kidding*," and promptly collapsed, and I yelled, "CREWMAN DEVLIN, YOU NEED TO GET YOUR OXYGEN MASK ON RIGHT NOW."

And then we were all unconscious.

☆

"I was only playing the Getting Around as Much of the Spaceship as Possible Without Touching the Floor game," said Carl later, when the three of us were outside the captain's cabin, waiting to be called inside.

"Oh," said Josephine, who had been trying to kill Carl using only her eyes for the last fifteen minutes.

"You were just playing. In the ventilation system. Which carries certain gases that we breathe. Like Somnolum X. And *oxygen*."

Carl spread his hands. "Okay. I thought *either* I'd find a way to stop them, *or* I'd have an unbeatable Getting Around as Much of the Spaceship as Possible Without Touching the Floor score. Either way, a win. I mean, knocking us out with Somnolum X is *wrong*, yeah? I saw what you wrote on my petition! It was great! So this is like I'm *resisting*, right? It's like a *revolution*!"

"I think it's more like *terrorism*," said Josephine icily.

Then Captain Mendez called us inside. He was probably about forty or so, but I had the impression that he'd looked younger when we started out.

"Do you realize you could have poisoned or suffocated everyone on the ship?" he asked.

"*We* didn't do anything," said Josephine. "It's not our fault he crashed out of the ceiling and nearly killed us."

"I don't care who did what," said the captain wearily.

"Well," I said, "you really ought to."

"That's enough out of you, Alistair; you're in enough trouble as it is."

"MY NAME IS NOT ALISTAIR," I said, but Josephine elbowed me in the ribs.

"And Josephine, it's no good pretending you weren't involved. What about your little manifesto the other day?"

"I agree with Carl's *goals*," said Josephine loftily. "But I have serious problems with his methods."

"And Crewman Devlin says this isn't the first time you've tried to sabotage the ship. You've been seen unscrewing fixings before."

Josephine started a bit. "Oh. Not on purpose."

"It's true," admitted Carl. "They didn't have anything to do with this. No one else did. It was just me."

Captain Mendez stared down at him. "How'd you end up on this ship, Carl? Exam, VIP, or did someone pull your name out of a hat?"

Carl looked uneasy. "My brother's name, actually," he said. That was how it worked. If your name came up in the lottery, your brother or sister got a place on the ship too.

"It didn't have to be that way, you know," said Captain Mendez. "When they were planning the evacuation lottery, not everyone thought they should take siblings. Some people thought it would be fairer if more families got a chance to have a kid out of the fighting."

"None of this is really fair either way, is it?" Carl said shortly.

Not fair to be taken, not fair to be left behind. I suppose I shouldn't have been surprised that he'd been thinking the same thing Josephine and I had from the beginning.

"No, it's not," agreed Mendez. "But suppose that vote had gone another way? Your brother would have been out here on his own."

Carl paled. "You're not going to . . . you wouldn't send me back and leave Noel on Mars by himself?"

"I'm saying," said Mendez, "that we're taking you all this way to keep you safe from the Morrors, and all those other kids on Earth have been left behind with the shock rays and the ice instead of you. It's the most dangerous time humanity's ever faced. And you seem to be doing the best you can to make it worse. I'm saying you're here by a billion-to-one chance. And this is what you decide to do with it."

Carl looked shaken. "I'm sorry," he said. "Alice and Josephine really didn't do anything."

Captain Mendez must have kind of believed that, because he stuck Carl in the escape shuttle for the rest of the voyage. But he must have also kind of *not* believed it, because he had all our tablets and games and stuff taken away, which caused Josephine to vow undying wrath against Carl.

"Gassing us was wrong, though," Carl called defiantly as the door was shut on him. "I was trying to do the right thing."

Mendez looked at him hard through the little window in the shuttle door. "You actually care about doing the right thing?" he asked. "Or do you just like the spotlight?"

I got a glimpse as Carl's mouth fell open in indignation, but no words came out. Captain Mendez turned away. "You think about that."

☆

It turned out that Carl had broken the Somnolum X system pretty thoroughly, so there was no more of it for the last two nights of the voyage. And frankly, no one got any sleep at all.

"Well, we'll sleep on Mars," I said to Josephine. I could see her glowering by the starlight from the windows as people whooped and ran around and sang and Sergeant Kawahara groaned for everyone to be quiet.

"You're disturbing Dr. Muldoon!" she tried when everything else had failed.

"Oh, this is all right by me," said Dr. Muldoon airily, watching the chaos with detached curiosity. "I only sleep once a week anyway." She gestured to her temples and smiled. "Cortical implants!"

So that was why her eyes looked a little bit too sparkly.

"What harm are they really doing?" she asked, and Sergeant Kawahara looked as though she thought that was easy to say for someone who didn't need sleep. "Let them have their fun," persisted Dr. Muldoon more quietly. "When are they going to have another chance? Isn't what we're doing to their lives enough?"

The planet was filling the dark ahead—red and purple and gold and silver.

5

Landing on a planet is worse than taking off, or at least I think so, because you're basically *falling*. For the first time in days, everyone on the ship mostly shut up. Opposite me, Josephine was gripping the edge of her seat.

The windows filled with fire as we burned through the atmosphere, and then suddenly, instead of blackness and stars around us, we were plunging through a pale purplish sky. The ship was once again urging us to breathe deeply and think of babbling brooks and sun-dappled beaches, and the being-hammered-by-tablespoons feeling was even worse than before.

The coppery ground flew up at us and the

spaceship started to slow down, but it didn't seem like it could possibly slow down enough, so we were still absolutely sure we were going to crash. How on Earth—how both *on* and *off* Earth—could my mum do this all the time?

Then we stopped moving. And everything went weirdly quiet.

We were on Mars.

There was a floaty feeling that felt as if it should wear off now that we'd stopped moving, but it didn't. It made you want to move. I was suddenly very, very impatient to get out of the spaceship, and I wriggled against the seat belt.

"Ow," said Josephine, because I'd accidentally kicked her in the shin. My foot just came up a lot higher than I'd meant it to. This wasn't the artificial gravity anymore. This was Mars's brand of gravity, and there was a lot less of it.

Kayleigh led a round of slightly hysterical cheering—theoretically for the crew, though really everyone just felt like clapping and screaming. The crew lurched around the main passenger cabin looking completely exhausted, making sure we'd all got oxygen masks, for acclimatizing. The oxygen canisters were pretty big, but they didn't feel heavy.

There was a thump from the escape shuttle where

Carl was still shut away in disgrace. I imagined he was either trying to get out or doing an experimental jump and hitting the ceiling.

When we had the oxygen masks fixed over our faces, the doors opened and a blast of thin air flowed in. It was cold, but as you know, I was used to that. And faster than the crew wanted, we all spilled down the ramp and onto the surface of Mars.

Beagle Base was a cluster of drum-shaped buildings on stilts and domes and windmills. The hills above the base were smooth, abrupt lumps with polished red sides, still bald, though there was thin blackish-green arctic grass growing on the plain.

But we weren't that concerned with where we were going to be living. We saw at once that we would never, ever, for a single second, be able to forget we were on a different world. The sun was too small and too pale. The horizon was too close and too curved. I don't think people would have ever thought the world was flat if they'd started off on Mars.

And the gravity. It was *amazing*. It felt like we'd suddenly gotten superpowers, because in a way we *had*. I jumped as high as I could, as high as my own head. It was almost as exciting as being able to fly, but kind of scary too, because that's a long way to come down. But I descended slowly enough to *see* the red horizon settling lazily back into place around me. Josephine looked up at me and took off herself. Soon everyone was doing it, three hundred kids all bouncing up and down on the alien plain like bubbles in a pan of boiling water.

Then there was a horrible blaring noise overhead, and everyone jumped or shrieked or giggled or fell over. Until then we hadn't noticed the three little flying silver ball things that had whooshed over from behind a cluster of red rocks and were now spinning around in a triangle formation above us. They shouted in one deep, annoyed American voice: "You will get in a line! You will be silent! You are all Exo-Defense Force cadets now! You will act like it!"

So we did, at least the getting-in-a-line part, and we were quick about it too, because those things were scary.

"EDF goads," said Josephine. "I read about them. . . ."

One of the goads plunged down out of the pinkish sky and hovered in front of us, shimmering. In the shimmer we could see the face of an old, angry-looking man, who bawled at Josephine: "SILENCE!" And then it swooped off along the line and bawled the same thing at a lot of other people, with variations like "STAND UP STRAIGHT!" and "WIPE

THAT SMIRK OFF YOUR FACE!" and one of the other goads swept along behind it, translating into various languages and sounding just as furious whether it was yelling *"SILENZIO!"* or *"CHEN MO!"* even though it was automated.

A large, strange shape was emerging over one of the hills; something huge and black with four legs, a bit like a horse and a bit like a dog and a bit like a monkey—except that it didn't have a head because, being a robot, it didn't need one. Astride its back was the man whose face we'd seen in the goad. He was even part robot himself, from the knees down. You could see this because even though he had to be at least seventy-five, and even though we were on *Mars* and it was chilly to say the least, he was wearing very short shorts.

He looked down at us from his steed, which you expected to rear up dramatically against the skyline.

"I AM COLONEL DIRK CLEAVER." He was very loud, even louder than Carl. But even if he hadn't been, the three little goads that were now whirling above amplified his voice all over the Martian plain.

"AND THERE ARE SOME THINGS YOU SHOULD KNOW ABOUT ME," he went on just as loudly. "I never *wanted* to wind up stuck on this rock, babysitting the likes of you, because some sniveling pen pusher thinks I'm too old to fight. But since I *am* here, by god, YOU WILL BECOME THE FINEST FIGHTING FORCE OF SEVEN- TO SIXTEEN-YEAR-OLDS THE WORLD HAS EVER SEEN. Those invisible scum buckets will *quail in terror* of you. But first, you will quail in terror of *me*!"

I was already quailing, maybe not in *terror*, but certainly in a general oh-god-what-is-this-ness kind of way. I sneaked a glance at Josephine. She was not quailing at all, but she was staring into the distance in a resigned manner, as if she was sizing up what the next four years were going to be like.

Dirk Cleaver pointed. "There are your barracks. I want you back out here in uniform in twenty minutes!" For a moment he looked vaguely disgusted. "The civilian robots will show you what to do." He didn't sound as if he thought much of the civilian robots. I was still keen to see what they'd be like, though the thing the Colonel was riding was exciting enough. He shouted, "Yah!" and the thing responded just as if it had been an animal; it charged down the hill with him sitting easily upright astride it. The headlessness was creepier when it moved—it could go in any direction without hesitating or looking where it was going; sometimes, when there was a big rock or something in the way, it would go straight from galloping like a horse to moving sideways like a crab. Once he was down on the plain, the Colonel rode along the line of children with his whirling goads sweeping after him, as we all tried to quail in suitable terror. "Go on! Get moving! March!"

So we marched off as best we could toward Beagle Base. Colonel Cleaver's voice continued to yell at us out of the goads, "Quick march! Left, right!" while another robot came to meet us, hovering above the ground like the goads. Except this one was shaped like a sunflower with a smiley face and was playing a jingly tune.

"Hi there!" it said in a friendly way. "¡Hola, chicos! Namaste, dosto! Nimen, hao! Wow, you're a long way from home! Welcome to Beagle Base! Why don't we take a look around?"

"You will become living weapons!" roared the Colonel. "You will be disciplined! You will be strong! You will be *ruthless*!"

"We're going to have a fun time together!" giggled the sunflower robot placidly.

"I don't think I like it here," said Josephine.

⋆

The Sunflower led us between a couple of buildings on stilts and down a tunnel into a huge, misty-looking, transparent dome. Inside, it was all green and warm and lovely and full of growing things. Little robots skittered about between beds of plants, spraying stuff on them or picking cauliflowers and beans while bees hummed overhead. The Sunflower led us through the gardens, rocking gently from side to side as it hovered, talking in Mandarin and then Spanish in the same happy tone.

"Look at all the healthy food we're growing!" it said when it went back to English. "And see, over there are some EDF scientists called *ecologists*! They're helping to make Mars a safe, green, living planet for us all!"

It was true; on the other side of the dome, standing between banks of strange plants that didn't look like anything I'd seen on Earth, there were some actual humans. Some of them were wearing lab coats and some were in overalls, but all had the Exo-Defense Force comet symbol on the chest. They were directing the little agricultural robots around or comparing results on their tablets. One of them was a woman riding a vehicle like a more delicate, spidery version of the Colonel's Beast, carrying her over the crops by elegantly placing its pointed feet into tiny spaces between plants. All these people ignored us completely—we were the Colonel's and the robots' responsibility. The beds of vegetables opened out around a big oval sports field framed by a running track. It had been a long time since I had seen anything like that that wasn't covered in snow.

"Let's meet my friends!" cooed the Sunflower.

Our teachers and caretakers for the next four years were waiting for us in the middle of the sports field—standing or hovering. They came forward, pleased to see us.

Like the Sunflower, they were designed to appeal to children, and they mostly looked like huge toys. There was a Cat and a Star and a Flamingo and a Goldfish. The older kids just had a plain hovering globe thing, like a slightly less aggressive version of the Colonel's goads. But I think something had gone wrong with the design of the robot for the smallest kids, or maybe it had become a bit broken on the way to Mars. It was a six-foot-tall Teddy Bear that lumbered forward and said, "HELLO, LITTLE CHILDREN" in a deep and awful voice. The four seven-year-olds burst into tears on the spot.

But little Noel Dalisay didn't cry, because he was too busy looking around for his brother.

"They've forgotten Carl!" I said to Josephine.

"Huh," snorted Josephine bitterly. "Tragic." She'd only had her tablet and its library of books back for a couple of hours, so she wasn't in any mood to be forgiving.

The robots seemed to know exactly who we all were and, more importantly, how old we were. They roamed about, looking at our faces and calling out names. Then, for the first time, we were divided up by age rather than by nationality or by whoever we felt like hanging out with. Josephine and I and the rest of the eleven- and twelve-year-olds got the Goldfish.

"Hey, kids!" it said to us. It had a livelier, jauntier way of talking than the Sunflower, which sounded permanently spaced out on the bliss of being a flower-shaped robot. "I can't wait for us all to get to know each other and start learning and having fun! Gosh, it's gonna be super."

"Um," I began. It felt weird to be talking to a fish. "I think Carl Dalisay should be in our year? And he's still on the ship."

"Aww, don't you worry, Alice!" it said fondly, as if it had known me for ages. "We'll find him!"

The Goldfish *was* a rather fascinating thing. It was orange and shiny and faintly translucent, with a light inside that slowly pulsed from dim to bright and big, glowing blue eyes. When it was talking English, it had an American accent, and like the goads and the Sunflower, it hovered above the ground. I thought it was programmed a bit too young for us, though. It hadn't been talking for two minutes before it became clear it was very keen on sharing and everyone using their imaginations.

"At some point," I whispered to Josephine, "that fish is going to make us sing."

"Well, I just bet you all want to know where you're going to sleep, and what your new uniforms look like!" chirped the Goldfish, as cheerfully as it said everything else. "Let's go, kids!"

It led us off across the sports field and to the edge of the dome, where we found there were classrooms and corridors looped all around the central garden in rings. We got occasional glimpses of smaller domes outside, clustered round the main dome like little bubbles in bathwater clinging to a big one.

"That's where they're growing wheat and soy!" the Goldfish told us happily. "In here for Assessment and Processing, kids!"

I was a little scared of being Assessed and Processed, but it herded us into a wide, bright chamber full of little cubicles where you got blasted with an unexpected sonic shower. The floor weighed you and something in the walls scanned you to measure how tall you were, and I think maybe it was checking to see if you had any diseases too.

"Hey," said somebody while things whirred busily behind the walls. I turned. Lilly was in the cubicle with me.

"Hello," I said, not too warmly.

But Lilly was smiling at me—a humble, earnest sort of smile, like I was a duchess and she was interviewing for a job as my butler. "I like the pink in your hair. I'd never dare to do that, but it looks awesome."

I blinked. "Thank you."

"I think your mom's totally amazing, by the way."

"Mmm-hmm."

Lilly stopped smiling and twisted her hands. "Look, I'm sorry about before, with the exam girl. We were all just joking around and, you know, I guess she can't help it, but she *does* come off as kind of strange, and maybe we got a little carried away."

I looked at her. Up till then, Lilly-and-Gavin-and-Christa-and-various-hangers-on had all been one blob of unpleasantness to me. But on her own, Lilly was very harmless looking. She was about my height, slim, dark-blond hair, pretty but not so you'd notice the first time you looked. Her shoulders were tense, and her fingernails were bitten down to the quick.

I didn't say anything. I wasn't sure what to think.

"Christa's actually really cool," added Lilly. "And I'm sure she wasn't trying to be mean either. And I was so scared those first few days on the spaceship. And Christa's, like, used to people who are celebrities and stuff, and it was so nice of her to hang out with us. So, you know."

". . . So you were trying to impress Christa," I summarized.

"I don't know." Lilly looked harassed, and I wondered if I was being too hard on her. She'd just said she was scared, after all. "I wasn't trying to do *anything*, I just . . . I really miss home, and is it that big a deal? Can we be cool?"

I considered this as two tightly folded uniforms came plonking out of a hole onto a shelf, like a chocolate bar out of a vending machine.

"Well," I said cautiously, "it's not me you should be apologizing to. It wasn't me you were picking on."

She flinched a bit, but then said, "Oh, okay, I'll totally apologize to Josephine too."

And I think, at the time, despite everything that happened later, she probably meant to.

☆

When everyone in our class had uniforms, we went off to the dorms to change. Girls and boys were divided up, and there were six of us to a room. Josephine and I stuck grimly to each other, because under these circumstances it seemed like a good idea to hang on to people and things that you know you like, or at least can put up with.

Our dorm on Vogel Corridor was obviously a lot more modern than what I was used to at Muckling Abbot, but really the general idea—a bed and a chest of drawers and a little pinboard to put posters on—is much the same whatever planet you're on. The ceilings were very high, though, because in this gravity, a decent jump would probably have knocked you out otherwise. The uniforms were at least slightly better than the sludge-green uniforms at Muckling Abbot, and they were the same for boys and girls. There were ordinary white T-shirts to wear next to your skin, gloves, and jackets and trousers that were black and glossy on the outside. They had a weird smooth texture like flexible glass, and a kind of soft webbing inside that could adjust to the warmth inside the dome as well as the cold, thin Martian air, so you were never uncomfortable. Of course they had that comet crest on the left side of the chest, and the EDF motto, which was RECLAIMING EARTH.

Josephine had gotten the machines to give her a toothbrush and some things for her hair. She was pretty glad to change out of the clothes she'd been wearing all week, and she said she liked wearing black. But she didn't like having to do her hair, which was very tangly now. Besides running her fingers through it or bundling it up in her scarf, Josephine hadn't done anything to it for the whole voyage. She sat on her new bed next to mine and began morosely trying to comb it. I tried to help, but fortunately some older girls from next door wandered through. One of them was called Chinenye, and she was from Nigeria and had similarish hair and a usefully bossy temperament. She took over.

"What have you been doing to yourself?" she scolded Josephine. "Look at this mess. Don't you know how to do your own hair?"

"In principle, yes. In practice, it's not one of my strengths," said Josephine, looking as if she was being martyred. She sighed and mumbled, "My sister does it, mostly."

"You never said you had a sister," I said. Actually, she hadn't said anything about her family. And I hadn't asked—not because I wasn't interested, but because it's a tricky subject in a war. Mostly people just don't.

Josephine became slightly frosty. "Well, I've only known you a week," she replied.

I was a little bit hurt. But as I say, family's a touchy thing when you're in a war, or maybe even when you're not, so I tried not to take it personally.

Chinenye hastily did Josephine's hair into two buns on top of her head like mouse ears and said, "There."

"You look nice," I said.

"How can I think straight with my head all pulled tight?" moaned Josephine. "Anyway, what about you? Are you allowed to have your hair dyed pink in the army?"

"No one said I couldn't," I said anxiously, and scraped my hair back so the pink bits didn't show. This dampened my morale, and I felt more sympathetic to Josephine's gloom.

I've just realized I never said what I look like, though we've already covered that I like pink and am good at glaring. Aside from that, my eyes are blue; my hair is short and brown. My face is rounder than it would be if I'd gotten to design it myself, but I look nice enough, in a sturdy kind of way.

"Quick! We've got to run," said Chinenye, because the dorm was empty by now except for us. I didn't want to find out what Colonel Cleaver would do if we were late, so we did, across the gardens and the sports field and out of the dome onto the plain, and hastily lined up with the rest of our group. We already made a tidier, more military-looking formation than we had before—I suppose putting on a uniform does something to you. But we had the Goldfish hovering beside us this time.

"Let me tell you this! Mars is tough! And it will MAKE YOU TOUGH!" roared Colonel Cleaver. "You will learn to survive!"

"Learning is fun!" piped up the Goldfish in agreement. The Colonel scowled, and one of his goads came whooshing over to us with his face glaring out of it. The Goldfish gazed back with its unblinking blue plastic eyes. It was impossible to tell if it was actually aware of taking part in a staring competition, but in any case, it won, because the goad bobbed irritably and flew back to the Colonel, looking somehow disgruntled.

Then the Goldfish went swimming off toward the *Mélisande* and said something to the haggard-looking crew, who were standing there watching us assemble. There was a small kerfuffle, and then Sergeant Kawahara went and opened the doors of the escape shuttle and Carl came soaring out.

The Colonel rode over on his Beast. "Hah!" he

said to the crew. "Looks like you nearly flew off with this one aboard!"

Captain Mendez shuddered visibly at the thought.

Carl began doing just what the rest of us had done as soon as we got outside—looking around and jumping up and down a lot. He didn't mind doing this in front of an audience of three hundred any more than he'd minded being dragged out of the sea with everyone watching.

"STOP THAT!" barked the Colonel. "STAND UP STRAIGHT!"

Carl obeyed instantly, even flinging the Colonel a salute.

"I'm ready to learn how to fight aliens, sir," he announced, and then looked at the robot beast as if he'd just fallen in love. "Oh, sir," he said. "When do we get one of *those*?"

There was a pause while Colonel Cleaver looked Carl up and down.

"I like you, kid," he announced finally.

Beside me, Josephine quietly hit herself in the face.

6

It was the older kids who got the brunt of the Colonel's training regimen, because they were going to be doing all this stuff for real in a year or two. So the fourteen- and fifteen-year-olds were doing flight sims and weapons drills and climbing over the Cydonian hills every day, while we younger ones were mostly indoors learning Wordsworth or comparisons in Spanish or medieval crop rotation with the Goldfish.

Sometimes, though, instead of telling us about the French Revolution, the Goldfish gave us lessons about the planet we were actually living on.

"Hey, kids," sang the Goldfish, glowing contentedly as it floated around the classroom. "Today we're going to be talking about the Labyrinth of Night!"

The name sent a pleasant shiver down my spine. I imagined a huge, dark maze full of ghosts. There were all these strange and lovely names on Mars. Memnonia, Mariner Valleys, the Golden Plain. And thinking about them made me wish I could go to those places and see if they looked anything like the way they did in my head.

"Do you think we could go there?" I said wistfully. "On a sort of . . . field trip?"

"Oh, no, Alice," said the Goldfish. "You kids need to stay here at Beagle where it's full of fun and oxygen! Until the terraforming's finished, Mars is too dangerous for exploring!"

I thought crossly that the EDF wasn't so worried about keeping us safe once we'd successfully been turned into living weapons. Meanwhile, the Goldfish hovered over to Gavin.

"So, Gavin, what can *you* tell us about the Labyrinth of Night?"

"Uh," said Gavin, biting his lip. "I guess it's . . . erm . . . on Mars. Somewhere."

"Aww," said the Goldfish sadly, after waiting in vain for more. "You need to put in more work by yourself, buddy! But never mind! See what you can learn in class today." It bustled over to Josephine. "Can you help us out, Josephine?"

Josephine didn't notice the Goldfish was talking to her. She was leaning back in her chair, dreamily gazing up at a bee circling under the transparent roof of the dome. The bees were *everywhere* on Beagle Base. Our classroom was in the inner ring around the garden dome, so there weren't any windows in its high white walls, but you could see the clouds through the curve of the ceiling. It had been raining heavily all morning—weird rain, falling so much more slowly than on Earth, making a purring, warbling noise on the roof. It was quite nice in a way: feeling hidden and safe, with no spaceships zapping each other overhead and nothing in the sky but rain. But on the other hand it made you feel shut in and very aware of how lonely Beagle Base was and how we really were very cut off from everything. We'd been on Mars nearly a month by now, and we hadn't had any kind of contact from Earth. Sometimes I wondered if the Morrors could have actually taken over the world by now, and when we would find out if they had. I also wondered if they'd killed my mum yet, but wondering about that wasn't anything new.

"Wakey wakey, Josephine," urged the Goldfish, nudging her arm with its nose, almost like a friendly dog.

"Mmmh," Josephine said sleepily. "Urgh. What?"

Gavin tittered nastily.

"The Labyrinth of Night," prompted the Goldfish patiently.

"Oh. *Noctis Labyrinthus*. It's a system of canyons by the equator at the west end of *Valles Marineris*— Mariner Valleys. It was formed by extensional tectonics in the Noachian period and erosion by rivers and collapse of grabens in the late Hesperian and Amazonian periods," said Josephine. Then she dropped her head onto her arms as if exhausted.

Josephine was the sort of person who stumbles into a lesson without her books or tablet or any apparent idea of what's going on, and almost never puts her hand up, but then seems to know more or less everything. It would have driven a human teacher at least slightly crazy, but being a robot, the Goldfish had infinite patience.

(Well, that's what I thought at first. We found out eventually that it *did* have its limits, and it *could* snap, but I'll come to that later.)

"That's great, Josephine, good job!" it said, completely satisfied, skimming back to the front of the classroom. "A *graben* is what happens when a block of land falls down in an earthquake and becomes the flat bottom of a new valley," it told the rest of us.

Josephine looked slightly mournful. It wasn't that she did this sort of thing for dramatic effect, but she would have liked some reaction. "You can't *surprise* it," she told me later.

She'd at least managed to surprise Gavin, and not in a pleasant way, because he muttered, "Freak."

Josephine rolled her eyes magnificently and otherwise ignored him, but the Goldfish didn't stand for that kind of thing at all. "Now, you cut that out, Gavin," it said sternly. "I'd like you to say sorry right now!"

Scowling, Gavin did.

"So, who else is out there?" asked Carl. "There's Zond Station, right? What are those guys up to?"

"Good question, Carl!" The Goldfish twinkled. It spun slightly to project a hologram of Mars from its mouth into the air. "Zond is aaaaaaaall the way over here by Mount Olympus, and that's not just the tallest mountain on Mars, it's the tallest mountain *in the solar system*! Don't you think that's nifty?" It zoomed in on the mountain to show that its peak rose all the way above the atmosphere, bare of snow and ice. "Zond Station is just a very small base for our brave Exo-Defense fighters! But there's also Schiaparelli Outpost—who can guess where *that* is?"

"Schiaparelli Crater," I said.

"Good job, Alice!" enthused the Goldfish, spinning the projection of Mars to show where that was. "And that's where some clever scientists are working hard to see how the new *ecosystem*'s doing! Does anyone remember what an *ecosystem* is?"

"So there's only a few hundred people on the whole planet, and most of them are us," concluded Carl, ignoring this question.

"That's right, Carl! And of course there's lots of my robot pals out there, enriching the soil and the air and planting seeds and making Mars a better place for you to enjoy!"

"Well, no, they're not," I said gloomily. "Not for *us*. You pretty much just said so. *We've* got to go and fight the war with the Morrors."

There was a slight pause, and the Goldfish hovered where it was, its plastic blue eyes looking somehow more blank than usual.

"Cheer up, Alice!" it said eventually, in its sunniest and most robotic way.

"So . . . . we're here, and there's no one around for thousands and thousands of miles, except maybe some robots?" said Carl. He thought for a second and then grinned. "Awesome."

After that lesson we had our supplements and stood under the UV lamp to stop the low gravity from doing bad things to our bone density, and played with the Goldfish. Besides projections of Mars and other school things like that, there were a lot of decent games on it. During breaks it would get us chasing holographic bumblebees or meteors around on the sports course. It was quite fun, even though the Goldfish kept chattering on about just how fun it was and how well we were all doing.

There was a lot of other stuff on the Goldfish too—well, all the robots knew basically everything. And although we couldn't get the proper internet across fifty million miles of space, Beagle Base did have its own network with email and books and the odd amusing cat video on it. But annoyingly, all the robots and all the computers also knew exactly how old everyone was, and so there was no way to get them to show you anything you were supposedly too young to see.

But we didn't get much time to think about it, what with all the lessons and all the exercising. The Goldfish made us run around a lot, and twice a week the Colonel had us for military training. And that was very different because, as you might have gathered, the Goldfish and the Colonel did not exactly see eye to eye on how to treat and motivate children. There was an assault course sprawled around the Cydonian hills, and it looked terrifying, like it had been made for giants—hurdles higher than your head and a climbing tower about the height of a skyscraper. But of course, in this gravity, it wasn't as hard as it looked, though you did need the extra oxygen strapped to your back.

One morning, I struggled up to the top of the tower and looked out over the lumpy hills. I pulled off my oxygen mask to get a better look—you weren't supposed to do that too often, but there was enough oxygen in the air that you could go easily twenty minutes before you even got dizzy. And after all, Mars was supposed to be Making Us Tough. The mirrors in the lavender sky were glittering icily behind rosy clouds, and against the near horizon there were a few dark pine trees. It was hard to tell if it was just the tighter curve of the planet or whether they really were impossibly tall, but against the sky their silhouettes looked something like a little kid's drawing, everything out of proportion.

"Hi, Alice," said Carl, climbing up beside me.

I wasn't sure if I had forgiven him over that Somnolum X stunt, so I gave him a sort of half-strength glare and said, "Hello."

He looked out at the view. "This whole planet," he said, "is basically pink. You must be in heaven."

I went up to three-quarters-strength glare and said, "It's really more a kind of peach."

"Nah, it's definitely pink. All it needs is for, like, a herd of unicorns to come galloping over the plain there. . . ."

I decided not to bother responding to this, so Carl changed tack. "When your parents decided to name you Alistair—"

Full-strength glare, on the spot. "If you call me that again, I'll push you off the tower."

Carl laughed and swung himself away from me, and at that point one of the Colonel's goads soared up to us and started yelling.

"Get going, you lazy little snots! I bet you think you're something special, just because you can jump a few feet higher than you could back on Earth. That's not *you*, you little morons, that's the gravity; you're still all as weak and sloppy as a pile of wet spaghetti, and in danger of getting *worse*! Your muscles'll get lazy if you don't make 'em WORK! So MOVE!"

He was kind of right—I'd never been very good at monkey bars before, and now it was almost pathetically easy. Josephine had gotten into a habit of putting a book on the floor and reading it while standing effortlessly on her hands in a corner of the dormitory. After a while of this you do start to feel rather smug and like you're going to go back to Earth and show off what an amazing athlete you've become. But then the Colonel would go up the tower hand over hand, without his prosthetic legs on, just to show us what being tough was really like.

Carl and I put our oxygen masks back on and started clambering down the tower. Carl's method of doing this was basically to jump off and then catch himself by grabbing a rung from time to time as he fell slowly past them.

"The sea's just over that horizon," he said, waiting for me as I climbed down in my more cautious way. "If we were on Earth, we'd be able to see it from here."

"Hmph," I said. "So?"

"So it must be cool, that's all. The sea on Mars!"

"Very *cool*," I said. "Partially *frozen*, actually. But you're probably foolish enough to go for a swim in it anyway."

"We should at least get to see it," insisted Carl blithely.

There was some kind of fuss happening on the ground among the little kids, who were supposed to be doing their own training exercises under the supervision of the Teddy and the Sunflower. At first

Carl and I were too busy with bouncing down the climbing tower and being yelled at by the goads to pay much attention. But when we got down, the Teddy was waddling around making a honking noise and bellowing, "NOEL DALISAY."

"What? Where's Noel? What's going on?" Carl asked, that huge voice suddenly small and strangled. He started running. One of the Colonel's goads came whizzing after him, and to my alarm, Carl actually HIT it and said, "That's my *brother*."

Then the Colonel himself came pouncing out of nowhere on his robot beast and jumped down to the ground. Thankfully he ignored Carl and said, "You. Bear. What is this?"

"NOEL DALISAY IS MISSING," explained the Teddy in its horrifying voice.

7

"**W**ell, how did you let *that* happen?" yelled the Colonel, and then looked disgusted at himself for talking to a six-foot Teddy Bear and stalked off.

"NOEL!" boomed Carl. "NOEL!"

"He can't have gone far," I said. But I got a horrid cold-watery feeling, because since we'd gotten to Mars, we'd all had it drummed into us that Wandering Off on Your Own had replaced Getting into Cars with Strangers as top of the list of things that were incredibly bad to do. Mostly because you'd run out of oxygen, somewhat because you'd die of hypothermia, and a little because the atmosphere was still too thin to filter out the radiation that would give you cancer.

"I promised Mum and Dad I'd look after him," said Carl, his eyes unfocused, as if he wasn't talking to anyone in particular.

The Colonel mounted a little rise; his goads sprang into the air and he bawled, "Stop what you're doing!" through them. "This is now a search-and-rescue operation. All you with the"—he grimaced as if he felt sick—"the *flower thing* and that *damn bear*, get inside, look for him there. Everyone else, I want you in pairs or groups of three. No one make a *move* on your own! I want you to spread out *slowly*, in a circle. If you do get separated, stop moving and yell. But DON'T get separated, UNDERSTAND?

"Don't worry, Dalisay," the Colonel's voice added to Carl via one of the goads, while the Colonel himself went bounding off over the rocks. "Got heat vision on these things—he'll show up."

And the goads went spiraling about overhead, scanning the ground.

But half an hour later we still hadn't found him, and it was getting awfully cold. I had run out of ways to say that Noel would totally be fine, and Carl had gotten very quiet, which was particularly unnerving because it was so unlike him.

Then we heard sad, swoopy music, like the Martian tundra had somehow turned into the pavement outside a Parisian café from the olden days. Of course it was Josephine, sitting cross-legged on a rock, gazing thoughtfully at the sky and playing her harmonica.

Carl stopped and stared at her. "You're not even going to help?"

"No point carrying on that way," said Josephine. "He's not there. We'd see his tracks in the salt crust— you can see ours. And I *am* helping." She took a swig of oxygen from her canister and went on playing.

"How is that racket going to help?" Carl cried.

"It's '*Clair de Lune*,'" said Josephine reproachfully.

"This isn't really the time," I said. "And you're supposed to be in a group."

"I don't want to be in a group," said Josephine.

"Well, you're in one now," I told her firmly.

To my surprise, she sighed and got up and joined us. But though she gave up on "*Clair de Lune*," she kept playing, her hands fluttering over the harmonica, so a brisk bluesy soundtrack accompanied us as we bobbed and glided along our worried way.

"You shouldn't use up your breath like that out here; you'll run out of oxygen," I said.

"Hmm," said Josephine vaguely. "It's actually quite an interesting feeling."

I was worried her lungs would swell up and she'd get pneumonia, and I also wondered if she'd decided to get back at Carl by being as annoying as possible in her own particular style. I thought her timing was pretty mean if she had. But I was actually quite glad of the music, because it was so quiet without it, and she *was* good.

Carl was too worried to pay much attention to Josephine either way. "Stupid little tick!" he cried, leaping over a crater thinly lined with arctic grass. "I'm going to kill him!"

"It wouldn't be that hard to get lost," said Josephine. "You don't burn energy so fast in this gravity, so you can go a long way without feeling it. And then with the horizons being closer . . ."

"Yes, I *know*," snapped Carl. "I bet, when we find him, it turns out he was following a *bird* or something." A snow goose flapped slowly past, above our heads. "Yeah. One of those. An actual wild-goose chase! Him and his animals!"

Abruptly, Josephine stopped playing the blues, turned off to the left, and started marching away from us.

"Oh, what now?" I cried.

"He's been missing long enough to have realized he's gone too far and tried to walk back," said Josephine. "But no one's found him, so he must have gone the wrong way. He can't be anywhere to the north of us, because someone would have found his tracks. The geese are flying that way, toward the sea. Carl, you just said he might have followed one. They're certainly the most obvious animals around. And something must be stopping the goads from finding him. So if he started off toward the sea and tried to come back and ended up somewhere where he wouldn't leave obvious footprints, where could he be? He's over there, among those hills. They look enough like the ones around Beagle to have confused him."

There was a pause, and then I started yelling and waving my arms in the air, trying to get the attention of one of the goads.

"There," said Josephine rather maddeningly. "Music helps me think."

"You don't *really* know that's where he is," said Carl dubiously, while I tried to summarize to the goad what Josephine had just said. Soon we saw the Colonel hurtling toward us on his beast.

Josephine suddenly seemed to lose interest in the whole business. "Well, that's figured out," she said.

"Actually, I think I'm going to have a look at the sea."

"No! You know you can't go off on your own!" I protested, which didn't have any effect whatsoever.

"It's only over the dunes. I'll be back in a minute," Josephine said, and wandered off playing *"Clair de Lune"* again. Then the Colonel galloped past us toward the cluster of knobbly hills, and with just a quick nod, Carl went running off after him. I couldn't stick with both Josephine and Carl at once, and I did want to see if Noel was okay, so I sighed and made a roughly arrow-shaped heap of stones pointing the way Josephine had gone, in case she did collapse from oxygen deprivation and we needed to find her.

It took me a while to catch up with Carl, and by the time I did the Colonel was coming back toward us. He had Noel in front of him on the Beast, wrapped up in a silver blanket, and Noel was shivering and apologizing and looking a bit weepy.

The Colonel slowed beside us, and Carl bounded six feet in the air and exploded. "You stupid little dipstick! You've got the whole base looking for you, you know! Don't you realize you're in the middle of bleeding *Mars*? Why are you so fantastically moronic?"

"I'm sorry," said Noel, crying some more. "I didn't mean to. But after I got to the sea, then there was this thing on the beach, Kuya—I was trying to get close enough to take a picture of it on my tablet, but it was too fast—"

"I don't care about your flaming animals! Oh, Jesus," Carl added, "don't *cry* about it."

"It wasn't a normal animal," said Noel. "Sir," he appealed, turning to the Colonel. "It wasn't a normal animal."

Carl went on alternating between yelling at Noel and being nice to him as we went along, and then we passed my little marker of stones. I wondered if I'd better tell the Colonel we needed to start another search party, but then Josephine emerged over the dunes. "Hi," she said to me, strolling up. "Hi, Noel, glad you're okay."

"What are you doing on your own, Jerome?" blazed the Colonel. "Because it looks a lot like defying a direct order."

Josephine was not quite so unflappable as not to look a bit scared. She started stammering, "Oh, I was only . . . it was just for a few—"

Carl sighed. "Don't be too hard on her, sir," he said. He looked awfully tired now. "She was the one who figured out where Noel was."

The Colonel looked meditatively at Josephine and growled, "I'll overlook it. *This* time."

Josephine fell into step beside me and Carl, the Colonel's Beast treading slowly enough that we could keep up with it. "So what was the sea like?" I asked.

"Pink," said Josephine.

Carl had recovered enough to snort, "There, what did I say?" and elbow me in the ribs.

We went along in silence for a while. The sun was setting. The sea *would* be pink, I thought, a bit wistfully.

"What happened to your legs, sir?" asked Noel suddenly.

"Noel!" I said, scandalized. I didn't mean to start him off crying again, but unfortunately that looked as if it was going to be the effect.

"What?" said the Colonel irritably. "I'm a freaking cyborg, and he's not supposed to notice? You tell me, son—what do you think happened to them?"

"Um. The Morrors?" sniffed Noel.

"No, no, this was thirty years ago. See, there was some local trouble in the Pacific back then, and one day I was out on a patrol boat and we ran into pirates. And so we tangled with them, and as the pirates went down, they launched one last torpedo. Boat disintegrated around us. And as if that wasn't bad enough, up came a shark—"

"A shark!" Noel yelped involuntarily.

"And I fought that shark, one on one, to the death. He got my legs, and a one-way ticket to the bottom of the sea."

"You killed the shark? Even when pirates sank your ship and the shark had . . . had . . . ?" asked Noel, too amazed to keep crying.

"Oh, yeah," said the Colonel. "Knife between its eyes."

"Wow," said Carl respectfully.

"Is that . . . actually true?" asked Josephine tentatively.

"Ah, you caught me," said Cleaver cheerfully. "No, no, it wasn't really a shark. It was back at the beginning of the war. I was on a spacefighter carrier taking a consignment of the old Aurora models out to the moon, and we took a shock-ray hit to the bow. Lost my legs in the explosion, and just before I was blasted out of the wreckage, I let all the air out of my lungs and used a fire extinguisher to propel myself through the vacuum of space. Then I managed to catch hold of one of those Auroras and pull myself inside before I passed out."

I realized my mouth was hanging open. Josephine tilted her head slightly.

"*Or,*" said the Colonel, before any of us could say anything, "maybe it wasn't a spaceship, now I think about it, maybe it was a fighter plane and I was shot down over Tanzania during the Second Water War. Now, it wasn't my plane being blown up that was the problem, I was parachuting out of there, and everything seemed okay—until I realized I was coming down miles from anywhere, straight into the middle of a pride of lions."

"And it was the lions . . . ?" I asked.

"I spotted the biggest and toughest of the lions," said the Colonel, "and I steered around in the air and landed astride that lion's back, grabbed its mane, and rode it twenty miles across the Serengeti. But unfortunately we passed a river, and out of the river came a crocodile, headed straight for us. Now, by that time, the lion was my buddy, so, to *defend the lion* . . ."

There was another pause, and a bit nervously, Carl began laughing. And then the rest of us started off as well.

The Colonel grinned. "Something like that. I forget."

We were nearing Beagle Base now, and Noel was looking a lot better. "Carl," he said, "Carl. The animal I saw. It was kind of like a worm, but it could fly? But it didn't have wings, it had segments that went round and round, like . . . like a *drill*. And it buzzed . . . and it was this big, and it was eating the sand . . ."

"You'll have to ask Doc Muldoon about that," said Colonel Cleaver. "She's probably loosed a load of mutant freaks out here—it's the sort of thing she'd do. Even those geese have had their genes messed with."

He swung down from the Beast outside the gates of Beagle Base and deposited Noel on the ground.

"I lost Enrique," said Noel forlornly. "My snail," he explained.

"We'll get you another one," said Carl automatically, in the mindless tone of someone who's said the same thing a thousand times before.

"There aren't any other snails on Mars," said Noel.

⭐

"I wonder what that flying worm thing he saw was," mused Josephine when we were back in the dorm and had warmed up with hot showers.

"He was probably making it up," I said. "I mean, maybe not on purpose, but he was pretty scared, and I've heard your brain can do weird things when you're low on oxygen."

"He wasn't making it up," said Josephine. "When I was on the beach, I saw the tracks it made in the sand."

Our room didn't have windows except for the round skylights high in the ceiling, and for once I felt a little pleased that we couldn't see the emptiness of Mars spreading around us into the dark. Because that's when Josephine murmured, "There's something out there."

8

After all that happened, I started thinking of Carl as a friend. And Josephine went from despising him to having no views on him at all, so that was progress.

She did get along well with little Noel, though. They had an interest in common—the creature Noel said he'd seen on the beach. Josephine wasn't especially excited about animals in general, the way Noel was, but she did like things that were weird and unexplained, and flying worm things that might be unknown to science certainly qualified.

Since Noel hadn't managed to get a picture of the thing on his tablet, she made him draw it. But Noel was eight and not very good at drawing, and

Josephine didn't consider the results good enough to be useful for further study. So the two of them spent a couple of evenings in our dorm, taking notes and doing sketches, with Josephine interrogating Noel and making him describe everything about it.

I did not have much to contribute to this, so I left them to it and killed some time customizing my uniform in small, subtle, not-allowed ways, like gluing tiny pink jewels onto the EDF crest on my jacket.

A few days later we were walking to the sim deck for flight and combat training and Josephine said, "Look at this. Noel will have to check it again, but I think it's as close as we're going to get."

What she showed me was this:

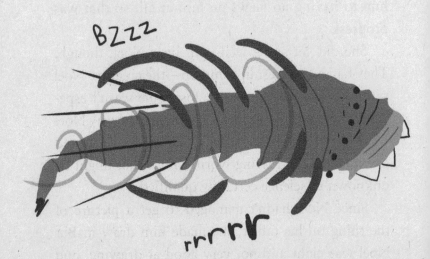

"Ugh," I said, shuddering. "Gross. You really think there's one of those out there?"

"No," said Josephine calmly. "I think there are several."

"Oh, don't," I said.

"Well, it's not likely Noel would have stumbled on the only one on the whole planet, is it?" said Josephine.

"You don't think they could be . . . actual *Martians*?" I said, feeling a bit stupid, because we *knew* there weren't any Martians, not actual alien ones that hadn't been genetically engineered by humans to make the terraforming work better.

But she didn't answer, because then we reached the sim deck, a big, semicircular underground chamber with a huge screen wrapped around its curved walls. Josephine suddenly looked alarmed and said, "Oh. Were we supposed to do . . . some sort of homework for this?"

"Flight and Combat Theory, yes," I said. We'd gone over the basics of flying with the Goldfish, but this was our first time doing combat flight with Colonel Cleaver.

"Oh," said Josephine again, and began trying to make herself invisible by standing behind me.

This didn't work very well, but she didn't get

yelled at. In fact, it didn't seem fair at all that the very first thing that happened was that the Colonel shouted, "Dare?"

"Yes, sir," I said, worrying about the little pink jewels on my uniform. But the Colonel hadn't noticed them. He was smiling at me in an odd way, sort of proud but a little bit sad.

"You're Stephanie Dare's kid, aren't you? She's one damn brave fighter. Cadets, you all know about the Battle of Kara?"

The President of the EEC's nephew is standing right there, I reminded myself, glancing over at him. It's not that big a deal.

There was a slightly groany chorus of yeses and the Colonel growled, "I can't hear you! Yes *WHAT*?"

"YES, SIR," everyone bawled dutifully.

Sometimes I think being in the army is just a little bit like being in a pantomime.

"Kara," sighed the Colonel to himself, and I was sure he was sad about being stuck here with us, away from the real fighting. "That was some fine flying. Well, get up there, Dare. Show us how it's done."

"Thank you, sir," I said stiffly.

I didn't want to go first. And Carl was practically levitating with longing to get behind the controls of anything remotely spaceship-like as soon as possible, so it was doubly unfair.

There were two simulator ships, but we were going one at a time to start off with. From outside they were big, beige, boxy things on a thick strut on which they could pivot and swing. But on the screen, a perfect digital replica of a Flarehawk was waiting on an icy Earth launch platform, and I didn't need to be told it would respond to everything I did in the cockpit. So everyone would be able to see exactly how I was doing.

Now, this was supposedly so we could all learn from each other, rather than for the purposes of ritual humiliation, but the army's good at doing two things at the same time.

I climbed into the simulator, and inside it was just like being in the cockpit of an actual Flarehawk. Through the viewport, the icy launch platform and the bleak gray sky looked completely real. There were snow-covered hills in the background. It could have been Suffolk.

"Hello, home," I said quietly.

"Go ahead, Dare," said the Colonel through the radio.

I fired the thrusters and lifted the ship up. It wobbled a bit, and I realized I was being too tentative with the control yoke. The artificial gravity created a very good imitation of that battering-spoons feeling as I rose through the atmosphere.

I wasn't quite clear what I wanted to happen. I didn't want to be *bad* at doing this. The Colonel and the EDF and my *mum* wanted Stephanie Dare's talent for flying spaceships and shooting aliens to be hereditary; if it wasn't, they'd all be disappointed. And more to the point, being bad at fighting aliens would not bode well for my long-term survival.

But on the other hand, if I *did* turn out to be some sort of spaceship prodigy, then it would feel like another way in which my life was all about a woman I never even actually got to *see*. Like I was actually *destined* to be in the space army instead of it being just the way things were.

The first thing I was supposed to do was just fly around with the computer-generated squadron and not crash into any of them. That was fine. Then I had to use the torpedoes to pick off a few of the light shields. I kind of *missed* the first one, which was embarrassing because it was hanging right in front of me, but at least I saw how I'd gotten the angle wrong, and it didn't happen again.

Then "Morrors" started attacking.

So this was my first taste of shooting aliens— although obviously it was really only a computer game. I remembered all the instructions about how in a dogfight you had to get on top of the enemy. Still, when one of the other Flarehawks in the squadron blew up, my first instinct was to screech various words I hoped the Colonel wasn't listening to while I hauled blindly on the control yoke, so I actually flew straight into a shock ray aimed at someone else. But the ship's systems seemed to be telling me the ray had just skimmed across the tail, and though everything jumped around a bit, apparently I was still in one piece.

Okay, I thought, trying to pull myself together. Torpedoes. Aliens. Time to apply one to the other. And while I wrestled and flailed the Flarehawk around, I watched the pale, glowing transparent shapes whizzing across the viewport and told myself, You've got to aim for where they're *going* to be. And although even Mum's special Morror-spotting sense wouldn't have helped in a simulation, I got a little bit of a sense of what it was *for*, how you had to fill in the gaps in the technology yourself, because though the sensors were supposed to pick up the Morror ships and project ghostly outlines of them onto the viewport, they always seemed a little off from where the ships really were.

Still, I got two of them. Then another one pounced

on me, and I couldn't get out of the way fast enough and I got hit again. And I did think it was a bit mean of the people who designed the simulation to actually make the ship shake and scream while flames filled the viewport before everything went black. I mean, I would have gotten the point that I'd just died without that.

When the lights came back on, the door opened and I got out. I felt rattled and I didn't think I'd done very well, but no one was laughing and the Colonel said, "Good work, Dare." Even if I thought he *did* look slightly disappointed I hadn't done anything spectacular, he also wasn't the sort to say that if he didn't mean it. Then he started talking about how I'd obviously panicked a bit when the Morrors came in but recovered well, and taking out two of them was good, and getting blown up was normal.

"You survived twelve minutes!" said the Colonel. "Not bad! Work on your turn diameters, and you'll get that figure *way* up."

I'd been starting to feel quite happy until he said that.

Then he said, "Okay, Dalisay, you're up," and Carl bounded up into the cockpit, barely bothering with the rungs on the ladder. I swear you could've told who was in the simulator just by watching the screen: the ship *jumped* into the sky, and soon he was rampaging all over the Morror ships like a really lethal two-year-old kicking down sandcastles.

He was so ridiculously good at it, I couldn't help thinking that was really how Stephanie Dare's kid was *supposed* to fly.

"He is going to be insufferable," whispered Josephine.

And indeed Carl didn't get killed even once and popped out of the simulator at the end muttering, "Awesome!" The Colonel didn't even say anything, just patted him on the back, smiling quietly and looking about fifteen years younger from sheer pride.

Then it was Gavin's turn, and gratifyingly, he wasn't very good at it. Then it was Lilly, who was better than I had been, which was annoying.

"Did she ever apologize to you?" I asked.

Josephine snorted a little. "No."

"She said she was going to."

Then the Colonel yelled, "JEROME," and charged over to where Josephine was lurking behind me. Josephine took a deep breath and accepted her fate.

"You'd better be about to tell me I've gotta call EDF command and say I've got a kid here who's just escaped a Morror kidnapping and spent the last week struggling her way across space to make it to my class on time. Because that's the *only* reason I can think of why your Flight and Combat Theory assignment wouldn't be on my tablet right now."

"I've been busy with something," said Josephine, though she didn't look particularly hopeful that saying this would help matters.

The Colonel stared at her coldly for a while, then said, "Well, you show us what happens when you don't prepare."

Josephine set her jaw and went and climbed into a simulator. On the screen, her Flarehawk rose lopsidedly from the ground and lumbered there in the air for about a second.

She looked a little clumsy up there, but I thought there was a fair chance she might surprise the Colonel. She was always stumbling into lessons half asleep and then revealing she already knew the whole subject backward or else she figured it out on the spot.

The Flarehawk spurted backward into the ground and burst into a cruelly well-rendered digital fireball.

Everyone laughed. I wanted to be loyal, but even I couldn't help smiling a bit.

"Again, Jerome," said the Colonel into one of his goads.

Josephine got a bit farther off the ground this time, and promptly bashed into one of the other Flarehawks. They *both* exploded.

On her third try, I could see the Morror ships closing in on her and I found myself yelling, "THEY'RE BEHIND YOU!" but she couldn't hear me because the simulator was soundproofed. Josephine just kept on exploding. I mean, I honestly started wondering if she was doing it on purpose, but when she came out of the simulator and I saw her face, I didn't think it was that funny anymore.

But plenty of other people did.

"How did you manage to torpedo *yourself*?" I couldn't help asking. *"Twice?"*

Josephine made a wordless growling noise.

"Jerome, I'd better have your Flight and Combat Theory assignment and an essay on the importance of preparation on my tablet by tomorrow," Colonel Cleaver said at the end. "Dare, you put up a damn good fight. Just keep at it, and you'll be as good as your mom."

As we left the sim deck, Josephine loomed up behind me, as much as a small person can, and said darkly, "You never *will* be as good as her, you know."

"Thanks," I said. I knew she wasn't happy, but

I wasn't in a good mood myself, despite the Colonel saying nice things to me. After the individual rounds, he had paired us up and made us fight each other one-on-one in the simulators, and Carl had killed me quite a lot.

"Your mum loves it," explained Josephine. "You don't."

✧

Gavin started making exploding noises at Josephine at lunch, and after about a second's hesitation, Lilly joined in.

"Oh, come on, Lilly," I said.

"Come on, Lilly!" echoed Gavin in a stupid baby voice. He clasped his hands. "Pwease, stop being *mean* to my *wickle fwend*, Lilly, or I'll go and tell a *gwown-up*!"

I stared wearily at Lilly but she just snickered like the conversation in the Processing chamber had never happened at all. I think even my full-strength glare was a bit weakened by the strain of the flying lesson, because I couldn't get them to stop. In fact, a few others joined in and started flicking bits of corn at us and tweaking Josephine's hair and so on. So we cleared out of the canteen as soon as we could.

"Let's do something nice," I said.

"Let's get a proper scientific opinion on the flying worm thing," said Josephine.

This wasn't necessarily my idea of a stress-relieving activity, but I wasn't going to argue. We rounded up Noel when he came out of the canteen and took him with us to the research section.

"Why do those kids have such a problem with you?" asked Noel as we walked through the gardens.

"Because I'm weird," replied Josephine stoically.

"No!" I snarled. "It is *not* because of what you're like, it's because of what *they're* like." And I might have stamped my foot, except that stamping looks particularly silly in low gravity.

Dr. Muldoon and all the other scientists turned out to be having some kind of party. It was very, very bright in their laboratory, with UV lamps around the walls and mirrors casting a cone of light into the middle of the dome. As we sidled in, something happened in the middle of the throng of scientists, and there was a lot of clapping.

"Not now," said Dr. Muldoon absently when we went and said we had to show her something.

"It's important and Colonel Cleaver is making me spend the rest of the day writing an essay on being prepared and focused," said Josephine plaintively.

I think Dr. Muldoon might already have had a lot

of the champagne, because she said, "Ahhh, mean old Colonel Cleaver," and suddenly became quite friendly. She wandered over to a bench, swept aside a tray of peculiar algae, perched herself on the edge, and sat there swinging her legs. "All right, what have you got?"

Josephine showed her the picture of the worm thing, and Dr. Muldoon screwed up her face and said violently, "Euurgh," which none of us thought was a very scientific sort of reaction to have.

"Well," she said, "that's completely hideous. What is it?"

"That's what we wanted to ask you," said Josephine.

"It's *not* hideous," interrupted Noel. "It's *interesting*."

"Noel doesn't think any animals are ugly," I explained.

Dr. Muldoon frowned at him thoughtfully. "Not even maggots?"

"Not even maggots," said Noel piously. Dr. Muldoon shrugged and drank her champagne.

"All right, we can assume you didn't make it, then," Josephine said.

"I'd hope I'd make a handsomer class of monster

than that," said Dr. Muldoon.

"It's *not* a monster," protested Noel. "It's an *animal*."

"Well, whatever you want to call it. We've engineered a few species of worm to help enrich the soil. But definitely nothing that goes '*Grrr.*' *There's* the main thing I've been working on lately."

She pointed, and we saw what the party was about. There were two men and a woman standing in the middle of all the light, also drinking champagne and looking very pleased. They were wearing sleeveless tops that revealed diamond-shaped patches of shiny, emerald-green skin all over their arms and shoulders. And they also looked very muscular, in a slightly weird way I couldn't quite put my finger on.

"Are they . . . *photosynthesizing*?" asked Josephine, sounding awed.

Dr. Muldoon grinned and nodded. "That, and a few other enhancements. How does it feel, Angela?" she called.

The woman spread her arms, tilting the bright-green patches to the light. "Lovely," she said.

Josephine gazed covetously at the people. I was rubbing my arms surreptitiously to make sure they were still normal.

"Gills," said Dr. Muldoon thoughtfully. "That's my next ambition. Getting gills on people. Imagine the applications! So useful for exploration! Lifesaving for our servicemen on submarines!"

I supposed it might be useful for Dad to have gills, but I couldn't say I liked the idea very much. Josephine, however, made a little moan of longing and looked as if she might be forgetting why we'd come in the first place, so Noel insisted, "My *animal*."

"The animal," agreed Josephine, turning reluctantly to her tablet.

Dr. Muldoon squinted at the picture. "Are those *eyes*? Good lord, look at its *teeth*. You've got a nicely gruesome imagination, I'll give you kids that— flying worms at the bottom of the garden, it's brilliant, but—"

"I didn't make it up!" Noel cried.

"He didn't," said Josephine. "And neither did I. I don't do *hoaxes*. They're unscientific. Listen, the risk is that this is a *Morror* animal. I wondered if it could be some sort of biological drone, for . . . spying, or sabotage or something."

Dr. Muldoon became more serious. "Hmm. It doesn't *look* like any specimen I've seen. They haven't introduced any flying animal into the biosphere that we know of—and I can't see how this creature of yours *could* fly. And the Morrors have shown no interest in Mars. . . ."

"What if it came from here?" I asked. Dr. Muldoon, Josephine, Noel, and even a random passing scientist all looked at me in a pitying way. I felt my face get hot. "I just mean, suppose there was something here that we didn't know about, and the terraforming sort of . . . woke it up?"

"That couldn't possibly happen," said Dr. Muldoon flatly. "There was nothing on Mars before us."

A section of the party near the back of the room got overexcited, and something made of glass crashed to the ground. Someone called out, "Er . . . Valerie!"

Dr. Muldoon took Josephine's tablet and emailed the picture to herself. "Got to go," she said. "Send me the rough coordinates for where you saw it, and then don't go hanging around in the open on your own again. And if you do see one, don't try and get close to it, not until we've gotten this cleared up. I'll look into it."

"I'm getting gills as soon as possible," said Josephine ruminatively as we walked back to the dorms. Noel and I shuddered. "Why would you not want them? Gills. Definitely gills."

✧

The Goldfish spent the rest of that afternoon making us do things with the radiuses of circles. Later I started composing an email to Dad, because we were getting close to one of the days when Beagle Base's computers opened up channels so you could send and receive messages from Earth. If we'd only known what was going to happen, we could have made a lot better use of that day, but we didn't. So I just wrote about how I didn't seem to be a space-pilot genius and how I preferred him not to get gills and how I missed him. It was nicer writing to him than to Mum, because I was about eighty percent certain most of the time that he was probably alive.

Meanwhile, Josephine got started on her essay, moaning a lot about it, and we all waited for Dr. Muldoon to get back to us.

Only she didn't. Because after that, all the adults disappeared.

9

I know it sounds bad, but at first we didn't actually notice.

We noticed when Colonel Cleaver went away, obviously—he wasn't the sort of person who blends into the background—and anyway, he told us he was going. In fact, he galloped through Beagle Base on his Beast, yelling through the goads that he was going on a short mission and would be back in a few days and everyone had better damn well remember they were EDF cadets and act as a credit to the force while he was gone.

Carl and I saw him soar away in his Flying Fox, off into the purple sky.

After that we had our flight and combat training with the Goldfish.

We were all very used to being looked after by the robots now. They got us up in the mornings (the walls started humming in a cheerful way at half past seven, and the Goldfish would hover from room to room to encourage us) and they herded us into the mess room, where more machines would dollop your food out onto trays, and they taught us our lessons, and broke up fights, and made sure everyone was more or less where they were supposed to be at night. There weren't that many adults around to *miss*, and so when we didn't see any, we all just assumed they were off around the corner doing something else.

We did ask sometimes exactly when the Colonel was coming back and what he was doing, but the robots plainly didn't know, so we stopped. In the meantime, it was quite nice having a break from being yelled at, even if it meant the Goldfish made us sing even more songs about teamwork and having a positive attitude.

⭐

I think I had a vague feeling of unease by the fourth day, but considering the war and being on another planet and there possibly being not one but several creepy flying worm things out there in the Martian wilderness, that was fairly normal. Also we were getting closer and closer to the day the channels opened up, which meant another opportunity to maybe hear that my mum was dead, so I was definitely distracted.

If only we'd realized a little bit earlier, it might not have been such a problem.

So, on this particular morning, we all got messages beamed to our tablets.

Mum's email was very short, but it was there, and I breathed a sigh of relief.

Darling—can't write much—have to run!
I hope you're having a wonderful time and
Mars is every bit as exciting as I imagine it.
Let me know how your flight training's going.
Are you enjoying it? I hear Dirk Cleaver is
training you—wonderful, the man's a legend!
But I hope he isn't pushing you too hard.
Everything's been a bit hairy down here—the
Morrors haven't given us much rest lately. But
I'm fine. Love you! Mum.

She was alive, anyway. Or had been two days ago. So that was good.

Dad's was a bit longer.

*Hello, love—hope Mars is treating you well.
Funny to think of you so far away. You can't
remember things being any other way, I
suppose, but if the day you were born someone
had told me you'd be training as a soldier on
Mars by the time you were twelve . . . well.
Hope you're making lots of friends, anyway.*

*Things are all right on the old sub, I
suppose; all rather dark and cold and boring.
Though we ran across a big school of those
Morror fish—well, of course they're not fish,
with all those legs. Though they're not exactly
legs either. But anyway, they were the prettiest
thing any of us had seen for a while down
here—transparent and all different colors. We
must have given the poor things a terrible scare.
Tried to catch a few for the scientists to look at,
but they were too fast. I suppose the Morrors
must catch them for food, though—must taste
nice if they're worth bringing all the way to
Earth.*

*I hear your mum's still the talk of the town.
We should be coming up for leave in a month
or two, so we might even get to see each other
for an afternoon. Won't be the same without
you, though.*

Miss you loads.
Dad

Meanwhile, Josephine read her messages, stared blankly at the screen, and then ran off crying. I could only think of one reason for anyone to react like that, and I got a horrible cold feeling in my chest where all the relief had been.

She was faster than me, so I hurried after her. I went into some of the classrooms in case she was under any of the desks. She wasn't. Then I went out to the biggest dome with the gardens and the sports field. All the usual robots were skittering among the plants, but the only people I could see were Christa Trommler and a large, muscular boy, playing a messy game of tennis on the sports field. Neither of them had had any bad news, clearly; they were laughing breathlessly as they lunged for the ball, as it hurtled back and forth, as it squeaked and tried to get away. . . .

It wasn't a ball, of course. It was a little hovering robot, and sometimes it would manage to catch itself in midvolley and bounce in the air as if half stunned, uttering confused chirps, until one of them hit it again.

"What are *you* staring at?" demanded the boy.

I *was* staring. I'd stopped dead without quite noticing. I wasn't sure the little robot was exactly *alive*—it probably *wasn't*, surely?—but it looked and sounded so much as if it was in pain, and that was exactly what they seemed to be *laughing* at. . . .

"Leave it alone," I said, and my voice came out small and feeble.

But the large boy heard me. "You want to mind your business, or you want to come here and join the game?" he said, and shifted his grip on the racquet in a way I didn't like at all. Christa stopped to gaze at him, still panting, her eyes shiny with devotion.

Then the little robot made a desperate spring into the air and Christa pounced on it, giggling. "Leon, help! It's getting away."

The boy turned back to the game with one last meaningful swing of his racquet in my direction, and I hurried into the gardens before they could take any more notice of me. I didn't find Josephine, but I did find the Teddy, which was clumping awfully down the path between the beans singing "Old MacDonald Had a Farm" in an extremely menacing way.

"HELLO, ALICE," it said when it saw me.

"Uh . . . hi," I replied, looking up at it. The Teddy was mostly blue, with a pattern of pink hearts on its tummy. Its face was fixed in a sinister grin. It freaked me out even more close up, and I gained new respect for the seven-year-olds who hadn't lost their minds completely since we'd arrived. "You haven't seen Josephine Jerome, have you?"

"YES. JOSEPHINE JEROME IS CRYING IN THE BEAN PATCH," said the Teddy. "I SANG HER A SONG. IT DIDN'T HELP."

"Right. No. I can see how that might have happened. I'll try instead then, okay?"

The Teddy tried to come with me, but I managed to get rid of it.

The bean plants were genetically engineered to be enormous, and Josephine was very well hidden under their leaves, but I did find her in the end.

"Hello," I said.

"Go away," said Josephine. But I didn't. After a while, Josephine sighed and wiped her nose. "No one's died," she told me.

I sat down beside her in a tent of leaves and scarlet flowers, wondering what else could be so awful. "Then what is it?"

Josephine sobbed a bit more and thrust the tablet at me. The email on the screen went like this:

Jrdigqwfi,

    X'cm zelz xte lrjbmzvum gfc ekisx fgb. M zngy bdm flpz arva taxkis.

    El rsl ajc oqaii, tdiekl oiik uoaikgk fbx xkj kfkzi oweui A enu ekyehtgf mcms wpr fwepxmzj avivlug xvbivpdak . . .

And it went on like that.

". . . What?"

"Oh," said Josephine wearily, taking the tablet back. "Sorry. I forgot. It's a code Lena and I use."

"Right," I said, managing not to yelp *"Why?"* "Lena's your sister, then?"

Josephine smiled crookedly at me. "Yes. She's eighteen. She's a bit . . . odd. But very clever. She mostly looked after me when I was little. She thought learning cryptography would help develop my brain. She also thinks it's very important to always carry duct tape."

I tried to imagine someone who was odd even by Josephine's standards, but I didn't say anything, and Josephine rubbed her eyes and then read out the message as easily as if it had been in proper English.

"Josephine,

"I've made the inquiries you asked for. I wish the news was better.

"As you are aware, things have changed for the worse since I was accepted into the military science program: back then, of course, no one seriously thought that evacuating children to Mars would ever become necessary. Now, with pressure from the Morrors so severe and the advance of the ice so extensive, the feeling is that no hand can be spared. Unfortunately, barring some dramatic change in the direction of the war, it's most unlikely you'll be allowed to continue academic studies or to serve as a scientist without completing at least some time in active duty first.

"This strikes me as a shortsighted policy, but there appears to be little either of us can do about it.

"I can only hope you have found flight and weapons training more congenial than you expected when you left us, as I must advise you to master these skills as swiftly and fully as possible.

"Father is well and sends his regards.

"Lena"

I wasn't absolutely sure I understood all of this even translated, but I knew Josephine had hoped she'd be able to do science for the EDF rather than any actual Morror fighting once she graduated in four years. And according to Lena, that just wasn't going to work out.

"You've seen what I'm like," she choked. "What do you think's going to happen when I have to do it for real? It's dangerous enough for people who are any good at it."

"It's a long way off yet," I said. "And you could do fine if you tried."

Josephine made a desperate snorting sound.

"You could! I don't think you're *used* to trying. I think normally either you're just good at things or you don't do them at all, right?"

Josephine looked rather angry for a second but then sighed. "Maybe. I will try, I suppose. But I've already *tried* to try and I *hate it so much*. And it's not just flying the ships and shooting and being so bad at it—it's *being in the army*. I'll lose my mind if I have to live like that."

"Maybe the war *will* be over by then, like you said," I said as confidently as I could.

"I always try to think it will," Josephine said, but her voice was wobbly.

We sat there for a while. "Hey, I don't think you translated everything," I said eventually. "What's that underlined bit?"

At the end of the message from Lena, it said CRXF PQID IYWL.

Josephine rolled her eyes and started to look a bit more like herself. "It says 'COMB YOUR HAIR.'"

A little fanfare played over the PA system, which meant it was lunch, and we could hear the cheerful calls of robots herding children to the mess room. Josephine groaned, but she got up, and we emerged from under the beanpoles.

As we made our way across the garden dome, I saw the broken remains of the little robot from before, smashed on the asphalt of the running track.

In the mess room, the walls were singing a happy song about vitamins.

I suppose you couldn't say the trouble *started* that lunchtime, as it had actually been going on for days, but this was when it started coming out. And it was all because of what happened with the spinach.

"Maybe Dr. Muldoon would help," I said when we'd found a couple of places together at one of the long tables. "Maybe she'd take you on as a sort of assistant, and then you could become indispensable, and then she'd do some sort of appeal so she could keep you."

"I could let her do experiments on me," said Josephine, sounding faintly hopeful. Then she looked at me in a wondering way. "But you'll still have to go. Don't *you* ever mind it at all?"

"Well, of course. But I don't hate it like you do, and I'm not bad at it. . . ." I shrugged. "And I never expected I might get to do anything else, so it's different."

"Don't you ever even think about what you could be, if you didn't have to be in the army?"

"No," I said firmly.

Then the trays of food started gliding down the conveyer belts on the tables, and everyone started groaning, just as Carl arrived suddenly and emphatically in the seat in front of us.

"Right," he said. "This has gone too far."

We both knew what he meant, even before we saw what was on the trays.

Spinach.

Now, back at Muckling Abbot, all the dinner ladies (except Mrs. Skilton, who usually just snarled) were always going on about how there was a war on and we couldn't be fussy, and in principle that's fair enough. And it's not that I hate spinach, because it can be all right. But lately some program in the kitchen computers had gotten completely fixated on spinach, and we'd been having little processed bricks of it, sort of half dry and half soggy, at every meal for *days*. And if you didn't eat it, you only got more at the next meal, and the robots sang even more songs about nutrition. Plus, it wasn't as if we didn't *have* other vegetables growing in the garden.

"I mean, does anyone seriously think the *grown-ups* are eating this?" Carl said. "I don't see any of them here, do you? Hey, are you okay?" he asked Josephine, whose eyes were still rather red.

Josephine gave a noncommittal growl.

"Good. You're in then, right?" said Carl, and bounced up to stand on his chair and announce passionately, "They can't make us eat this! Not over and over again. It's not fair!"

"Sit down, Carl, please," said the Goldfish, pleasantly but firmly.

"I want to talk to a *person*," said Carl. "Where is everyone?"

"He's right. The adults can't really be putting up with this," I said. "Some of them had *champagne*."

That caused a discontented grumble to ripple across the tables.

"Please sit down, Carl," said the Goldfish and

the Sunflower, in mildly sinister unison. When Carl didn't, the Goldfish and the Sunflower and the Star and the other floating robots sort of slowly closed in and hung there on either side of him, uncomfortably close, staring at him with their glowing plastic eyes.

I couldn't imagine they were really going to hurt him, but it was the creepiest thing I'd ever seen the robots do, and for a moment everyone in the mess room went quiet. Carl *might* have sat down and done as he was told, I think, and if he had maybe everything would have gone differently, at least for a while.

But then Kayleigh jumped up, and it all kicked off. "I want to talk to a person too!" she said. "It was my *birthday* yesterday! And the computers *still* won't let me watch *Untying Paolo* and you robots are still making me go to bed at ten, and I'm *not* fifteen, I'm *sixteen*, and if they're going to send me off to fight Morrors next year, I should at least get to watch whatever I like!"

All Kayleigh's friends applauded and went "Wooo!" and jumped up as well.

The Sunflower went whooshing over to stare creepily at Kayleigh—but that was a mistake, because it left a space between the other robots for Carl to slip through. And when they tried to close in around him again, Josephine reached up and yanked on the Goldfish's tail and said grimly, "He's asking to talk to a person—what's wrong with that?" And everyone started yelling, and there plainly weren't enough robots to surround *all* of us. So instead, the robots all made a nasty high-pitched shrieking noise that I think was meant to subdue us, but it only made us feel more justified in making a lot of noise of our own. So Carl yelled, "Come on!" and we all ran out of the mess room.

We kept on running.

The loudspeakers weren't making jolly little fanfares anymore; the robots must have signaled them, and now they were whooping angrily. I think a few of the older teenagers decided the whole thing was beneath them, but otherwise it was all three hundred cadets of Beagle Base, the finest fighting force of seven- to fifteen-year-olds in the solar system, on the rampage.

Carl stayed in the lead, though he'd managed to fish Noel out of the melee and was steering him along beside him. We went into the dorms, and then we tried to get into some of the labs, but they all turned out to be locked.

Theoretically we were looking for A Person, but really we expected A Person to find us: I think we all expected that *someone*—somebody scary and in charge and *human*—would appear and we would all be in very serious trouble. And the more we expected it and the more it didn't happen, the more worked up we got.

We spilled across the garden dome, bouncing along in swooping Martian leaps, and the Teddy appeared and lumbered after us, honking, as if catching one or two of us would do any good. The kids darted easily out of the way, then surged back and knocked the Teddy over. The Teddy couldn't get up again after that, and it lay there waggling its plastic legs like an upturned tortoise, and we all shrieked and laughed and bounced onward.

Nothing happened. Nobody came.

We zipped up our uniform jackets and went outside. Some of us grabbed oxygen canisters, but not everyone bothered. The sky was dull and powdery, and there was a scouring pinkish wind sweeping between the hills. We could still hear the hooting of the alarms from inside, but it sounded a lot farther away than it really was.

We went round to the hangar where the spacecraft were kept. The huge doors were firmly shut, but there was a row of thick windows, and the mass of kids spread along the nearest wall, peering inside.

A couple of Flying Foxes were still there, but . . .

"The Flarehawks are gone," breathed Josephine. All the fighter craft were missing.

"You know what?" said Carl, turning to face all three hundred cadets. His voice rang loud even there, out in the wind. "There isn't anyone here. They've all gone and left us."

There was a breathless pause, then a soft flurry of voices—no one really *reacting* yet, just repeating it, translating it, into Hindi, Mandarin, Spanish. . . .

"What are we going to do?" whispered a girl.

For a second Carl looked wide-eyed and tight-lipped and just plain scared. But then he grinned.

"*Anything we want,*" he said.

10

Look at it this way. We were stuck on an alien planet with no parents or teachers. We could go out of our minds with terror, or we could just, well, go out of our minds.

Kayleigh's birthday party lasted three days.

Obviously the first thing we wanted to do was stop those stupid alarms. Of course it ended up being Carl who hung from one hand among the struts at the top of the dome and whacked at the speaker with a broken chair leg. Finally it went quiet and we all cheered, and Carl hooked his knees over the strut and swung upside down with his arms outstretched, whooping.

Then we celebrated. We raided the kitchen to find

something nicer to eat than spinach, and though the best we could find was some vaguely chocolate-flavored gludge and some underripe raspberries from the garden, it was certainly an improvement on the meal we'd been having when everything went down. Some of the older kids broke into the offices and labs to see if they could find any alcohol. They didn't find any champagne, only a couple of bottles of beer in a fridge, so no one got more than a mouthful, but it was the principle of the thing, I guess.

Josephine stood there in the middle of all this, looking like a computer program crashing, or like a person who does not have to do any flight and combat training for the immediate future, but who also doesn't like it when alarms go off and mobs of people run around shouting. That is to say, she didn't move or say much, until eventually, when pressed, she said, "Arrgh," and ran off.

By this time the robots had stopped hooting or staring and instead started following us around pitifully like unloved dogs, if unloved dogs were constantly trying to teach you algebra.

"Aww, kids, equations can be fun," pleaded the Goldfish, bobbing unhappily in the air.

"No, they can't," said Carl firmly, but not unkindly. And pretty soon we'd herded all the teacher robots into classrooms or closets and barricaded them shut. There was just the Teddy left, still lying on the sports field, flashing its eyes and waggling its legs. It wasn't particularly trying to teach us anything, but looking at it got kind of depressing, so we dragged it off to one side and threw gym mats over it.

But when things quieted down a bit, I took a plate of the chocolate gludge and wandered around listening for the sound of a doleful harmonica until I found Josephine in the rhubarb patch.

"Here," I said, "why don't you come out and play that? We need some music."

She looked dubious but followed me over to the sports field, where a hundred or so assorted kids were now sprawled in a daze of disbelief and accomplishment, and she never stopped playing, just gradually shifted the tone to something more cheerful. "Wooo, Josephine!" yelled Kayleigh, lazily raising an arm, and a lot of kids who normally weren't sure what to make of Josephine gave her a round of applause. Josephine didn't look up but smiled cautiously around the harmonica, and some of the other musical kids joined in. There weren't many musical instruments at Beagle, because you weren't allowed to take very much with you on the spaceship. But I guess the President of the EDF's nephew was a special case, because he had a guitar, and there was a girl who said she was a drummer in a band back on Earth, and she started whacking plastic chairs because we didn't have any drums. Kayleigh started dancing, and everyone joined in, and that was the nicest part of the adult-free phase on Beagle Base.

By the third day, a few things were slightly on fire.

I woke up sometime around noon in the supply closet. Christa and her boyfriend, Leon, had taken over our dorm room the night before, though we'd at least managed to rescue our duvets. It wasn't so bad. It was a big closet, and there is something to be said for having a ready supply of star-shaped stickers.

Getting to sleep as long as you liked, provided you could find a quiet place to do it, was a novelty on Beagle Base, and I only woke up because Josephine was shaking me awake.

"We've got to move," she said. "Gavin knows we're in here."

"So *what*?" I groaned, burrowing under the shelf with the highlighter pens and the Sticky Tack.

"Because he and his friends are coming and it's *bad news*," insisted Josephine, yanking at my arm. Neither Colonel Cleaver nor Miss Clatworthy would have approved of her current appearance: she now had her red scarf tied round her forehead like a pirate, hair erupting from underneath in a distinctly nonmilitary way. She also had a grim expression and a bloody lip.

"WHAT THE HELL?" I said when I saw it, sitting up at once.

"Gavin," said Josephine.

"Wha—?"

"Because he could," explained Josephine, in a maddeningly patient way, apparently finding me very dense. "And he doesn't like you very much either."

"*Right*," I growled, not quite sure whether to concentrate on the first-aid kit that I was sure I'd seen somewhere or on the dreadful things that ought to happen to Gavin. He might be fairly horrible, and have some horrible friends, and the same went for Christa and her crew, but it wasn't as if we were completely defenseless. I didn't think that we should let anyone push us around anymore; getting kicked out of our room was quite enough. Carl would be on our side, and he was more or less the king of a sizeable faction of kids. . . .

"Civil war of some kind is inevitable. Let's not *precipitate* it, shall we?" said Josephine, apparently reading my mind. She grabbed her bag from the floor and threw a handful of highlighter pens into it, just because they were there. "We need to talk about what we're going to *do*."

Regretfully, I let her lug me out of the stationery closet.

"Hang on a minute," I said.

Josephine dragged me down a passage of empty classrooms. Sure enough, I could hear some unpleasant laughter approaching that sounded a lot like Gavin and Lilly's gang.

"Where are we going?" I asked. Josephine hurried me through an unexpected outer door into the wind and dust of Mars, and I was glad that I was still dragging a duvet with me. I threw it over my shoulders like an awkward cloak.

"Up there," she said grimly, pointing across the scrubby ground at the communications tower—a great spindly cone of metal latticework blurred by the sandy wind. There was a drum-shaped cabin, presumably some kind of control or maintenance station, just below the final length of the antenna. And that was evidently where Josephine was headed, for in a few good running leaps she was over at the tower and climbing up hand over hand with a determination that would have made Colonel Cleaver proud.

I had gotten so much into the habit of running after her that I was soon following, even as I said,

"I am *not* holing up with you in some *bird's nest* on top of a *pole*."

"It's only temporary," said Josephine. "I can't get any of the comms working, but we can keep trying to get a message to Zond Station, and we'll at least have the high ground while we figure out what we're doing. And no one else is going to kick us out! *No one* wants to stay there."

Well, I could at least agree with her on that much.

"Look," I pleaded, "if you don't want to have a fight with Gavin, then all right, but can't we just . . . *not do* whatever it is you're doing? Why don't we stick with Carl's gang—"

"*Carl's gang,*" snorted Josephine derisively.

"Well, we'll be all right with them until the Colonel or . . . or *somebody* comes back. We're already in as much trouble as we can possibly be. We might as well enjoy what time we've got. They were going to go down to the sea today anyway and try to build a raft."

"Alice!" cried Josephine. "What if being in trouble is the least of our problems? *What if no one is coming?*"

We both stopped moving. She'd swung round and was staring down at me.

"They wouldn't just—" I began.

"*Exactly!* They *wouldn't just*. They didn't abandon us for *fun*. Don't you think something's happened to them? What if that thing happens to *us*?"

I looked down at the ground. I had been having nervous thoughts about just how long the food would last and whether the garden robots would keep on growing it; I just hadn't wanted to concentrate on them. I mumbled, "I guess we ought to get a bit more organized."

Josephine sighed so enormously she must have used up most of what little oxygen was in the air. "You're not going to be able to *organize* Gavin and Lilly into being productive members of a self-sufficient little farming community."

"Oh, come on!" I said. "The channels to Earth'll open up again automatically in another couple of months; we've only got to hang on till then. What are *you* suggesting?"

"*Leaving* and going for *help*, obviously," said Josephine witheringly.

"I don't know whether you've noticed, but we're on *Mars*," I said. "We can't exactly pop round to the neighbors for a cup of sugar."

"That's why we need to figure out how to get into the hangar," said Josephine.

I forgot about saving oxygen and made a long,

alarming noise that was sort of a laugh and a groan at the same time. "You want us to steal a *spaceship*," I translated.

"Only a little one," said Josephine. "I haven't figured out how to get past the locks yet, but we'll think of something. Obviously you'll have to do most of the piloting."

I dropped my forehead against the cold metal of the tower. "*Please tell me* you're not thinking I can fly you back to Earth."

"Well, probably not, but—"

"Probably!"

"I should think you're easily good enough to get us to Zond Station; that's only three thousand miles—"

"Three thousand miles!"

"Stop repeating everything. Zond's a proper military base. We'll tell them what's happened—we'll find out what's gone wrong! Either they'll be able to sort it out, or they can fly back to Earth before the channels open, and at least we'll be *away* from all of *this*." She waved a hand down at Beagle Base. Then she said more quietly, "And I want to know what happened to Dr. Muldoon."

"This is insane, Josephine," I moaned.

"There isn't a risk-free option! Just sitting around

here and hoping it all works out is the *most* dangerous thing we can do."

"Oh, you don't know that," I shouted. "I think crashing a Flarehawk in the middle of the Terra Sabaea sounds pretty dangerous!"

"Alice," said Josephine, more quietly than before. "People are going to start killing each other."

There was a long pause. The tower hummed in the wind.

"Now come on," she urged me at last, and started to climb again.

After a moment I started climbing too—but the other way, down to the ground. She called my name, but she didn't stop going her way, and I didn't stop going mine.

11

Over in the garden dome, Carl's gang of about fifty kids, mostly younger than thirteen, had built a camp in the middle of the sports field with mattresses and crash mats and a few tents made out of blankets and gym horses and things. It was a bit smellier and messier than it had been the day before, but it still looked festive, like some sort of carnival, what with the flags and paintings people had made. But I did notice there didn't seem to be as many kids around as before, and there was an argument going on among the ones who were left.

"We can't sit on our bums here forever—where's the fun in that?" Carl was saying.

"It's a bad idea to go anywhere," said a boy called

Ramesh. "We've got to protect our territory."

"We're not *dogs*," objected Carl, who was looking much more harassed than I'd ever seen him.

"I just don't think Christa and Leon were kidding about wanting us out of the dome," said Ramesh.

"Well, so we'll leave guards," said Carl.

But though several people seemed not to want to go down to the sea, nobody wanted to sit around and be a guard either, especially since guarding anything implies you're expecting to be attacked.

"Let's draw lots," Carl proposed.

"I notice *you're* not volunteering to stay," grumbled a girl called Mei.

"This whole thing with the boat is *my idea*!" cried Carl in exasperation. But he still grinned when he saw me. "Oh, hey, Alice, welcome to Carltopia," he greeted me. "You and Jo not joined at the hip after all, then?"

"I wouldn't call her that where she can hear you," I said. And I suppose I should have sat down for a sensible discussion about what we were going to do about Christa and Leon and Gavin and Lilly and all the horribleness that was brewing at Beagle Base. But I still couldn't really believe things could be all that bad after just three days without adults and robots. Anyway, nothing dramatically dreadful was happening right there where I could see it. I didn't want to be thinking about *territory* and *factions* and *guarding things* any more than Carl did, so I said, "What about building this boat?"

"Good question. What about it?" he asked the rest of the assembled kids. "Because *I'm* going to the sea. The rest of you can do what you like."

So it started out as a bad-tempered, muddled expedition, without anyone making any decisions about guarding the camp, and people just going or staying depending on what they felt like. And those of us who were going fought quite a lot about what we would make the raft out of and whether or not we should take sheets to make a sail with.

Noel said something about driftwood, but of course there wasn't any; the seas of Mars were too new for that. And though there must have been some hammers and nails and things in Beagle Base somewhere, we hadn't found them. But we did find plenty of empty barrels near the hangar that had once held liquid oxygen, and we had a table and some strips of plastic paneling that were torn off a wall at some point in all the excitement. Then Carl found some tough plastic-covered string stuff in the garden and decided we were ready.

"*Cavemen* could make boats without nailing

things," he said to the slightly demoralized band he was leading across the Martian countryside. "And so can we."

Somewhere between Beagle Base and the sea, the faraway little sun came out from behind a purple-gray sheet of cloud. The wind had died down, and though it wasn't *warm*, it wasn't freezing either. Cydonia was having its spring. Mei squeaked, "Rabbits!" and Noel corrected, "Arctic hares!" And whatever you called them, they were white and fluffy and adorable and hopping about the Martian tundra.

"They're there so their droppings add biomass to the soil," said Noel happily.

"And so we can hunt them," said Carl.

"Oh my god, I want one," said Mei, and we all agreed catching a baby one and keeping it as a pet would be the next order of business.

By the time we dragged our raw materials to the dunes, we were all much more cheerful, and the actual raft building was just as lovely as I'd hoped it would be.

"WE ARE THE FIRST MARINERS OF MARS!" yelled Carl into the silent lavender sky as soon as the amethyst sea opened before us. And I've never read about any of the earlier scientists or explorers using boats on the Borealian or the

Utopian seas, so he was probably right. We dropped everything and ran down to the water to start kicking it about and shrieking at how cold it was. I found tiny white flowers growing among the red rocks and thought it was wonderful that even with a gigantic war going on, humans could make flowers grow on a planet that used to be dead.

Obviously, when we lashed the table to the barrels with the string, the resulting raft was not particularly seaworthy and it fell apart before very long, but it *did* last until everyone had had a ride on it. And as I was lying on the tabletop, looking up at the passing snow geese, with Carl using a pole from the gardens to punt through the shallows, I thought that being kids alone with an entire kid-sized planet to play with really wasn't so bad.

Then I wondered what Josephine was doing, and that made me feel uneasy and a bit guilty, so I tried to stop.

The string holding the raft together came undone again, and no one felt like fixing it this time so we left its ruins on the shore as a monument to the expedition. Even then, although we'd all started shivering a bit and Mei said her hands had gone numb even inside her gloves, we weren't in a great rush to head back. No one wanted to say that we were scared we wouldn't like what we'd find. And anyway, Noel wouldn't let us leave until everyone had had a look for his flying worm thing, but we didn't find any sign of it.

But eventually it started to get dark. We were all very cold and wet, despite the fact that our suits and boots were supposed to be waterproof, and we were also a little bit oxygen deprived, which might have been why we got slightly lost on the way back to Beagle Base. It didn't last all that long, but it was enough to spook us, and even when we did see the domes rise over the horizon at last, the relief felt unsatisfactory and achy because we weren't really home, everything was sort of a mess, and we didn't actually know what would be going on inside.

I looked up at the communications tower. Josephine couldn't really be planning to spend the night up there, could she? I decided I'd look for a decent spot on a crash mat somewhere in "Carltopia" and get something to eat and then try to find her, though I really didn't fancy climbing the mast in the dark.

The sliding doors opened for us, the same as ever, and we got a nice head-clearing rush of oxygen and warmth.

Then we smelled the smoke.

In the middle of the sports field, Carltopia was a

wreck—all torn apart and scattered, and to make a point, someone had set fire to one of the crash mats, which was pouring awful-smelling smoke everywhere.

Carl gave a yell of indignation and rushed straight for his ruined kingdom, and at that a lot of unfriendly-looking kids appeared, namely Gavin and Lilly and plenty of others, all of whom seemed remarkably much bigger than us, though that might have been the effect of the chair legs—and the legs of dismembered garden robots—that they were carrying as weapons.

"Hey, idiots," said Gavin. "New rules. None of you get to come in the dome anymore."

"Yeah, that's totally something you get to decide," scoffed Carl. But he sounded uncertain.

"Leon made a list, you're not on it," said Gavin.

"Don't be stupid," I said, and they all snickered. "Lilly—Lilly, let's just go and talk, okay?"

But she looked at me as if she didn't know who I was, as if something awful had gotten inside her and eaten away the person I'd thought so normal-looking the first day we arrived on Mars. She didn't look normal anymore; none of them did. They all had an expression I'd never seen before, but it was a little like the look on Christa's and Leon's faces when they were hitting that little robot until they broke it—flushed and breathless like that, but much wilder and more desperate, and I wasn't sure they could stop now even if they wanted to.

"Lilly," I tried again, backing away as the gang of kids advanced.

"Wait, not yet," said Lilly to Gavin, and for a moment I thought it might be all right. But then she said, "Get their tablets and stuff off them first."

The next part wasn't pleasant. By the time it was finished, I was missing my tablet along with a clump of my hair, and my shin was bleeding where Lilly had hit me with a robot's leg. I would have thought Carl would stay and fight like anything, but when at last Lilly shoved me back and the gang laughed and withdrew, Carl and Noel had already vanished. Mei and the rest were scattering too.

I limped after them at first. But then we passed the communications tower and I broke off and called, "Josephine!" up at it.

It came out sounding feeble. The wind was picking up again, and I didn't think she'd have heard. I climbed a few experimental steps up the frame, but my leg hurt a lot and I couldn't even see the top of the tower. I mostly thought Josephine probably wasn't up there anyway. So I came back down.

Mei and everyone else had disappeared into the dark by this time. I supposed the sensible thing would be to camp in the wheat dome or the soy dome and hope things looked better in the morning. Some kids were sleeping in them already, and I knew it was all right, if kind of scratchy. Or maybe someone had managed to get into the grown-ups' block, and then we could really be comfortable, at least until Leon and Christa kicked us out of there too. But had they really taken over the whole center of the base—the ring with its segments, as well as the dome? And what about the kitchen and the food storage buildings?

I was getting extremely hungry, apart from anything else.

What I decided I'd do was creep around the external doors and see how things looked, and if I could get in without being seen and find any food.

And I did still have the idea that if it came to it, everyone else might start being sensible if I could just be sensible enough toward them. I could find Kayleigh, I thought, or maybe Chinenye. Kayleigh wasn't necessarily that sensible all the time, but she was older and probably on my side and she had a lot of friends, and she *had* managed to get Gavin and Lilly to back down when we were all on the

Mélisande. The scarier kids wouldn't have things nearly so easy if all the reasonably nice people stuck together and looked after each other. Maybe the scarier kids would see that and they'd settle down and be vaguely normal.

Although if they didn't, it did sound a bit like two rival gangs poised for something close to the civil war Josephine had predicted. . . .

I went back to the door Josephine had dragged me out through hours before, and after peering warily through the windows, I put my hand on the sensor panel and went inside.

No one was about. It felt so wonderfully warm after being outside. Finding a bathroom was equally welcome. Then I ran on tiptoe through Beagle Base, peeking round corners as I went.

There was some kind of noisy fight going on in the garden dome.

While I hadn't run into anyone unpleasant, I wasn't finding the confident crew of nice people I'd been hoping for either.

In a classroom in the southwest segment, a group of girls was sitting on desks and chatting, but none of them was Kayleigh or Chinenye and I thought I'd seen at least a couple of them hanging out with Christa, so I didn't talk to them. And though I did find nice, safe-looking hideaways in dorm rooms and laundries, I kept thinking I didn't fancy it on my own and that if anyone did find me there, I'd be trapped.

That made me think of the simulation deck, which I was pretty sure had a door of its own to the outside. I crept down the dark corridor, expecting the deck would probably be locked, but when I got close enough, I saw someone had jammed the door open with a fire extinguisher. Without moving it, I poked my head through the gap and looked inside.

I had the immediate impression of furtive whispers going quiet, so I called, "Um, hello? It's just Alice."

Somebody shrieked, and Kayleigh scrambled out from behind a bank of seating. She looked dirty and red-eyed even before she hugged me and burst into tears.

"I thought you were Christa or someone," she said. She started back to look at my injuries. "Oh my god, you poor thing. Are they *looking* for you?"

"Shhhh . . . shh!" hissed someone else from behind the seats.

"Shh!" repeated Kayleigh to me unnecessarily, looking around with exaggerated caution, and we crept behind the seating, where Kayleigh and Chinenye and four other teenagers had made a kind of camp. It was not a very good camp, just a pile of blankets and a few empty food wrappers, the dim glow of a tablet for light, and a dismal unwashed smell in the air. Kayleigh looked pale and flinchy and Chinenye was curled in an exhausted ball, with one of the Russian boys mechanically patting her hair.

"I was looking for you," I said.

"Oh, wow," said Kayleigh, dragging her hands through her hair. "That's nice. But you're sure *they* don't know where you are? We really can't take any more trouble. Not after today."

I stared at her, feeling all my bruises start aching again. "Do you want me to go, then?"

"Oh, no," Kayleigh said, and she hugged me again and even tousled the pink bits she'd put in my hair. "Of course not. You can hide with us if you want. Alice can stay here, can't she?"

None of the others looked wildly enthusiastic, although Chinenye did manage to look up and sort of smile at me.

"You'll have to bring your own food, though," said one of the boys. "We haven't got any."

"I was thinking of getting some food anyway," I said.

"Oh, god!" said Kayleigh fretfully, twisting her fingers. "Be careful."

"Maybe you could come with me?" I suggested. "Or someone else."

There was an awkward silence. Chinenye dropped her head back into the Russian boy's lap. "We just can't," she said, without opening her eyes. "We can't go out again tonight. It's not worth it."

"We think lying low here until the Colonel gets back is our best bet," Kayleigh explained.

"Even if you *starve*?" I said, beginning to get irritated with them all. They didn't answer. "I was thinking we should start making plans in the case that nobody *does* come back."

"Oh, don't say that!" Kayleigh said, starting to cry again. "They will. They have to."

I wondered if somehow I'd been imagining her as bigger than she was, because now she seemed sort of shrunken.

"I'll come back later," I told her. And then added, "Maybe," and went back to the corridor. I'd get into the food store from outside, I decided. That would be safer, and then I'd take whatever I could find over to the wheat dome, and maybe somehow everything would look a bit better in the morning.

I went back to the air lock. There was an oxygen pump there, so I refilled my canister and put the mask on before I went outside.

It was black and cloudy and I only had the glow of the dome to find my way by, but I managed to get into the food store beside the kitchens. I couldn't find the lights at first, and a couple of larder robots whirred past my shoulder in the dark, carrying a tub of soybean oil over to a shelf, and I clapped my hand over my mouth to keep from yelling out in shock.

When I'd got my breath back, I collected some dried Smeat bars and fruit, a block of cheese, some noodles and a tub of chocolate gludge, and then a few slightly more random things that had survived the other kids' raids, like a tub of sprinkles and some tomato ketchup. I put everything in a wire crate I found in a rack and carried it awkwardly outside and hid it behind one of the twisty pine trees near the entrance to the base. Even though I could lift such a lot in the low gravity, it was annoyingly bulky and the things inside kept sliding around, so it was too awkward to carry much farther on my own.

I should have gone straight to the wheat dome and gotten someone to help me carry everything. Unfortunately I decided I'd make another scouting trip and try to get some wipes and toothbrushes.

I went back in through the food store and the kitchens. They were close to the Processing Chamber where we'd had our uniforms dispensed to us on the first day, and with a bit of luck, I thought I might be able to make it and get something out of the machines. But this time, just as I was opening the door from the kitchen to Vogel Corridor, I heard someone coming.

All the internal doors on Beagle Base were old-fashioned ones with hinges and door handles like back at Muckling Abbot, so that no one got stuck if there was ever a power outage. It was only the doors to the air locks and outside that slid open and shut. I drew back into the kitchen, and the door clicked.

"What's that?" said a girl's voice.

"Just one of the kitchen robots," said a boy.

"No, it wasn't. It's one of those kids trying to hide. Come on." Their footsteps speeded up.

It was Christa and Leon wanting a snack, I suppose.

I retreated farther into the kitchen in the beginnings of a panic. I was sure they were coming inside, but there wasn't time to run back through the food store. I decided I didn't want to be found hiding in a closet, so I set my shoulders, pushed the door open, and walked out. "Hello," I said.

"You don't take a hint, do you?" said Christa.

"I wanted to talk to you," I said reasonably. "I know we've never gotten on that well, but things are different now. We've got to cooperate. We don't know if the grown-ups are even coming back."

"We're the grown-ups now," said Leon. "And you'd better learn to do as you're told."

"We need to at least work out how we're going to organize the food," I pleaded, backing away as they came closer. Not that I meant to be pleading, but pleading seemed to be what came out. "We've got to make sure the wheat and soy and everything gets harvested. We don't even know how long the robots will keep going or how to fix them if they break, and if this goes on for weeks, people could *starve*."

Leon grabbed my arm and dragged me down Vogel Corridor toward the garden dome. It was horrible how *easy* it was for him, that I was fighting as hard as I could and it didn't really do a thing. I'd had all that training to toughen me up. But so had he.

At this point Lilly and Gavin and all their gang came running to see what the noise was about, and they brought their chair legs and bits of robots.

"Hey, Lilly?" shouted Christa. "Isn't this a friend of yours?"

I did manage at this point to kick Leon in the knee as hard as I could. And he let me go—by throwing me toward Gavin and Lilly, and what with the gravity I went flying a scarily long way down the passage, even if I didn't land as hard as I would have on Earth.

This time, when they started hitting and kicking me, it was even worse than before, and for a while I ended up on the floor with my arms over my head thinking about what Josephine had said, that "people are going to start killing each other." But it didn't go on that long, I suppose, although it felt like it, and when they backed off I was not dead. They did not stop there, though. I scrambled up and tried to break away and Lilly and Gavin laughed at me for running. Leon grabbed me and said, "No, no, you wanted to get in, didn't you?"

He hauled me a ways down the passage and pulled out an old scaffolding pole or something jammed into the frame of a door, and flung me inside a dark classroom. I could hear them all laughing outside as they wedged the pole back in place to hold the door shut.

The classroom was a mess, all tumbled desks and chairs and burned gym mats someone had thrown in there. Not that I spent much time looking at any of that. I did what people trapped in rooms usually do: started banging on the door and shouting, "Let me out!" even though I knew it wouldn't get me anywhere.

After a while, I stopped and considered my situation. I reflected that it was just as well I'd been to the bathroom recently, but it wouldn't be much fun if I was still in here by the time I needed to go again.

Also I was still very hungry, and thirsty too.

I told myself they wouldn't *actually* leave me in there until I died, but I wasn't absolutely convinced. Even if they didn't really mean to do it, they might wander off to a different part of the base and forget I was there.

I stood with my forehead against the door and my eyes shut, and was just coming to the conclusion that I might as well have a little cry, when something came up behind me and boomed, "HEY THERE, ALICE," in my ear. I screamed.

It was the Goldfish. It was hovering delightedly right in front of my face.

I flopped limply against the door and swore, at length.

"Now, EDF cadets don't use language like that, do they, Alice?" the Goldfish scolded me, but it seemed too excitable to stick to the subject. "I sure am glad to see you, Alice!" it rejoiced. "We have so much to catch up on! Say! What about those quadratic equations?"

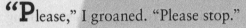

12

"**P**lease," I groaned. "Please stop."

I was lying on my back on a desk. I would have been staring hopelessly at the ceiling, but the Goldfish was bouncing about in the air above me, and it shone algebra problems into my eyes whenever I opened them.

It was also singing.

"Oh, little old x and negative b,
They can be equal, you will see.
When you plus or minus the square root,
Divide it all by 2a so it's neat and cute.
It's the fun that never ends,
Quadratic equations are our friends!

"Sing with me, Alice!"

It wasn't the Goldfish's *fault* that it was programmed to teach children the EEC standard syllabus, or that, in its roboty way, it seemed to feel terrible whenever it couldn't. On the whole, I was glad it was there. For one thing, it glowed, and it would have been very dark in the classroom without it, as someone had smashed the lights. It took my mind off how long it would take to die of hunger and thirst, and made me focus instead on just how well educated a person could be *before* she died of hunger and thirst.

It was very annoying, though.

"Can't you just *try* and get us out of here?" I begged, picking at a bandage on my hand. The Goldfish had at least helped me find the first-aid kit. I had patched up my various injuries very thoroughly, because the Goldfish didn't try to teach me anything while I was doing it.

"I already have, Alice," said the Goldfish sadly. "But hey! At least we've got plenty of time to *learn*! Now, what do you think that *x* might be?"

"Four," I said sulkily, screwing my eyes shut.

"Aww, come on, Alice! I know you can do better than that."

I sighed and opened my eyes a crack. "Nine," I admitted.

"Great work, Alice!" the Goldfish cheered, and emitted a stream of sparkling stars over me like confetti. "So, let's try another equation. . . ."

"Oh, god, please," I said desperately. "Please, can't we at least do something else? Can't we do . . . biology? I *like* biology."

The Goldfish seemed to hesitate. It tilted slightly in the air, as if it was putting its head on one side.

"Biology?" it repeated, almost warily, as if I might be playing a trick on it.

"Yes," I begged. "What about . . . cells. You know, the difference between plant and animal cells, and . . . and DNA and everything. Because I think all that's *fantastic*."

The light behind the Goldfish's eyes pulsed thoughtfully. "*Fine*," it said in a very grim voice for such a cheerful robot, and the glowing equations hanging in the air vanished and were replaced by friendly diagrams of eukaryotic cells.

I felt pathetically grateful. I really do like biology, even if it was fairly low on the list of things I wanted to be doing just then.

"Can I go to sleep afterward?" I asked. "It's ever so late."

"Okay, Alice," said the Goldfish, sounding a

little mournful, and I wondered if it was thinking about how neither biology nor quadratic equations was going to give us a better morning to wake up to.

"And Goldfish," I said forlornly, "when we've done the parts of the cell, and if I really concentrate, could you maybe . . . tell me a story? Or even sing a song, so long as it's not about algebra?"

The Goldfish came closer, and I actually leaned my face against it. "Sure," it said gently.

Half an hour and plenty of organelles and cytoplasm later, I was curled up on the desk while the Goldfish glowed and sang softly in Mandarin.

This is going to be embarrassing if anyone finds out about it, I thought. But then I realized that if I was ever in a position where getting teased for asking a robot fish to sing me a lullaby was my most pressing problem, life would have improved immeasurably and I'd have no business complaining.

"What does it mean, Goldfish?" I murmured sleepily, hoping it wouldn't see it as an opportunity to be educational.

The Goldfish obligingly projected subtitles into the air without stopping singing, and I was too tired to read them all the way through, but it was something about the moon and a river and being a long way from home.

And so I fell asleep.

✩

I don't think I slept very long. It was just as dark and felt just as empty around the classroom, except something was happening outside the door. The pole was scraping and creaking in the doorframe, and someone was grunting with effort to pull it free.

Someone laid the pole quietly and carefully on the ground. I sat up.

Josephine stood in the doorway, her eyes wild under her pirate scarf. "Alice," she said. "Do you still have any objections to stealing a spaceship and getting the hell out of here?"

Later I couldn't help but wonder if she might have practiced saying that, but whether she had or not, the effect was excellent. All I said was "None at all," and ran to join her, thinking I'd never been so glad to see anyone in my life. I grabbed the first-aid kit on the way, because I had the feeling that where we were going, we might need it.

The Goldfish came sailing after me into the corridor, just as glad as I was to be free.

"Stop *glowing*, anyway," I hissed when it didn't go away.

I don't think the Goldfish was physically able to stop glowing altogether, but it did dim itself until only its eyes were hovering points of blue light in the dark.

"How did you find me?" I panted as we ran.

"A kitchen robot saw it all happen," said Josephine. "Sorry it took me a while to get to you."

"But . . . what? The kitchen robots don't even talk!"

"No, but the Sunflower does," said Josephine. "It was shut in the laundry. I persuaded it to access all the visual records from the security cameras and the other working robots until it found you. It told me the code to get into the hangar too."

"How?" I asked. "Why should it do any of that?"

"Because I had something it wanted." We'd reached the main entrance lobby. Josephine slammed her hand onto the sensor panel to open the doors. "I let it teach me Spanish for four hours." She looked at me and grinned. "*¡Hola!*"

The night air was freezing by now, and as it hit me in the face, so did the reality of what was happening. Oh, god, I thought, she wants me to pilot a *spaceship*, in the *dark*, and fly off to find help that might well not exist, thousands of miles away *on Mars*.

It felt even more alarming when I actually *saw* the spaceship—well, technically it was barely a spaceship: it was another Flying Fox, which was only designed to zoom around sub-atmo but could have probably gotten us to Phobos if we'd wanted. But what was worrying me was that Josephine had managed to pilot it out of the hangar herself, but had promptly veered off the runway and crashed it into the obstacle course. The Flying Fox seemed to be okay, though the monkey bars didn't.

"Wait," I said, swallowing a cold feeling in my throat. "What about—how are we actually going to do this? What about supplies?"

"I've got everything we need!" insisted Josephine, swinging her shoulder bag, full, as I knew, of duct tape, rocks, and a stock of highlighter pens.

"What about food? What about oxygen?"

"What about your biology textbooks?" added the Goldfish, concerned.

"Go *away*, Goldfish!" I snapped, swatting at it.

"Oh," said Josephine, deflating slightly. "Well, there's an oxygen pump in the Flying Fox, but . . . I didn't really think about food."

"It's all right," I said. "I've got a whole crate hidden. Look, get in the ship and have some proper oxygen. I'll go and grab it."

Josephine looked a bit dubious, but she did as I said, and I scrambled off over the rocks and between the scrubby bushes of Beagle Base.

The Goldfish was still with me. I felt a bit mean about trying to shoo it off, because it had been nice to me in its own way while I was alone in the classroom, but it was clearly only going to be a nuisance.

"What are you doing, Goldfish?"

"I'm looking after you kids, Alice," it said, as perkily as ever. "That's what I'm here to do!"

"Well, not to be rude," I said, dragging the crate out from its hiding place, "but you haven't done a very good job of it so far."

The Goldfish sank in the air and the lights in its eyes got very dim indeed. I felt mildly awful, because the Goldfish and the other robots shouldn't really have been expected to handle three hundred rioting kids all by themselves, but after the day I'd had, I thought I had some excuse.

Then it brightened up, both literally and figuratively. "Then, by golly, I'm going to do *better*," it resolved, and stuck to me with even greater determination.

"Alice!" someone hissed, a few feet away.

"*Oh, what now?*" I said, having had quite enough of sudden surprises for one night.

"What are you doing?" asked Carl, appearing out of the dark. He looked pale and disheveled. I wondered for the first time how *I* looked.

"Never you mind," I sniffed, gathering up the crate.

"But you're all right, though? They didn't rough you up too bad?"

"No thanks to you." I was not very happy about the way he'd disappeared when Lilly and Gavin's gang jumped us.

Carl looked unhappy about it too. "I'm sorry! I had to get Noel out of there. I *had* to," he said. "I thought you were behind me. I've been looking for you, I swear."

"Well, fine," I said, in that disgruntled way when you see someone's point but aren't in the mood to be nice to them yet.

"Are you running away?" said Carl, looking me over. "You are, aren't you? Awesome. Where are you going? How are you doing it?"

"None of your business," I grumbled, trying to stalk away from him and finding myself hampered by the fact he'd taken hold of one end of the crate and was trying to help me carry it.

"Where are we going?" he asked. "Hold on a sec, and I'll get Noel. He's in the soy dome. I'll be two minutes."

"You're not coming!" I cried.

Carl skipped the yes-we-are/no-you're-not part of the conversation and just asked, "How are you going to stop us?"

"We'll all stick together," announced the Goldfish. "TEAM! It stands for Together Everyone Achieves More!"

"Oh, for god's sake, go away, Goldfish," Carl ordered it. "We're *running away*. That means not bringing teachers."

"Well, it's like you said to Alice, Carl," said the Goldfish airily, though I felt there was a suggestion of menace in its voice. "*How are you going to stop me?*"

The two of them stared each other down for a moment before Carl decided that dealing with the Goldfish was my problem. "I'm getting Noel."

I didn't wait. I went on hurrying back to the Flying Fox with the Goldfish skimming along beside me, but I had to keep putting the crate down all the time to change my grip, so Carl and Noel caught up quite easily.

"Hello, Alice. Goldfish," said Noel politely, as if running away in the middle of the night was a perfectly routine thing to be doing.

Josephine popped out of the Flying Fox as we approached, and scowled as she saw the crew of tagalongs I'd picked up.

"Why did you bring *them*?" she demanded.

"I didn't *bring* anyone!"

"She's right," said Carl easily. "We invited ourselves."

Josephine didn't stop scowling.

"Well, Carl is a good pilot." I sighed. "And the Goldfish . . . knows stuff."

"*I* know stuff," said Josephine, aggrieved.

"Yes, of course you do," I agreed soothingly, "but you know the Sunflower was useful already."

In a way, none of it mattered, because the Goldfish, Carl, and Noel were all piling into the Flying Fox whether we liked it or not, and it would have taken a serious physical fight to even try to get them out. I for one was not up for that.

Carl and I did fight a little over who got the controls of the Flying Fox. For some reason, I wanted to be the one to do it. An awful lot of things seemed to have happened *to* me recently, and I wanted something to be happening because *I* was doing it, for a change.

Finally Carl let me have the pilot's seat. I backed the ship out of the obstacle course. Bits of it crunched worryingly around us, and I had time for more elaborately detailed visions of fiery death than even the best simulator in the world could come up with.

"You're doing great, Alice," said the Goldfish, hovering behind my head. "You can fire the thrusters now."

So I did, and for that second or so I could *feel* the ship fighting gravity—and it won; we won, and we took off into the dark sky. And then we were flying over the nighttime valleys and hills of Mars.

13

I went very slowly for what the Flying Fox was capable of—which is to say, about four hundred miles an hour. I screamed only occasionally, even though there was a ferocious wet wind coming the other way, scouring over the Gulf of Chryse. The Goldfish helped me, and Carl tried to help me too. At least, that's what he said he was doing. In practice it was more that the Goldfish would suggest I do something and I would try, and Carl would say, "No, no, not like *that*," and "Are you *sure* you don't want me to take over?"

Then Josephine sighed, leaned across, and quietly *did* something to him I couldn't see on account of not daring to take my eyes off the viewport. Carl yelped, "OW! What did you do that for? I'm only trying to help," and though he was not actually quiet after that, at least he wasn't bothering *me*.

But I was not going to keep this up for very long in the dark. It was about two in the morning or something equally awful by now. We were on our way, and far beyond Leon and Christa and Lilly and Gavin, and that was the main thing.

"We've got to stop and rest. I need something nice and flat to land on, Goldfish," I warned, trying not to sound panicky about it. We *were* flying over something nice and flat at the time, but it was the sea.

"That's okay, Alice, just bear south-southwest, forty k," it said soothingly. It was interfacing with the Flying Fox's computer, which was handy.

I skimmed over the dark coast, activated the lifters, and lumbered down on them before dropping the Flying Fox rather awkwardly onto something. It bounced around a bit before it stopped completely, and we all yelled, except for the Goldfish, and Noel, who slept right through it.

Silence settled in around us.

"Are we there yet?" asked Noel, waking up.

I thought we would have to sleep wherever we could cram ourselves on the floor, but it turned out the Flying Fox was better equipped than that. You pressed a button and the hatch to outside popped open, and an egg-shaped pod with smooth, firm walls of glossy fabric ballooned itself out of a cavity in the wall, with little legs unfolding to the ground to support it. Or rather, the Goldfish pressed the button with its nose; we'd never have found it otherwise. I thought the Goldfish looked even smugger than usual after that, which should have been impossible as its expression couldn't really change and it always looked smug. The Goldfish called its discovery a Sleep Capsule and I called it an unusually impressive tent, but either way all we had to do was fasten some toggles and get the sleeping bags out of compartments under the seats.

We had Smeat bars and dried apricots for supper, and then we flopped into the tent. Carl dragged his sleeping bag over to the far wall and, with a dramatic huff, lay down as far from Josephine as possible.

"What did you *do* to him earlier?" I whispered to her when the Goldfish had turned out the lights and settled into standby mode.

"Nerve clusters," she replied darkly, and instantly went to sleep, leaving me wondering, rather anxiously, just why she knew about *those*.

But in the end I went to sleep too, without really

having much of a clue where we were, besides hundreds of miles from the nearest human being.

☆

When I woke up, I was alone in the tent, though I could hear Josephine's harmonica nearby, so I knew nothing too awful had happened.

Someone had opened a slit in the rear wall of the tent, and I poked my head out of it.

Hundreds of perfectly round little lakes and ponds were scattered across the red plain, shining in the sunlight as though someone had dropped handfuls of silver coins. And bright-green moss was growing on the rocks.

The Goldfish was resting on a hump of moss in the sunshine. Noel was lying on his front, letting a beetle run across his ungloved fingers and talking to it softly. Josephine was perched on the wing of the Flying Fox, swinging her legs and playing the harmonica.

"We thought we should let you sleep, seeing as you got so bashed up last night," Noel told me as I lowered myself down to the ground.

"Are you feeling better, Alice?" the Goldfish asked.

In one way I was feeling worse, because all the places I'd been hit had gotten more achy in the night, but the sun and the solar mirrors were bright in the lilac sky, the light was sparkling on the water, I'd successfully avoided crashing the spaceship into anything the night before, and we could now be completely confident of being left alone by Gavin and Lilly and Company, so I felt pretty good about life. "Yes, thanks," I said. Josephine tossed me a pack of crackers and dried fruit, and I started my breakfast.

Carl walked up from behind the Flying Fox. "Where are we, Goldfish?"

The Goldfish was very happy to be asked. "This is the Acidalian Plain, Carl," it began.

"The *Acidalia Planitia*," grumbled Josephine, who preferred the old Latin names.

"And look, you see those ponds and lakes?" went on the Goldfish. "Those are all craters left by meteor strikes, filled with water now because of terraforming! We're still north of the Martian dichotomy line, which is why the ground was nice and smooth for Alice to land on. If we keep heading south, things are going to get a whole lot more bumpy."

I started worrying about that, but Carl had other concerns. "Has anyone ever been here before us?"

The Goldfish tilted to one side. "Well, I don't have articles about every exploratory trip before terraforming . . . but no, Carl, probably not."

I might have had a nice little moment of awe about us being the first people ever to be there, but before I could really get it going, Carl flung his arms wide in triumph. "THEN I AM THE FIRST PERSON TO DO A PEE ON THE *ACIDALIA PLANITIA*," he announced to the universe.

Josephine dropped her harmonica to utter a scoff of disgust, which only made Carl even more pleased with himself.

The Goldfish, however, seemed to take this as a prompt to start being even more teacherly and motivational. "Right, gang," it said, "anyone else need to go? No? All got your teeth clean? Good. Then . . ." It did a joyous swirl in the air. "*Iiiiiit's history time!*"

"Oh, not this again," I said.

"Goldfish, if you can't understand why it isn't history time, then you'd better go home," said Josephine, jumping down from the wing of the Flying Fox. "Our priority is survival. We can't keep having this conversation."

"There's always time for the fall of the Roman Empire," said the Goldfish, its cheerful tone somehow stiffening.

"Look, none of that teacher stuff applies anymore," said Carl. "We're not doing lessons. You can't make us."

The Goldfish hung motionless for a moment, the light inside it quietly throbbing. "Can't I?"

Then its eyes flashed red, and we all jumped as something whipped through the air around the Goldfish and stung us like an electric shock.

"Ow!" we cried in unison, and then stood there staring at the Goldfish and at each other, and couldn't believe it had actually happened.

"Was that *corporal punishment*?" Josephine asked, incredulous.

"That's against the law!" cried Carl.

"Would you like to make a complaint?" inquired the Goldfish sunnily.

"Yes!" I said.

"Your complaint has been logged! Your feedback is important! NOW," roared the Goldfish in a blaring robotic voice, stripped of all perkiness and about two octaves lower than normal, "YOU WILL DO YOUR HISTORY COURSEWORK."

All we could really do was make outraged noises as we sat down on the ground and got out our tablets, or rather Josephine and Noel got out theirs, because the kids back at Beagle had stolen Carl's and mine.

"*I* never said I didn't want to do lessons," said Noel piously. "You didn't need to zap *me*."

I wondered if the Goldfish was planning to do a

full seven-hour schoolday right there on the *Acidalia Planitia*, or if it would just keep on teaching forever, zapping us whenever we tried to escape, until we all died of hunger or radiation. But after an hour, when Josephine groaned, "We've got to get *moving*, Goldfish," the Goldfish agreed brightly, "Okay, time to go!" and floated off into the Flying Fox, content.

An hour of schoolwork a day, then, I thought. It wasn't an unreasonable price to keep it happy.

So we started packing up, and I looked into the food situation. There was still quite a lot left.

"I guess we should be at Zond by this evening," Noel said.

"We should save some of this stuff anyway," said Carl. "In case anything goes wrong."

And it was just as well we did.

"I wish there could be toast," I said.

"I wish there could be champorado," said Carl.

I glanced at him. "Hmm?"

"It's this kind of chocolate rice porridge—you have it for breakfast with dried fish."

"Oh. That sounds nice!" I said, trying to make a face like I meant it.

"Yeah, I know, you think it sounds disgusting," said Carl tolerantly. "All white people do, and you're all wrong. We really only have it now when Auntie

Marikit comes round. Well, we *did* have it then, I guess." He rifled through the stock of Smeat bars and dried apricots, but there was nothing in there like Auntie Marikit's champorado, and he sighed.

"I miss popcorn," said Noel.

"You're kidding," Carl said. "Mars wouldn't be far enough to get away from that stuff."

"I miss the smell," said Noel, a faint quaver in the back of his voice, and Carl's expression tightened before he forced a grin and scrubbed his hand annoyingly over Noel's hair.

"Your parents work in a cinema?" Josephine deduced.

"They *run* the cinema," said Noel proudly.

"Yeah, I've been sweeping popcorn off carpets since I was six. We all practically bleed the stuff now," said Carl. "Guess you can take the boy out of the cinema, but you can't take the cinema out of the boy." He jostled Noel's shoulder, then obviously remembered he was talking to Stephanie Dare's daughter. He looked a little defensive. "Mum's in the reserves *too*. And Dad's a shock-ray warden. And Dad *used* to be in the regulars. But he got hit over the South Shetlands, and it messed up his nervous system."

I grimaced sympathetically.

"It's not that bad. He just shakes sometimes, can't always hold stuff, that's all. I'll get the Morrors back for him when I have the chance."

He cleared his throat and frowned into space, and we all went back to focusing firmly on packing up our supplies. We didn't have anything left to drink, though there were water-purifying tablets and a filtration kit (which was slightly disappointing to Noel, who had been looking forward to boiling drinking water over a fire, even though it's really hard to get water hot in an atmosphere as thin as that).

We walked down with our empty bottles to the nearest lake. It was all so beautiful, with the glitter on the water getting into the air and everything so new and untouched and quiet.

"Has this got a name?" wondered Carl, filling the bottle up.

"*Jerome Lake,*" said Josephine instantaneously.

Carl frowned and brooded on this for a moment. "Fine," he said, and took a swooping leap to land boot deep in the next pool. He called back, "But *this* is Dalisay Waterhole."

"And *this one's* Dare's Pond!" I said.

And then we were all boinging about and leaping from pool to lake and racing each other to name things. This game wasn't as much fun for Noel because of course he and Carl had the same last name, and he couldn't keep up with the rest of us that well, but then he got distracted by some shrimpy things he found in a puddle anyway.

After claiming Jerome Lake, Josephine seemed to be making much slower progress than Carl and me, but the two of us mostly lost track of which ponds were supposed to be ours pretty quickly. It turned out that Josephine had been using the pens she'd stolen from the supply closet to write her name on rocks before putting them back to mark the spot, as well as logging names, coordinates, and pictures into her tablet for posterity.

Carl looked down at the slogan LOCH LENA neatly printed onto the broad red rock at Josephine's feet and then gave her an aggrieved stare. "Lend me a pen, then," he said.

"No," replied Josephine serenely.

"Please," said Carl, making his eyes very big and sad.

Josephine tapped a pen thoughtfully against her teeth. "All right. But on the understanding that this whole area," she waved her arm, "is called the Jeromiana Waterlands. Except for whatever bit you peed on. I don't want that."

So we took the pens and kept on boinging around

until we'd given everything in sight names that got fancier and fancier, and then Carl wondered if the gravity was low enough to let you run across the water like a skimming stone, if you were fast enough.

"It won't work," said Josephine, and started to talk about gravity and velocity and stuff, but then Carl splashed her so she pretty much had to retaliate. And we almost forgot about Morrors and missing grown-ups and everything but being free.

This was all pretty absorbing, so it was a while before we noticed that Noel wasn't playing anymore. Instead he was waving and pointing at something in the sky and asking, "What's *that*?"

(Okay, possibly we had noticed but weren't paying much attention because he was the little one.)

"All right, what's what?" said Josephine finally.

"*There,*" said Noel, and we looked up. I couldn't see anything at first, just the mirrors tilting lazily on their slow drift past. Then I made out a streak of motion almost straight above us: five little dark specks falling out of the thin pastel sky.

No, not falling, *flying*—sweeping in at a steep angle toward the ground.

Spaceships? Maybe the adults had finally remembered about us?

Then, as I saw the color of the things—a dull

gray-green like the uniforms at Muckling Abbot—and my eyes worked out the perspective and I realized they were both a lot smaller and a lot closer than I'd thought, I took a step back on instinct. Foot-long conical things—just a bit, I thought, like airborne cucumbers on the warpath. But then they were closer still, and you could see the spinning segments and hear the dull grinding noise as they bored through the air.

One of them plunged into Crystal Mirror (mine) and one into the Cauldron of Doom (Carl's) and the splash sent up great white pillars of water into the air, descending in Martian slow motion. The other worm things went straight into the ground—drilling into the rock as soon as they hit it, as if it were as soft as sawdust. The Jeromiana Waterlands shook and we grabbed at each other so as not to fall over. Before we had much time to figure out how to react to any of this, three crooked furrows spread out from the three holes where the things had landed, as if something was plowing up the ground from underneath, and the buzzing sound got louder.

The worm things broke the surface, devouring everything in front of them, everything disintegrating under blunt, impossibly hard, impossibly *revolving* teeth.

"*Those* are my animals," said Noel, with a faint air of triumph.

We watched Noel's Animals, chewing up soil and plants and rock. A cloud of colorless dust rose behind them and floated away on the breeze.

"I don't like them," I said.

"They're interesting," insisted Noel loyally.

The two Animals that had landed in the water were not, apparently, any the worse for getting wet. They buzzed their way to land and began feasting on everything they found. They were, I suppose, too hungry to be picky.

"No," conceded Noel, tilting his head to one side. "I don't like them either."

"Uh," said Carl, in a slightly strangled voice, pointing upward. More specks were descending from the sky.

We had all drawn closer together. "Well, we could be taking some fascinating pictures about now," remarked Josephine, "or we could be running away."

The nearest worm thing reared up, and I could see the ring of tiny black eyes, motionless behind the whirring teeth. It was looking at us.

"I vote run," I said.

"Yes," agreed Josephine, "I think run."

"Why is this something we are *talking* about?"

demanded Carl, grabbing Noel's hand, just as Noel's Animals decided that we were probably better to eat than rocks and stones. Suddenly they sprang into the air and flew straight at us.

And so we ran. And thank god we were on Mars, where running was easy, and thank god we'd all had so much physical training. On the other hand, I wished we hadn't already been jumping about using up oxygen and energy so recklessly.

And if only we'd packed the tent back into the spaceship. It was still standing on its struts, bulging out the side of the ship.

I didn't look back, though the buzzing seemed to be practically in my hair now, and my own breathing and heartbeat were almost as loud. I bounded up and through the slit in the tent, and Carl threw Noel up after me and I dragged him inside. Then Josephine and Carl climbed in too, neither of them missing any pieces yet, but Noel's Animals were *right there* behind them. We charged into the ship, and Josephine and I started fiddling with the buttons to fold the tent back in, but at this point one of Noel's Animals drilled through the wall of the Flying Fox. It buzzed and bounced around inside like a very large flesh-eating wasp, so we got more preoccupied with screaming and looking for things to hit it with.

"Hey, what's going on, guys?" asked the Goldfish pleasantly, as the Animal bounced off the opposite wall, chewing a chunk out of it as it went.

"KILL IT, KILL IT, DO THE ZAPPY THING," I howled, ducking as the Animal flew at my face.

Carl hurled himself into the pilot's seat, grabbed the controls, and very rapidly got us out of there, which was great, except we were now lurching around in a small spaceship above Mars with:

a) the door still open

b) a big, bulgy tent hanging out of one side

c) a horrifying flying monster thing inside and trying to eat us

d) the rest of the horrifying flying monsters still coming after us.

The Goldfish gamely started trying to zap the Animal, but it isn't easy shooting a moving target in a confined space that is also moving, with a number of children you're programmed to protect right there. The air filled with the smell of scorched metal, and the Animal remained perfectly healthy. It lunged at

Josephine and ate a hank of her hair as she dodged out of its way.

"Get the tent in—I can't steady her," yelled Carl, unaware that this wasn't as much of a problem as the Animal on a beeline for his head. Josephine grabbed her bag, swung it by the strap, and batted the creature away from him. I was never going to complain about anyone carrying a bag full of rocks with them anywhere again. The Goldfish took another shot, but the Animal was too fast for it. Then, just to make everything even better, the ship swung over sideways so the wall became the floor, and Noel fell through the door into the tent, which was of course still open to the air at the far end.

"Noel!" I bawled, hurling myself toward it. Noel was still there, thank god, clinging to one of the dangling struts.

"Noel? What's happening?" asked Carl anxiously, dragging the Flying Fox through a terrifying swerve, which I was almost sure was going to shake Noel off. I heard the ship's guns go off, so I supposed Carl was firing at one of the Animals *outside* the ship.

"Nothing! Everything's fine!" I said in a ridiculously cheerful way, feeling that giving the pilot anything more to worry about wouldn't be productive.

"Uh, help, please?" said Noel, sounding vaguely embarrassed as the tent bounced and thrashed in the whirling air.

I really couldn't get near him. Fortunately we had somebody there who could fly.

"Get him, Goldfish!" I yelled, and the Goldfish stopped trying to shoot the Animal and dived into the tent.

Which left me and Josephine to tackle the Animal on our own.

Josephine swung her bag again, and this time it exploded against those whirring teeth in a shower of interesting stones and highlighter pens.

I swung a bottle of water (it was at least moderately heavy), and Josephine hurled one of her stones with excellent aim for someone who was so terrible at Flight and Combat Training. The Animal actually dropped to the ground for a second before bouncing back up at us again, and so for a while it was just a matter of us both yelling, *"Aaaaargh!"* and throwing anything that wasn't tied down. Most of what we threw got eaten, which at least slowed the Animal down. Then it came at me again, and as

I threw myself out of the way I knocked into the food crate, which I grabbed and emptied everything out of. Then I threw the crate over the Animal and jumped on top of it.

This happened so fast that even before I'd finished doing it, I was thinking, I'm not sure I thought that through, because the crate was made of plastic and the thing could chew through *rock*. Still, I guess suddenly being in a small space, especially after having been bashed on the head with a number of stones, must have slightly confused the Animal. It knocked about like a wasp in an upside-down glass for longer than I expected before it remembered its own *killer spinning teeth*. I had no idea what to do next when it bored through the side of the crate, but Josephine *stepped on its back* and pinned it to the floor, those awful teeth gnawing the air as it twisted and struggled and tried to get its maw to her feet. Then the Goldfish hovered back into the ship with Noel wrapped around it like a baby monkey, and I grabbed its nose and aimed it at the appalling thing under Josephine's feet, and shouted "FIRE!" and the Goldfish did exactly that.

The Animal twitched mightily and went still.

Josephine sat down abruptly on the floor. Someone, possibly me, must have finally gotten the tent inside, but I don't really remember much about it. The important thing was that Carl got proper control of the ship, and we shot away at top speed with a flying worm from outer space lying dead in Josephine's lap.

14

"**S**pace Locusts," said Noel. "We should call them Space Locusts."

"That's a good name for them," agreed Josephine. "Ow," she added, pulling her hand away from me.

"I've got to disinfect it," I said. "It might have . . . space germs."

The spaceship had rattled its way through a few hundred miles of sky before Carl had to drop us on a flat-topped mountain above a maze of jagged rifts and canyons scribbled in an angry mess over the ground. I'd gotten the first-aid kit out and was doing my best to patch everyone up: we were all a bit bloody, but the slice the Space Locust had taken out of Josephine seemed to be the worst. And then there were the jaggedy tears it had made in our uniforms—special high-tech made-for-Mars fabric isn't much good with holes in it. But duct tape turned out to be excellent for both problems.

Meanwhile, Noel, under Josephine's direction, had laid the worm on a rock and was trying to dissect it. He had taken pictures of its eyes (seven) and segments (nine), but the knife Josephine had found in the ship's survival kit couldn't get through the hard shell to find out what its insides were like.

"Okay, I admit I see the point of taking duct tape into space now," I said, using a piece of it to stick some gauze to the back of Josephine's hand.

"I told you, that was Lena's idea. And she's almost always right," said Josephine, sounding mildly disgruntled. "Goldfish, can you *very carefully* shoot a seam through the creature's exoskeleton?"

But the Goldfish couldn't.

We heard something go *clank* inside the spaceship, and Carl swearing. He had pulled off a panel (it was almost falling off anyway) and was burrowing around in the engines, so I guess it was a good thing he'd gotten some getting-into-the-guts-of-spaceships experience back on the *Mélisande* after all.

Josephine gave up on cutting open the Space Locust with a sigh. "I wish I could see what was going on inside this thing. But I suppose it doesn't really matter." She wrapped up the Space Locust in a towel and contented herself with patching the ruins of her bag together with duct tape and a staple gun, so that she had somewhere to put it. "Either the Morrors are breeding these things as weapons *or they aren't,* and this is a completely new problem. We've got to get it to the government."

"Yeah, that's great," said Carl, dropping out of the bottom of the Flying Fox. "But I don't know if we're going anywhere in this thing."

I'd actually been avoiding looking at the spaceship. It was fairly easy to do when there were people shaking and bleeding and a dead Space Locust there to concentrate on. But it turns out that when Space Locusts eat holes in your spaceship, the spaceship does not like it very much.

The Flying Fox was riddled with holes. There were important-looking cables that had been chewed through sticking out of it, and it was giving off an unhappy singed smell.

Carl went in and poked some buttons on the dashboard, and the ship whirred miserably and its lights flickered for a second before going out again.

"Carl, are we . . . stuck?" asked Noel. And being a bright but not particularly optimistic kid, he put the rest of it together pretty fast. "Are we going to run out of oxygen and die?"

"We're fine, Noel," said Carl grimly. "We're going to be fine."

"But what are we going to do?" asked Noel.

"*Math!*" blurted the Goldfish. But then it shook itself and said, "I do have some tutorials on spaceship repair."

So the Goldfish projected plans and talked us through the things that needed to be welded together and the leaks that needed to be plugged. Our problems were twofold. First, the people who made the tutorials had never really thought about being partially eaten by flying worms. Second, I soon got the idea that the main principle for learning spaceship repair is: Don't be crashed miles from anywhere on the surface of Mars when you need to do it.

Still, we stuck everything back together that we could, and Josephine worked out how to reroute the power around the broken bits, and the lights came on. Then Carl jiggled the controls around for about a thousand years and figured out that you now had to hold the control yoke at a special angle, and we finally got back into the sky. We all cheered, and the Goldfish covered us in sparkles. There is a limit to how pleased you can honestly feel about having to go flying in a ship that now resembles a colander, but you have to take what you can get.

But sure enough, about an hour later, smoke started wafting gently out of the paneling. And then we were heading for the ground at a few hundred miles an hour, out of control and on fire.

Valleys gouged between jagged red rock walls blurred underneath us at a nasty angle. Carl wrenched at the controls, which had stopped working altogether, and yelled, *"Somebody hold it!"* I crawled underneath the yoke and tried to hold it solidly at the special position so he could actually steer.

We came within a second of flying straight into a cliff face. Somehow we hit the valley floor instead. Bounced with an awful noise of crunching metal. Skidded. Stopped.

We sat there for a while, hyperventilating. Then, when we didn't really have an excuse for not doing it anymore, we got out to look at the damage.

It was awful. There was a trail of blackened bits of Flying Fox strewn back along the valley, and the ship was lying tilted over, propped on one fin, and even at a glance you could see three of its thrusters were crumpled like used chip packets.

"How far are we from Zond, Goldfish?" I asked.

"Oh, I make it one thousand three hundred and twenty-seven miles, Alice," the Goldfish said.

There didn't seem to be much to say about that. "We'd better get started," I said. And we got out our meager collection of tools and began again.

The thing about trying to fix plasma compression engines with a staple gun, duct tape, and highlighter pens is: you can't.

We kept trying, though. Even when the light faded and our fingers went numb, and we got weak and dizzy from the low-oxygen air and had to keep topping up our canisters from the ship's supply. At least that was still working.

"How long will that last?" I asked the Goldfish airily, as though the answer wasn't particularly important.

"Five days, three hours, forty-seven minutes, give or take," the Goldfish replied.

I kept on trying to work out if the three chunks of twisted metal in my lap could be made to resemble an inertial compensator if I applied enough superglue.

"Those things are still out there," muttered Noel.

We looked at the sky. There didn't seem to be any Space Locusts in it, but we'd seen how fast they could move.

There didn't seem to be much to say about that either.

Eventually Carl said in a weird, forced, cheerful voice that didn't sound like him at all, "Guess there's nothing more we can do tonight! Let's get some rest while we can. We'll get straight back to it come first light."

There was a big hole in the tent, and none of us had the heart to try to get it set up anyway, so we just packed together for warmth into an unhappy pile of people at the bottom of the spaceship and tried to sleep.

I dreamed Mum flew down into the valley in her Flarehawk, and said she'd been looking for us for ages. It seemed so real that though I woke up a lot of times during the night, I found that I could shut my eyes and go on dreaming that we were on our way back to Earth. We landed on a sunny base somewhere in Africa, and Josephine was showing some military scientists the Space Locust, and Dad was there and we were drinking tea while I told them about everything that had happened. . . .

(I didn't go as far as dreaming the war was over and everything was completely fine. I guess that would have seemed too unrealistic and I'd have woken up.)

But eventually I did wake up, because something was making a pounding noise, sharp and ringing like someone hammering metal, annoyingly close.

"Whassat?" I groaned into a grubby fold of Space Locust–chewed sleeping bag.

"That's Carl," said Josephine dully. I sat up and looked at her. She was sitting in the pilot's seat, motionless. She somehow looked as if she'd been there a long time, and I wondered if she'd slept at all. "He's been doing it for hours."

I went outside to look. It was barely light. The two little moons were still pale in the sky, and the valley was striped with weird shadows from the columns of twisted rock that stood along its walls. Carl was kneeling on the ground, using a flat rock as an anvil and trying to bang some part of the engine back into shape with a stone.

"Are any of you going to *help*, or what?" he exploded.

Josephine appeared at my side, soundless as a ghost. "It's hopeless, Carl," she said softly.

Carl let out a strangled yell and hurled the bit of engine at the rock wall with all his strength so it bounced off with a noise like *SPANG* and the echoes clattered around the valley. Carl swiped one hand across his eyes. Then he turned round and said, so brightly he sounded almost like the Goldfish, "Okay! So we're going to have to get rescued."

Josephine put on her oxygen mask and quietly wandered away along the valley. I don't think Carl paid much attention. It wasn't Josephine he was talking to. He was talking to Noel, even though he couldn't quite look at him—Noel, who was sitting on the edge of the Flying Fox's wing, very still and huge-eyed and quiet. Carl went and pushed him off and wrestled with him a bit in a pointedly brotherly way. "Kind of embarrassing. We're never going to hear the end of it when we get home." His voice was even louder than usual. "What we need to do is work out how to get attention. There's probably a mirror somewhere in the ship we can use, to flash in Morse code or something."

"Goldfish, can you send out a signal that we're here and we need help?" asked Noel.

"Already doing it, Noel," said the Goldfish.

Carl looked briefly deflated.

"So there's nothing to do but wait," whispered Noel, looking at the ground.

Carl gave him what I guess was supposed to be an affectionately boisterous shove and yelled, "We're not going to just wait. That'd be . . . that'd be feeble!

Let's make a sign. You know. Just in *case* no one picks up what the Goldfish's doing."

We gathered stones and laid them on the ground to spell out HELP in big letters. Then we thought of adding an arrow pointing to where we were.

Then we ate a dismal lunch of Smeat and energy bars. Carl kept talking breathlessly the whole time: "This stuff is gross. What do they get paid for in those labs? I bet you I could synthesize something better out of sawdust, or . . . or Sticky Tack. I could murder a hamburger made of actual dead cow, I don't care what you say, Noel."

Noel was in fact saying nothing, so I felt I had to fill in some of the gaps. "You know, what I'd really like is spaghetti carbonara. I haven't had decent pasta in forever—they couldn't do it properly at Muckling Abbot either. My gran makes it with cream . . ."

I wished I hadn't thought about my gran. Or about spaghetti carbonara, come to that. And Noel still didn't say anything until at last we were finished. Then he looked over at our sign and asked, "What shall we do now?"

"Add an exclamation mark?" I said.

"Nothing left but to pass the time until they get here," said Carl shrilly.

So we played cricket. That was Carl's idea, obviously. Carl had a tennis ball, but cricket does not work very well with three people in low gravity with broken bits of spaceship for bats and wickets. Carl was blatantly letting Noel win, which was so unnerving that I got worried about Josephine and went looking for her.

She was perched on top of a twisted stack of red rock, high above the valley floor, her legs dangling. Her harmonica was lying on her lap, but she wasn't playing it. She was just staring into the distance.

"Um, hi," I yelled up at her.

"It's so huge," she said blankly. "You can't see from down there."

"Huh?"

"The Labyrinth. It goes on for miles."

The Labyrinth of Night. I hadn't quite realized we were in it.

"Come back," I said. "There might be Space Locusts."

Josephine hung her head. "I don't know," she said. "I don't know if I can do it."

"Do what?"

"Pretend to Noel that we're not going to die."

I felt a bit like kicking her and a bit like screaming.

I *did* know, in one way, that this was what Carl was doing, and what I was doing too. You don't want an eight-year-old to figure out that he's part of a small group of people who are all going to run out of oxygen soon. You probably don't want twelve-year-olds to figure it out either, but unfortunately no one was in a position to do much about it. But I didn't like her just *saying* it. "Well, someone *might* find us," I said desperately. "Where there's life there's hope."

Josephine sort of half smiled and gazed at nothing.

"It's cold out here," I said.

She climbed down and walked back with me in silence. We found Carl on the brink of volcanic overreaction to Noel having lost the tennis ball, and Noel was possibly about to burst into tears. Josephine shut her eyes at the sight of them before strolling over and saying with forced energy, "Let's get back inside. I know a game."

Actually she knew about a million extremely complicated word games, which I guess Lena had taught her on long car journeys. Josephine got very eye rolly when we forgot the rules, but she kept us occupied, and this was about as perfect for our horrible situation as anything could have been. She managed to keep typing something on her tablet while we were struggling to come up with a three-word phrase made up of words beginning with S in the form of a question, and eventually Noel curled up into a ball of half-shredded sleeping bags and went to sleep.

Carl looked at him and said, "Oh, god," and then lurched out of the ship. Josephine and I went too, and next thing I knew, Carl and Josephine were both collapsed against the wreck, practically cuddling each other.

"Thanks," he said. "Thanks for all of that. I couldn't. I can't." He put his head in his hands and said in a broken little voice, "Mum and Dad are going to be so angry with me."

"They're not," said Josephine. "They'll think you were amazing. I've written down everything that happened."

She showed him her tablet. Carl grinned shakily. "See, you're guilting them into making Jeromiana Waterlands official." He paused, reading on. "That's nice. Thank you."

"Your parents will be proud of you," said Josephine. "They'll be right to be."

Carl smiled, but began crying again too. "They're going to be *wrecked*."

Josephine swallowed. "I'm sorry. I was the one who wanted to run away. I stole the ship. This is all because of me. We should have stayed back at Beagle."

"Oh, that's bull, Jo. Everything had gone to hell back there—you didn't make that happen. You didn't munch a load of holes in the spaceship either. Everything was messed up to start with; you tried to do something about it. It's not your fault it worked out like this."

Josephine gave a crumpled laugh. "I guess at least it looks like I won't have to be in the bloody army."

"Ahh, if they gave you a chance and a decent laboratory, you'd probably win the whole war in, like, a day."

They went on telling each other in heartfelt terms how awesome the other was, and I didn't know why I couldn't bring myself to be part of this conversation. Part of me wanted to go and hug them and tell them they were amazing and that whatever happened, I was glad I was with them. But somehow I also felt like banging their heads together.

The Goldfish was a little ways off, hovering twenty feet above the valley floor, and I decided I'd go and chat. "How's the signaling going?" I called up.

The Goldfish's glow was very dull, and even its permanent smile seemed like a kind of torture, like someone had forcibly carved it onto its plastic cheeks. "I'm so sorry, Alice," it whispered.

"And evidently you can't think of anything to get us out of this," I added.

The Goldfish waggled dolefully in the air, and I understood it was shaking its head. "I guess I'm just not programmed for this."

"Me neither," I growled, and stomped back past Carl and Josephine, climbed into the spaceship, lay down, and pulled the sleeping-bag rags over my head.

"Alice," whispered Noel, "we're not getting out of here, are we?"

I knocked my head gently against the floor. "Of course we are," I said brightly.

"It's all right. You don't have to pretend right now. Except . . . except please go on doing it when Carl's around," whispered Noel. "I don't want him to know I know." And he burrowed into an even smaller ball.

I knocked my head against the floor more vigorously.

All that work we'd put into trying to fool him, and

apparently the only person still being fooled was me.

And that was even though, in the far distance beyond the hovering Goldfish, I'd seen many high-drifting plumes of dust, which probably marked the destruction the Space Locusts left in their wake.

In the morning (three days, sixteen hours, seven minutes of oxygen left) Josephine started playing her harmonica again. I'd never heard a harmonica sound so beautiful before, or so despairing. It was as though all the emptiness and shadow in the Labyrinth of Night was mourning for itself through her, using her mouth and lungs and the little metal box she held to pour itself into heartbroken sound.

And very annoying it was too.

"You're using up oxygen," I said.

Josephine gave a one-shouldered shrug and a sad smile, and might as well have yelled, *"I PREFER TO DIE A LITTLE FASTER DOING SOMETHING I LOVE"* for how subtle that was.

And somehow that did it. "OH, FOR GOD'S SAKE," I said.

"What's going on?" asked Noel, who'd been listlessly absorbed in some game on his tablet. By now I was shouldering my oxygen canister and wrapping up the nearest odds and ends and Smeat bars in a sleeping bag.

"I have had *enough*," I announced. "*You* can all sit around being tragic if you want. *I* am going . . . THAT WAY, to look for a way out of this. So." A little hiccup of mad laughter found its way up my throat. "Yes. I'm going outside. I may be some time."

"What the hell, Alice?" Carl said. But I jumped out of the spaceship and started marching off in what I thought was the direction of Zond.

The others tagged along, trying to reason with me or point out that I was an idiot.

"You can't *walk* a thousand miles on one tank of oxygen," Josephine snapped.

"Well, I'm going to give it a try," I said. "You can do what you like. You can come along and be *useful* if you want. But—" I waved my arms. "I'm *done* with this entire doom thing."

Josephine sighed. "Carl," she said apologetically and quietly, as if having gone loony I wouldn't be able to hear her. "I don't want her to go on her own. All right, Alice," she said more loudly, in a patient and noble sort of way. "I'll come with you."

"No!" I yelled. "You can come with me if you're

going to *help*. If all you're going to do is trail along looking like you just dropped your ice cream, then you're not allowed!"

"What do you *want* me to do?" snapped Josephine, and she sounded just a bit more alive.

"Think," I said. "You're some sort of bloody genius, aren't you? What's the use of that if you just sit there and wait to die? Just *try*, can't you?"

"I can't!" Josephine cried. "It's not fair to put that on me. What do you think *I* can do that you can't? *You* haven't got any ideas either!"

"Yes, I have!" I said. "*I've* got the idea of walking that way until I somehow bump into something that'll help. And if you think that's stupid, then *you* could at least try and think of something better!"

"*There isn't anything better!*" shouted Josephine. "God! Just because I'm not bad at exams . . . doesn't mean I can do *magic*, Alice. We don't have any oxygen, we don't have enough food—there was hardly anyone or anything to help on this planet even before they all ditched us, and now there's *nothing* out here except—"

And she stopped. There was total silence.

". . . except?" I breathed.

"Except . . . ," said Josephine again, though I

don't think she even heard herself or knew she was still talking. She turned slowly, eyes wide and unfocused, facing back the way we'd come.

"*What?*" Carl asked, earsplittingly.

"Robot pals," whispered Josephine. "Robot pals! Goldfish!" She started jumping and waving, and the Goldfish swooped down from its signaling station above the valley floor. "That lesson," she went on breathlessly. "Do you remember? We were learning about *Noctis Labyrinthus* and . . . Goldfish! Carl said there were only a few hundred people on the planet, most of them us, and Goldfish, you said there were plenty of your *robot pals.*"

"Sure, Josephine," said the Goldfish, startled out of its gloom and as happy she'd remembered a lesson as if we were all still back in the classroom.

Josephine grabbed the Goldfish and stared into its plastic eyes. "Are there any of your robot pals near here now, Goldfish? *Big* robots?"

Lights flickered in the Goldfish's eyes as it thought—or rather, I supposed, scanned—for nearby robots. "There are some seed planters and soil testers and earth movers about ten miles off—"

"HA!" yelled Josephine. She kissed the Goldfish's plastic face and turned an unexpected cartwheel.

"We're going to do *what*, exactly, with the robot

pals?" asked Carl, in a slightly snarky way that was obviously the result of trying not to be too hopeful.

Josephine came right side up again, eyes shining. She said, "We're going to *catch* one."

15

The Goldfish raced along as if it were swimming downstream with a strong current behind it, and we chased after it.

We slogged along the twisting valleys and climbed black-red slopes of gravel and razor-edged walls of stone, up onto the broken islands of rock called horsts and then, dishearteningly, we'd have to scramble down the other side and do it all again. Finally we found ourselves standing on a flat roof of rock with such a deep crevasse between us and the (apparently) unbroken ground that we wanted to get to that Josephine, all keyed up and jittery on hope and adrenaline, said, "Oh, to hell with it," and backed up before launching into a run and soaring off the edge of the precipice into a horrifying leap that carried her thirty feet to land in a little puff of dust on the other side. JUST.

While I dealt with my minor heart attack, Carl was only irritated that he hadn't done it first and went right after her. He teetered for a moment on the edge, but a second later he'd recovered his cool completely, and then he and Josephine were just hanging out over there, as if being worried about jumping across chasms was so last year.

Noel and I looked at each other. "Er," I said.

"Well," Noel said, and shrugged, and then almost went for it before I grabbed his collar. "Yeah, no," I said firmly.

Josephine and Carl gazed back at us with what looked awfully like smugness. "You can climb down with him, right? We can wait," called Carl airily across the gap.

"Typical," I grumbled. "No, I flipping won't!" I yelled back. "Here, Goldfish . . . you carried him before?"

The Goldfish was hanging in the middle of the gap, three hundred feet above the canyon bottom. It was funny—despite the fact that it almost never touched the ground, so long as it was hovering around head height I'd never really thought of what it did as *flying*. But it flew obligingly back, though it did say, "I'm not really built for *riding*, kids," as it let Noel crawl onto its back.

Noel's previous flight, into a spaceship besieged by Space Locusts, hadn't exactly been an experience to savor. This time, after a nervous squeak as the Goldfish took off, he grinned and waved and yelled, "*Wooo!*" and I felt a bit envious. I was already pretty sure I was too heavy for the Goldfish to carry.

Carl hadn't *seen* Noel riding the Goldfish before and winced, but Noel landed safely at his side, and I realized I had committed myself to getting across by the long-jump method.

"You can do it, Alice! Yay, Alice!" Carl yelled.

"Oh, shut up," I said irritably, backed off for as much of a run-up as possible, and resisted a ridiculous temptation to close my eyes.

I was in the air for unnaturally long; more than long enough to think how stupid this was and just barely long enough for it to be exciting. I only just got one foot on the very edge of the damn cliff, but Josephine and Carl grabbed my arms and I managed not to collapse in a little heap. And there we all were, out of the Labyrinth of Night and on, as the Goldfish immediately informed us, the Plain of Syria, which is a stupid name because Syria is a country on Earth with nothing to do with Mars. But there you go; they weren't consulting me when they named it.

The Goldfish skimmed forward over the plain, and we ran after it again. The ground was pocked with craters and scars, but in the distance it bulged into wide, low hills like bubbles in heating oatmeal. The valley we'd crashed into had seemed as bare and lifeless as if Mars had never been terraformed at all. Now we began to see little signs of life again: patches of purple lichen and emerald moss on rocks, and tufts of arctic grass.

"Look!" cried Carl, pouncing on something.

A small robot, about the size of a chicken, was crawling doggedly across the ground on four angular legs. Carl picked it up, and its legs waggled pitifully in the air.

"What?" Josephine was already breathless from running, but now her breathing hitched with panic. "I said *big* robots, Goldfish. . . ."

"I don't mean that little guy, Josephine," the Goldfish said indulgently. "Come on, gang!"

"Don't call us that," muttered Josephine, but we followed it over a rise and it jabbed forward with its nose in the air, pointing.

There, roaming placidly across the tundra like

grazing bison, were the Goldfish's robot pals.

Or, as you and I would call them, "the giant metal spiders."

"Oh," I said.

"*Perfect,*" breathed Josephine.

"Really?" asked Carl.

The robot spiders were easily as big as elephants. Technically, I suppose, they had six legs rather than eight, projecting from black metal bodies about the size of a car. But I don't think anyone could look at the way they moved, one poky black leg at a time, and not think "giant spiders." Sometimes they would stop moving and lower that boxy abdomen toward the ground, raising huge, multijointed knees toward the sky—and plop seeds into the soil as if they were laying eggs. Some of them sprayed out finer clouds of seeds or puffs of liquid from dispensers on their flanks. Sometimes they'd scoop up little samples of soil on long spoony things that then retracted back into the body.

"What's their top speed, Goldfish?" asked Josephine in a tense whisper, as if afraid of disturbing wild animals.

"Well . . . I don't actually have that information in my system," said the Goldfish. "But looking at them, I'd guess twenty-five miles per hour?"

"Then we'd only have to travel fifteen hours a day, and we could make it to Zond within three days!" cried Josephine. She pointed to the nearest spider as it ambled southward, sowing seeds and minding its own business. "That one's *ours*," she decided fiercely, and went running after it, as intent on her prey as a caveperson hunting down a woolly mammoth.

We followed, although I don't think any of us were very clear about what we were going to do with a giant spider even if we caught up with one.

The spider did not recognize the Goldfish as a robot pal, or us as something that shouldn't be run over. Josephine dodged a huge foot as it crashed down almost on top of her.

"Goldfish!" she ordered. "Fly up there and *interface* with it—make it do what you say!"

"I'll *try*," said the Goldfish, and maybe it was my imagination, but its perky voice had begun to sound a little harassed. Still, it did as she said—flew up to hover above the spider's thorax, and its eyes flashed rapidly as it beamed an invisible flow of information into the other robot's computer.

The spider was just as keen on doing its job as the Goldfish was on teaching us math. So I guess it wasn't surprising that it seemed confused and suspicious about the stream of new data telling it to stop what it knew it was supposed to be doing. It slowed down for a moment but then twitched crossly and stamped its way onward. The Goldfish bobbed wearily in the air in a way that somehow suggested a visible sigh, then flew after it and tried again.

This time the spider stopped moving, reached up irritably with a foreleg, and flicked the Goldfish away. The Goldfish hit the ground at high speed, with a resounding *smack*. The spider scuttled away, covering us in a fine dust of scratchy, sneezy seeds like ink from an escaping squid.

"Goldfish!" cried Noel, running to the fallen robot.

"I'm okay, kids!" said the Goldfish indefatigably, as it bounced up from the ground. But there was a nasty scuff along its side and a dent in its cheerful face.

"Oh, Goldfish," Noel said sadly, stroking the battered place.

"What's going wrong?" demanded Josephine.

"Well, guys, that is not a very *sophisticated* robot!" said the Goldfish, and might have said it through its teeth if it'd had any. "I can't get through its firewall. It just thinks I'm a threat."

"What if we could open up the casing—get into the CPU? Could you do a direct link?" Josephine asked.

"Well, sure, I might be able to force a reboot," said the Goldfish. "But . . ."

"But it won't exactly hold still for us to do that," Carl finished.

Josephine gnawed her lip anxiously as the spider and its central processing unit stomped away at a very brisk twenty-five miles an hour, but whether she would have come up with some new idea we never found out, because Noel announced, "I can get up there! Come on, Goldfish!" And he jumped astride the Goldfish's back and made a sort of giddyup clack against its sides with his heels. Now, I might have expected the Goldfish not to be totally thrilled with this, but I suppose it really did know how few options we had left, because it took off like a rocket. There was just the echo of Noel's excited whoop left behind.

"Bloody *Noel*," said Carl.

"He's really getting *into* this Goldfish-riding thing," I said, thinking also that the Dalisay brothers had more in common than I'd thought.

We ran and leaped to catch up. Ahead, we saw the Goldfish tip Noel carefully onto the spider's back. Frankly, at the rate it was going, it might have carried Noel off into the sunset without us getting anywhere near it. But after a while, when it realized no one seemed to be trying to reprogram it again, it relaxed a bit and slowed down, and we managed to catch up.

Noel was rattling and sliding about on top of the spider and saying silly things like "*Oh*, wow. This is, erm, yeah, *wow*."

"You all right?" Carl called up anxiously.

"Oh, hi," said Noel. "There's nothing to hold on to."

"Grip with your knees!" Carl suggested.

"They don't bend that way!"

"Get into the central processing unit!" Josephine bawled.

Noel was now lying spread-eagled on the spider's thorax, trying to grip the sides. "I can't—I don't see anything to open! It's just smooth!"

The Goldfish ducked between the spider's legs, under its belly, and up the other side.

"The access panel is underneath," it informed us.

"Well, then it's just badly designed!" exploded Josephine.

"It wasn't designed for *these circumstances*," the Goldfish said.

"Well, maybe I *could* reach under there," mused Noel, who was clearly very determined to be helpful now.

"No, don't be an idiot," Carl told him. But Noel didn't listen—he tried to lean under the spider's belly and, sure enough, nearly toppled straight off. In this gravity, falling from that height probably wouldn't hurt him much, but going under one of the spider's massive feet certainly would.

"*Noel!*" Carl shouted, helpless.

Noel managed to grab one of the spider's legs. There were an awful few seconds when there was nothing we could really do but make hissing noises through our teeth and watch him dangle as the spider thundered along before the Goldfish flew in and somehow nudged him onto the spider's back.

"Oof!" said Noel, landing and sliding and scrabbling. "So," he added conversationally, "what should I do now?"

"Hit it with something!" I yelled, and "Shoot it, Goldfish!" shouted Josephine.

"I don't *have* anything to hit it with," Noel complained.

"We didn't really think this through," I said breathlessly, throwing myself into another leap after the spider. Even at its slower pace, if it hadn't stopped from time to time to plant its seeds, we'd have lost it by now.

Carl picked up a stone and threw it. Noel looked surprised and completely failed to even try to catch it.

"Oh, for god's sake," said Carl, and tried again. This time, Noel caught it, nearly slithered off the spider's back again, and then started banging hopefully at the smooth plastic.

"Isn't it going to notice?" I asked anxiously.

"Hope not . . . doesn't seem as if it's got any pressure sensors up there," Josephine said, though she was biting her lip again.

The spider spurted forward, and we had another breathless struggle to keep up with it. When we did, we found Noel had managed to bash a hole in the casing. "Ow. Ow," he said, pulling at sharp bits of broken plastic. "Okay! I can see . . . computer stuff!"

The Goldfish promptly spat out a cable. It hung from its mouth (I hadn't even noticed there was actually a hole there) like a long noodle. Of course, having its mouth full didn't affect its talking, though the effect was somehow weirder than usual.

"Good going, Noel!" it said. "Now, you should be able to see a cable port in there somewhere."

"Well, maybe I should, but I can't!"

The Goldfish ducked closer and glowed as hard as it could into the hole Noel had made, and muttered more instructions while Noel grabbed the cable and felt around inside the cavity with it.

"I think I got it!" he crowed at last.

For a moment nothing seemed to happen. Then Noel was yelling *"Aaaah!"* as the spider collapsed in a heap underneath him.

"We didn't want you to *break* it!" protested Carl as Noel bounced free of the sad-looking pile of black metal legs. We all skidded to a stop. It felt like we'd been in constant motion for a long time, and I started to feel the lack of oxygen. Josephine sucked in an anxious breath.

"Poor spider," said Noel regretfully.

"I'm *rebooting* it, guys," said the Goldfish patiently, and a humming noise started up somewhere inside the spider. The spider slowly rose from the ground. It was oddly creepy, like watching something rise from the dead. *"Zombie* robot spider," I muttered.

"Can you control it now?" Josephine asked the Goldfish, her voice taut with anticipation. Her hands were locked into fists.

"Let's see," the Goldfish said. Its eyes flashed. The spider lumbered forward. It swung to the right, then to the left. It ran round us in a circle.

"You're doing it!" Josephine cried.

"Not quite there yet . . . ," the Goldfish said. It sucked away the cable. The spider stopped moving and stood trembling weirdly for a second or two. Then it extended one foreleg, then another. It bounced cautiously, as if doing squats, then ran in another circle before crouching in front of us.

"Well, what are you waiting for, kids? Climb aboard!" the Goldfish exclaimed.

We cheered. It was ragged and breathless, but it was only an hour or so ago that we'd thought we'd never cheer about anything again. "Back to the ship, Goldfish," commanded Josephine, settling cross-legged on the spider's back. "We need to salvage as much as we can carry. Especially the oxygen cells." She proved her point by swaying rather alarmingly as the spider lurched into a crawl. Carl and I grabbed her at the same time, and somehow it turned into a general, messy, celebratory hug.

"I'm going to call her Monica," said Noel, patting the spider's back.

Monica carried us back toward the Labyrinth of Night while Noel sang reedily, "'She swallowed the bird to catch the spider . . . that wriggled and jiggled and tickled inside her.'"

In the far distance, I could see Space Locusts dropping from the purple sky, a scattered dark haze like backward smoke pouring toward the ground. They looked a long way off, but then I remembered things about calculating distance and how close the horizon was on Mars, and I wished the Goldfish wasn't such a good teacher.

But nobody said anything about them. What was there to say?

16

Riding Monica wasn't the smoothest way to travel. She could crawl over just about anything, which was all very well, but sheer drops and vertical walls didn't mean a thing to her and made quite a difference to us. The Goldfish did get better at steering her after we all fell off the first few times, but that didn't do anything to fix the fact that it was really *cold*. There was nothing between us and the wind whipping past, and what with that and the lightheadedness from not enough oxygen, we were all on the point of toppling off yet again by the time we reached the wreck of the Flying Fox. We had to spend a long time just flopping around inside and *breathing* and getting as close to warm as the circumstances would allow before we could even start on the work of getting everything we needed out of the ship and onto Monica.

Taking the spaceship apart was a lot easier than trying to fix it, but still not actually easy: we didn't have enough tools and we were rapidly running out of duct tape. Still, eventually we'd built a sort of rickety platform on Monica's back, for us to sit on with the food crates and oxygen canisters. We hacked the remains of the tent-capsule thing in two: one part to wad around us on the platform so we weren't so cold, and the other slung underneath like a hammock to hold the rest of the dry oxygen rods and some of the other things. The platform fell apart and the hammock fell off several times before we were finished, and the friends-forever, group-hugs mood got badly eroded. In fact, we came fairly close to a general massacre, but at last, nursing our various broken nails and hurt feelings, we were on our way, even if Josephine was not speaking to anyone unless you count occasionally muttering to herself that she was the one who'd thought of catching a robot in the first place so you'd think she'd get more respect.

I was so tired that we hadn't been moving for very long before I went to sleep, which I wouldn't have expected to even be possible. When I woke up, the mood had thawed enough for someone to put my oxygen mask over my face. I pushed it off and sat up. Josephine was leaning over the side, making quiet retching sounds.

"You all right?" I asked blurrily.

"Travel sick," she said. "God, I've had enough of this spider."

"There, there, Monica," said Noel, patting the spider consolingly.

"Where are we?"

"Just getting into Tharsis," said Carl.

We were crossing an ancient lava field. It was just as well we had Monica; on foot it would have taken forever—there wasn't a patch of level ground anywhere. Around us were the remains of small, strangely blobby volcanoes. The rock below Monica's scuttling feet had been whipped into curlicues and swirls and bubbles, then cracked and broken like meringue. But now everything was green and velvety with moss, and there were little streams of rainwater snaking through the cracks. And to the west, the horizon swelled weirdly, like it was having a bad allergic reaction to something, and that was the bulge of Tharsis, where the biggest volcanoes in the solar system were.

"Where's the Goldfish?" I asked.

"It's up there," said Carl soberly, pointing to the sky. "Watching for Space Locusts."

The Goldfish was no bigger than a grain of rice among the clouds, which I noticed were worryingly dark—less purple and more a deep and bloody umber. Just as I looked up, it plunged down to hover close above us.

"So hey, kids, there's something kind of quirky about half a mile north," it said, with the particular type of cheeriness we'd come to understand meant trouble.

"Space Locusts?" I asked.

"Not exactly. Not *now*," said the Goldfish. "But I think it might be where they've *been*."

"Let's go around it, then," I said.

"Well, sure! We can do that! But here's the thing," said the Goldfish apologetically. "It's a little on the large side. If we go around, it's probably going to add more than an hour."

"We've got to get another hundred miles closer to Zond before dark," said Josephine at once.

So we went straight on. Before we even saw the scale of what the Space Locusts had done, we felt the traces of it in the air. Fine dust came sweeping over us on the wind, such thick clouds of it that we had to put our masks on again just to breathe and see. And all the vegetation gave out. There were pale scars gouged into the rock where moss or flowering lichens or little shrubs had been torn up.

Then we came to it: an enormous wound in the surface of the planet. The chaos of rocks and streams gave way to great banks of dust, sloping down, down, down into nothing. You couldn't see the other side of that awful gap. It must have been easily the size of the Grand Canyon, but instead of being full of inner peaks and cliffs carved by a river over millions of years, there was *nothing* in it but eddies of dust and pools of red mud where the little new Martian streams had leaked into it. One day, I thought hopefully, perhaps it would be an enormous lake, and people could sail boats and fish could live in it. But it was just horrible to look at now, and we were the only things alive there.

"Get her to speed up, will you, Goldfish?" Carl said after we stared at it for a while. Monica carried us down the scarp. Agile as she was, she foundered from time to time, and I wondered what on earth we'd do if she got stuck. The wind picked up and dust whipped around us like smoke, so before we even reached the bottom, it got so dark I could only just see the blue glow of the Goldfish's eyes through the murk, and I hoped it really knew where we were going.

No one said much until we were out the other side of it. I'm sure the Goldfish and Monica tried their best, but we couldn't go close to top speed, so it took easily an hour.

The faraway sun had dipped a lot lower while we'd been down there in the dust, so we emerged into twilight.

"Maybe we should have gone round after all," said Josephine when Monica finally scuttled us up the other side.

"There must be such a *lot* of them now," I said.

Josephine made faces. "The question is, are they arriving, or are they *breeding*?"

"Ugh . . . brrr!" I shuddered.

There was nothing we could do but keep on, of course. Josephine felt better enough to play her harmonica for a bit, but then Noel rather tactlessly wondered aloud how far the sound carried and if maybe the Space Locusts could hear her. So she stopped.

The signs of the Space Locusts faded away from the landscape. Patches of green reappeared on the rocks, and eventually they were fuzzy and mossy again.

"We should make camp," I said.

"When we find somewhere flat enough," agreed Carl.

Then we saw something else up ahead—something pale, streaming up into the purplish air.

"Is that *them*?" asked Noel anxiously, all of us thinking of the plumes of dust we'd seen rising from the ground where the Space Locusts had been.

"That looks more like *steam*," said Josephine. And indeed the column of vapor seemed to wisp into nothing, in a way that wasn't like rising dust.

"Maybe there's somebody here!" said Noel excitedly.

Somehow, even though we'd come all this way just so we could try to find somebody, this was surprisingly unnerving. We were used to having miles and miles of emptiness all to ourselves, and this wasn't where we were expecting to find any people. We were silent, watching the steam.

"Can you see what's causing it?" Josephine asked the Goldfish.

The Goldfish soared up to have a better look but soon dipped back down to us. "Darndest thing—it looks as though it's coming right out of thin air. I'm going to check it out, kids. You wait here," it said, and bustled away.

We were left kicking our heels on Monica's back.

"Christ, it's freezing," said Carl.

"It's Mars," I said. "It's always freezing."

"It wasn't *this* bad before," Carl grumbled. "Not even with the wind going."

He was right. The moss on the rocks around us was crusted with frost. I noticed little white pockets of ice in the hollows between them. Our breath misted the dry cold air like that white thread of steam up ahead.

We decided we'd get down from Monica and move around a bit to warm up, so we were stamping and blowing into our hands and then someone blurted out: "What's that?" To my surprise, I realized it was me.

"What's what?" asked Noel, reasonably enough.

"I . . . thought I saw someone, just there by those rocks. But obviously there isn't. Ha-ha." I didn't like how babbly and weird I sounded and was in the process of shutting up when there was—or at least I thought there was—this *flickering* on the edge of my vision. I said, "Oh, there, it moved! Wait, no. Sorry. Having a funny turn, apparently! Oh, dear."

"You do sound a bit oxygen deprived," Noel

said sympathetically. "Put your mask back on for a while."

"Alice," said Josephine quietly. "Can you still see it?"

Josephine was making herself look and sound extremely calm, but I knew she wasn't. She had gone very still, except she was breathing faster than normal and her hands were screwed into fists. I looked over at the perfectly ordinary patch of Martian ground. "Nope. Nothing," I said decidedly.

But Josephine reached out and took hold of my shoulders, to make me face her.

"Alice," she said firmly, "look at me. Do you see it now? Out of the corner of your eye?"

The iciness in the air wormed its way under my skin, gnawing and wriggling like the Space Locusts chewing up soil. I wanted to squirm away. I whispered, "Sort of."

"And what's it doing?" Josephine asked impassively.

"Standing on the rock," I stuttered. "Watching us. *No.*"

Carl breathed, "It *couldn't* be . . . ," and he and Josephine exchanged a look. I wasn't an idiot; I knew what they were thinking. They were thinking that even if Mum's genius for flying spaceships wasn't particularly hereditary, maybe other things about her *were*. In which case . . .

"No, it *couldn't*," I agreed, and I lurched forward, bounded off the rock, and stumbled straight toward what *wasn't, couldn't possibly be there*. It had to be my imagination that something had seen me coming and was *backing away*.

"Alice, wait!" Carl called, and he and Josephine came hurrying after me.

But they couldn't stop me in time, and the *thing that wasn't there* couldn't get away from me. There was nothing, there had to be nothing, I had to *prove* there was nothing—so I ran into it, something solid and invisible and very cold. I almost fell over, and I grabbed by instinct . . . and felt swathes of smooth, icy fabric under my fingers, which slid away from the shape underneath.

For a moment, I was face-to-face with something like a salamander with a mane of glassy fur, its head impossibly hanging in midair, where the invisible fabric still cloaked the rest of it. Its eyes were huge and transparent and veined with subtle color, like glass paperweights.

Then the Goldfish swooped down like the wrath

of god. It came flashing and making a howling noise I would never have thought it *could* make. And it did the zapping thing it had done to us, only much, much harder.

The Morror fell over and didn't get up.

17

"**Y**ou killed it!" said Noel. "It wasn't doing anything! That's not fair!"

I would have told him to shut up, except that I still felt too sick and trembly from having touched the thing. Honestly, I wouldn't have been too unhappy if the Morror was dead, because even if it *was* unfair, it wouldn't have been our fault. It wouldn't even have been the Goldfish's fault, really, seeing as it's a robot and was only trying to protect us. And we wouldn't have been stuck with a Morror that could go invisible when it wanted and might do anything. And what with being lost on the wrong planet already because of these guys, I don't think it's exactly surprising if I didn't feel very friendly.

But then the Morror moved, and I thought, Oh, this isn't going to be that easy.

"Oh, you only stunned it," said Noel, relieved.

"MY AIM WAS NOT TO STUN IT, MY AIM WAS TO *ELIMINATE* IT," said the Goldfish, sounding completely deranged. And then it zapped it again.

This time nothing much happened. The Morror just made a sound like it was in pain, because it obviously was, and the Goldfish beeped in confusion and zapped it another time. By this point it was fairly clear that the Goldfish was trying as hard as it could and only succeeding in hurting the thing.

"We could probably kill it with rocks," suggested Carl.

So I said, "Oh, for god's sake, we are not killing anything with rocks. I'm pretty sure that is actually a *war crime*."

"It's helpless, Goldfish," said Josephine quietly. "And it's true: we're soldiers. It's a prisoner of war."

"You're *children*," insisted the Goldfish, still sounding pretty scary.

"Exo-Defense Force cadets," said Carl grudgingly.

The Goldfish thought for a moment. "Teacher robots are not subject to international military law," it concluded, and was about to have another zap when Noel flung himself in front of the Morror.

"Stop it!" he cried. "Stop hurting it! You're being horrible!"

"Killing it would be a waste," said Josephine. Her voice was oddly expressionless. "No one's ever even seen a Morror before. And we're going to leave the first live captive rotting somewhere on Tharsis? Without learning anything about it?"

The Goldfish made a frustrated electronic groaning sound, and its eyes went from red back to blue. "Well, kids, I think you might be biting off more than you can chew," it said brightly. "But it's great to see you all compromising and working as a team! And if that Morror takes one step out of line . . . !"

There was a brief red flash in its eyes, but it backed off a bit.

"Well, what then?" said Carl.

So we stood there and stared at it. Or rather at its fallen, disembodied head, which was not getting any less creepy to look at.

"We should get the rest of the invisible thing off," I said eventually. "We can't have it running off in that thing."

The invisible suit seemed more like a kind of sack than anything else; heaven knows how the Morrors managed to walk around in it without tripping over it all the time. I could sort of not quite see it out of the corner of my eye (the effect was starting to make me feel slightly sick), and the others couldn't at all, but of course we could all feel it. It was very fine and silky and clingy under our hands as we dragged it off.

"So that's what they look like," breathed Carl.

"That's what *this one* looks like," corrected Josephine.

There was the first Morror human eyes had ever seen. The translucent mane covered its newt-like head, extended over its neck and shoulders, and stretched across its cheeks into tapering panels of shorter strands beneath its eyes. The mane wasn't really *fur*, of course; it was made up of tendril things, sort of like what sea anemones have. The strands of the mane got shorter and shorter as they approached bare skin, until they were just glossy round dots that spotted the Morror all over like a leopard, covering its chest and the six long, slender tentacles—three on each side—that hung from its shoulders. Between the dots . . . I suppose you'd have to call it gray, but such a complicated, mottled gray, sort of bluish or greenish or purplish, depending on how you looked at it. Each tentacle might have reached its knees, assuming it had them. But we couldn't see what it had in the way of legs, because though it was bare from the waist up, it was wearing a kind of long skirt made from stiff, dark-red papery stuff.

Its eyes were shut, but I'd already seen them: as big as my fists, glossy transparent round the edges and wells of deep black in the middle.

The Morror was still moaning quietly. It flicked up a couple of tentacles to cover its face, but it didn't seem to be actually awake.

"So does this work on humans?" Carl wondered, and put a fold of the invisibility cloak over his head and went, "Wooo. Wooo." It worked very well, but it turned out that a headless boy capering about was one more thing than I could properly cope with.

"Oh, bloody hell, don't," I said. Everything around me got swimmy and floaty and I realized I might possibly be falling over. Then someone got their arms round me and was making me sit down on a mossy rock.

"You're all right," said Josephine firmly. "You're just in shock. Drink some of this."

She was holding that silver bottle of perfume I'd seen on the *Mélisande*.

"What're you making me drink perfume for?" I croaked, the higher intellectual functions being beyond me at present.

"It's not perfume," said Josephine. "It's rum. It's

my dad's hip flask. Have some, there's a good girl."

I did as I was told, and Josephine patted my head approvingly while Carl laughed in a way that suggested he might be a bit in shock himself. "We've got a Morror prisoner," he said, giggling. "And Josephine's a twelve-year-old alkie. . . ."

"I'm nothing of the sort. I'm just extremely well prepared," sniffed Josephine, hugging her bag of peculiar objects proudly to her side. She passed Carl the little flask. "You'll note it's *full*."

Carl had a little swig, and then Josephine took it back and did the same, and Noel looked at her expectantly.

"You're not having any," Carl said flatly.

"So, what, I've got to just *stay* in shock?" Noel asked in indignation.

"Yes," said the rest of us.

Something strange happened to the Morror. The tendrils of its mane rippled and flared, and color pulsed through them, bands of purple and deep flame orange that welled up in its leopard dots and swept all across its skin. This freaked us all out except for Josephine, who put her chin into her hands and watched for a moment, then got out her tablet and started filming it.

"Is it *supposed* to do that?" asked Noel anxiously.

"Hey," said Carl. "Hey, Morror."

The Morror keened quietly and opened its eyes. There were faint threads of orange and purple in the transparency around its pupils.

"Are you *all right*, Morror?" Noel inquired.

The Morror sat up and wrapped its tentacles around itself. It looked at us in silence.

"We're army cadets, and this is our Goldfish, and I'm not going to let it hurt you anymore, but you're our prisoner, so we're taking you to the nearest military base, and we won't hurt you either, but don't try anything," Noel summarized helpfully, running out of breath a bit toward the end.

More silence.

"Do they . . . talk?" asked Noel uncertainly, and I figured that they must, because clearly they'd communicated with humans at the start of the invasion and we must have gotten the name Morror from somewhere, but I didn't think they'd had anything to say all the time I'd been alive.

The Morror said something. And meanwhile it changed color. Blues and turquoises and yellows and reds quivered across its spots and tendrils, and its voice sounded like wind in trees and all the syllables sounded like sighing. It said—and this is the closest I can manage and really there could easily be more

A's in there: "*Haaaa'thraaaa vsaaaa* Mo-*raaa* uha-*raaa* . . .*"

There was a pause. "Well, let's tie it up," said Carl briskly.

The Morror did not want to be tied up. It was very wriggly and its tentacles flapped and whipped and it changed color a lot. We were a bit worried about touching it, because for all we knew it was poisonous. But it was four against one—five against one, really, because the Goldfish was still hovering there as menacingly as it could, so eventually we got its tentacles bound to its chest in duct tape. We'd tried to make some kind of handcuffs to tie the ends of its tentacles together behind it, but we didn't have enough tape left. And as far as we could tell we hadn't been poisoned, so that was something.

"Damn, where's the invisible suit?" Carl said after we were finished. Everyone looked at me.

"*I* don't know," I protested. "It's getting dark, anyway, how am I supposed to . . ." But they made me turn round and round, trying to see it out of the corner of my eye, until I started feeling wobbly again. I didn't find it, actually; Noel did, by walking into it so that the tip of his boot disappeared.

"How are we not going to *lose* this?" I said. The Goldfish suddenly sprang open a compartment we hadn't known it had had in its side, but it didn't say anything. I don't know if it was trying to overcome the moral conflict between its programming and our decision, or if it was just sulking.

We put the cloak inside, and the compartment snapped shut.

"It *is* getting dark, though," I repeated. The rum had helped, but I didn't feel I could face traveling much farther. Still, I wondered how anyone was going to get much rest around a silent tied-up Morror changing color like a set of traffic lights all the time.

"I assume that was its ship you found, Goldfish?" said Josephine. "Let's go and look at that."

We tried to tie the Morror to Monica's leg, but we didn't have enough duct tape left. So in the end we left the Goldfish to make sure the Morror didn't get up to anything, and Noel to make sure the Goldfish didn't get up to anything, and the rest of us started scrambling over the rocks toward the plume of steam.

Something occurred to me on the way. "Does your dad *know* you've got his hip flask?" I asked Josephine.

"Yes, he's probably figured it out by now," Josephine said.

✧

The Morror ship, obviously, didn't seem to be there. The steam just poured out of empty air, into empty air, about fifteen feet above the bottom of the little valley. Except—and they were subtle enough that you might not have seen them normally—here and there were these little transparent patches of crusted ice, on the invisible contours of *nothing*, and cold was rolling off it.

The ground was a bit flatter—just where you'd aim for if you were crashing and trying to find somewhere to do an emergency landing. But I was pretty sure it had bashed into the high rocks we were standing on.

Thinking about Morrors crashing and trying to save themselves made me feel a bit weird. Then I wondered if our Morror was the pilot, and rather belatedly asked myself how big the ship was and if it was likely to have more Morrors inside it, waiting to spring to the defense of their colleague.

"How do we 'take a look at this,' exactly?" I said regardless.

"You tell us, magic-eye girl," said Carl.

So I had to do my corner-of-the-eye trick again. "It's about a third bigger than a Flarehawk, I guess," I told the others, after waggling my head around and swiveling my eyes until I felt like a total moron. "It's shaped sort of like . . . well, it's in two round bits joined together in the middle, like an hourglass. But I also think it's kind of spiky. Or . . . hairy. The front bit is all caved in."

"And can you see a door?"

"No!" I said crossly. "I can't really see the stupid thing at all!"

I told myself I couldn't reasonably be frightened of touching a Morror spacecraft after touching an actual Morror, so I went and cautiously patted at midair. I felt something surprisingly ridged and slightly damp, and continued stroking my way along the side of the thing. Then my hand suddenly pushed empty space and, from the point of view of everyone outside, including me, vanished.

I yelped and pulled my hand back, freaked out even though I could feel it hadn't actually ceased to *exist* or anything and I knew I'd really just found the door.

The others came closer as I stuck my head through, and I heard Carl saying, "*Christ*, that looks awful," at my apparently headless body from outside.

I blundered into some kind of ramp, hurt my leg, and climbed up inside.

It was cold, but not that much colder than outside. Some sort of machinery was croaking to itself in an unhappy way, which made me think the steam we'd seen was coming from the ruins of whatever was supposed to keep the ship at a Morror-friendly temperature.

The chamber lit up to greet me. After seeing the Morror, I suppose I shouldn't have been surprised at how colorful everything was. The walls were rounded and banded with stripes of color that whorled and curved like the lines in a fingerprint; mostly icy blues and sea greens on the left, giving way to some purples near the door to flamey reds and oranges on the right. Some of the colors lit up, some didn't.

Josephine followed me first. She was still filming everything in this ultradetached way that was becoming slightly scary. She lingered over some coils of white symbols in a swirl of dark red and said, "It's writing."

There were these oval alcove things set into the walls, each about two feet high and padded.

"Do you think this is for passengers?" I said. "I guess the front bit must be for piloting."

We leaned into the wreck of what must have been the helm. The view screen was all smashed, and half the control deck was caved in. What remained of the controls were all spaced and angled in such a way that they'd be horrible for a human to work, but you could see that they *were* controls. There were more wheely-slidy things, and banks of spongy leaflike things, where we'd have had banks of screens and buttons. But still. And whereas all the business parts of a human ship tend to come in sensible black or gray, with maybe a bit of blue or orange backlighting if you're lucky, these were as colorful as everything else in the ship. It almost looked like someone had dumped their jewelry collection on a counter and then decided to fly a spaceship with it.

"Never thought Morrors would be so *festive*," I said.

"If those are chairs, there should be a crew of three," said Josephine, looking at some hexagonal plinthlike things. She said this close to her tablet, for the benefit of the film. For the benefit of me, she added, "Just because it *can* take that many doesn't necessarily mean it did."

Somehow I did get the feeling our Morror was on its own; the way it'd been hanging around by itself and the way no one seemed to be trying to rescue it. Still, the possibility of lots of Morrors running around, when a minute ago you hadn't been expecting any, isn't something you just get over.

Carl pulled himself up into the ship. "So," he

said, "what can we swipe?"

The idea of pinching stuff from the Morrors was bizarrely cheering. It felt like getting a little of our own back, even though you'd think having a real live Morror prisoner was a much better way of doing it, but that wasn't fun at all as it involved a lot more responsibility.

So we poked around very thoroughly, and Carl got himself sprayed with some sort of bright blue liquid, which terrified us for a while but did not seem to do anything when wiped off except leave him a little cleaner. Eventually it turned out the Morror approach to storage was to have lots of hexagonal compartments built into the floor and walls.

We found some green-and-brown lumpy things, and some blue shredded stuff, all of which we decided was almost certainly food. One of the compartments was full of frozen lumps of meat—at least in the sense that we were somehow pretty sure it was bits of animal, despite being bluey gray—though whether the animals were more like fish or more like mammals, we weren't sure. This raised the what-if-it's-poisonous-to-humans issue again, and also made me feel weird, because suddenly I was imagining Morrors getting squirted with blue stuff and sitting around eating, which wasn't something I'd ever been able to do before.

We also found some weapons. Some of them were easy to recognize: semicircular blades with a hole, presumably for Morrors to slot their tentacles into, and a couple of curvy staffs, which Carl used to poke and prod, and ended up shock-raying a hole into the roof.

We left the food for the time being, but we thought we'd hang on to the weapons, especially with all the alarming things we'd encountered lately.

"The most important thing is the oxygen," said Josephine, because the ship was full of the stuff and we were breathing perfectly happily without our masks on. "Look, why don't we make camp here? We can't go much farther anyway, and that way we won't use up any of our own supply overnight."

"It's too cold," I said. "And too weird. But mainly too cold."

"I didn't mean we'd actually sleep *in* the ship. But we could trap the Morror in here and put the tent up outside and channel the oxygen in from here."

So that's what we did. Putting up a tent is no mean feat when it was never designed to stand up without being attached to a spaceship and has been partially eaten by Space Locusts. And getting an alien spaceship to blow oxygen into it is also pretty difficult. But we were becoming increasingly good at taking things apart and putting them together again in ingenious ways. We pitched the tent over two of Monica's legs, and the Morror ship's ventilation system turned out to be another thing that wasn't *that* different from anything we were used to.

The Morror didn't make a sound when we marched it into the ship, and didn't seem to have anything you'd call a facial expression. Its changing colors were a little hypnotic, though; I kept finding myself staring at it, and then I got scared that perhaps it was some kind of psychological weapon meant to make you dopey so it could attack. I tried not to look at it directly after that.

"Hey! Keep your . . . tentacles where I can see them," said Carl, brandishing his shock-ray staff as the Morror lifted a length of one finger-arm beneath the bindings round its torso. The Morror paused, stared blankly at Carl, and then squirted some blue stuff from the wall onto itself, which it then started flicking and smoothing over its tendrils as best it could. Even though it was pretty awkward being tied up, the effect was like a bird preening itself or a cat washing.

Then it suddenly managed to fold itself into one

of the padded alcoves and sat there, roosting like an owl. It gazed at us disconcertingly for a while; then it murmured some more whispery syllables to itself and closed its eyes.

Noel tried to feed the Morror some of the stuff we'd found, but it didn't want any. Carl was dead keen to try some of the Morror food, but we persuaded him that we should only resort to it on the brink of actual starvation, as we weren't equipped for a medical emergency. So, trying to pretend the Morror wasn't there, we ate some of our own stuff, and eventually we got into our tattered sleeping bags and bundled up together for warmth. It was our third night out on the surface of Mars.

Even though we knew the Goldfish would have zapped it silly and screamed the place down if the alien made a wrong move, none of us slept very well.

It wasn't just that it was there. It was that we still had no real plan for what to do with it.

18

"Okay, everyone try not to freak out," I said the next morning, "but I think there are more of them."

Everyone commenced freaking out.

We'd been in the process of discussing what to do with the one Morror we already had, and were leaning toward just taking careful note of the coordinates and leaving it tied up where it was. It wouldn't die before we got to Zond, and then we could tell someone to go back and get it.

Noel, of course, thought this was cruel.

But now I'd gotten everyone scared of extra Morrors. "Where? How many? What are they doing?" they all said, and Josephine and Carl brandished their newfound weapons. Carl still had the shock-ray staff, and Josephine had taken the curved blades and looked more piratical than ever.

"Over there, and *nothing*—there are three or four of them, I can't be sure, just lying down. I think they might be dead."

We hesitated, everyone trying to look at the things I'd pointed out and no one actually succeeding.

"It might be a trap," Noel said.

Josephine shook her head. "If they were alive, they'd have done something while we were asleep."

Carl lowered the shock-ray staff a little. "Well, let's have a look."

Then the Morror—our Morror, obviously—lurched out of the invisible spaceship, making a wailing noise and waggling its tentacles as best it was able.

Josephine and Carl had their weapons raised in a second, and the Goldfish was plainly gearing up for a good hard zap. The Morror stopped in its tracks and spread the ends of its tentacles.

"*Leeeeeeee-eeeeee,*" sigh-wailed the Morror. "*Leeeeee 'm alooooooo.*" Then it seemed to make an effort, pulling itself together, and it said much more clearly: "*Leave them alone.*"

There was a pause. Carl said flatly, "What?"

"*Leeeeeeeeeeve them alooone,*" repeated the

Morror. "They *aaaaaaahaaaaaaaaaahhhrrrr* already *deaaaaad. Leeeeeeeeeeee in peeeeeeeeece . . .*"

"You talk English!" crowed Noel.

No one else was as pleased about it as that, but Josephine's eyebrows jumped with intrigue.

"Yeeeeee-*eeeessss*." The Morror sighed, then shook itself slightly. "Yes. We are trained in your languages."

"What an interesting development," Josephine said softly.

"So you can spy on us," I said. "Lovely."

"It's good that you understand," said Carl, "because now I can tell you what bum-kettling invisible bastards I think you all are."

The Morror's colors rippled purple-black-blue. It said, "That is a natural response. You could not comprehend our reasons."

This did not endear it to us very much; even Noel snorted angrily.

"Why don't you find out for yourself whether we can comprehend?" asked Josephine. "Go on. Explain."

The Morror rippled orange and pink and reverted to the way of talking it evidently found more comfortable.

"Leee-heeeeeeeeve meeee. I aaaam ooo-ooonly

one Mo-*raaa* uha-*raaa*, I aaaaaam nooooot a threeeeeeaaaattt. . . ."

Then it scuttled back inside the spaceship, and thereby disappeared.

"Guard it, Goldfish," Josephine ordered, while gesturing fiercely at the rest of us to come out of Morror earshot.

"Fill the oxygen tanks and continue on toward Zond," she hissed at us when we'd put twenty yards or so between us and the Morror ship. "I'm staying here with it."

"What?" I exclaimed.

"We have to be realistic," Josephine said. "We've got limited oxygen; there's a planet of Space Locusts trying to eat us; we can't be *certain* there's anyone at Zond. We could all be dead in a few days, the Morror too. But we've got the first Morror anyone's ever seen. If I die, I want to find out as much as possible first. I want to leave a record. It could be crucial to the war *and* to science." She looked at us to see if we were getting the point and judged that we weren't. "I want to interrogate it," she finished.

"Do you have to be so *grim*, Jo?" complained Carl.

"Yes," said Josephine, inevitably.

"Well, we're not going to waltz off and leave you

stranded alone with it. You can forget that right now."

"It's tied up and I'm armed! I'll cope perfectly well."

"Yeah, this is not a thing that's getting negotiated," said Carl. "Is it, Alice?"

"No, it's not," I agreed. And, because Josephine looked as if she could probably keep arguing for a while: "And no one's dying. We'll bring it with us. You can interrogate it as we go, if you have to. And if, that is *when*, we find people . . . if we find Dr. Muldoon, she'll know what to do with it."

"What wonderful company it's going to be," said Carl, sighing.

✫

Noel, on the other hand, was thrilled, and scampered back toward the spaceship calling, "Morror! We're going to take you with us, Morror, and we'll feed you and look after you and make sure you're okay!"

The Morror was even less keen on this than Carl, and it made the long waily *leeeeeee* sounds that came out when it couldn't get its mouth around "Leave me alone." However, once the Goldfish had prodded it out of the ship and it saw Monica, it seemed resigned to its fate. Possibly it reflected that, while it might not like being a prisoner of war, being the stranded survivor of a spaceship crash wasn't necessarily a better bet.

We did go and have a look at the dead Morrors before we left, just in case there was any funny business going on. But they really were dead, lying under one large sheet of the invisible fabric, in a neat row. One looked more or less like the living Morror in the spaceship: same newt face and tendrils, though it was bigger and the face was squarer and the mane was longer and straighter. The other two were different; one had a much frillier mane, and the last was about twice the size of the others and didn't have a mane at all, just larger patches and spots over a rounder head.

The dead Morrors didn't have any colors. Their skins were dark gray, their glassy tendrils empty. But there were colored pebbles strewn all over the ground around them.

After we'd looked at them, Carl, without saying anything, quietly put the invisible sheet back.

So we packed up everything else and refilled our oxygen canisters from the ship, climbed onto Monica, and lurched west with our prisoner.

☆

Josephine and Noel were doing a Good Cop, Bad Cop routine with the Morror. No prizes for guessing who was who.

"Why are you invading Earth? How many of you are there? And why are you *here*? There's nothing on Mars but kids and scientists. Are you trying to take over the whole solar system, or is there something else to it? You needn't expect any food or water until you start cooperating."

"I'm Noel, and this is Josephine and Alice and Carl. So you know *our* names, can't you tell us yours?"

"Unnnntiiiiie meeeee," the Morror moaned. "Untie me." Its vowels were getting shorter and easier to understand; that was about the only progress we were making. It sat aboard Monica in that weird huddled-up roosting position, clutching something against its torso wrapped in its tentacles—it must have managed to pick it up inside its ship. It was a pale, irregularly shaped shiny thing about the size of a football, and as the Morror stared at it, colors and patterns started to stream across the surface. They were, at first, completely different colors (rose, amber, turquoise) from the ones rippling across the Morror itself (black, yellow, and purple), but gradually they started to sync up (lavender, slate gray and scarlet, sage green), though they never became exactly the same; the Morror always had odd little patches of some completely different color on its body somewhere, and the patterns on the object seemed more orderly and deliberate.

"What *is* that?" Noel asked the Morror. "What do *you* think it is?" he asked everyone else, when the Morror continued to pretend he wasn't there.

"Good question," said Josephine, and grabbed for it. The Morror struggled valiantly, but Josephine was determined and it couldn't move its tentacles properly.

"Tell us about this," she demanded, holding it out of the Morror's reach.

"It is nothing that could interest you," said the Morror.

"Oh, but I am interested," said Josephine. "I like weird things. I have a whole collection of them I carry around with me everywhere."

"You caaaaan't haaaaave it," said the Morror, getting all long voweled again in its distress.

"Is it a weapon? A communications device? Or . . . something religious, maybe?"

"*No,*" insisted the Morror, tentacles straining to get the object back. I couldn't help feeling a little sorry for it, though you've got to admit that having shiny things taken away from you is pretty mild as interrogation techniques go.

"Why don't you just say what your name is?

Where's the harm in that?" urged Noel.

The Morror sighed. Well, it always sounded as if it was sighing, but that one sounded particularly deliberate. "I am . . . Th*saaa*."

"That's a nice name," said Noel encouragingly.

"All right, Th*saaa*," Josephine said. "Start with what you're doing on Mars. Are you colonizing it?"

"No."

Carl butted into the interrogation: "Well, why the hell not? It was right here. No one was living on it. Surely you could have terraformed it as well as we can. If you needed a planet, why couldn't you damn well take this one and leave us alone?"

"This planet is unbearable," said the Morror softly. "I cannot even feel where I am or what direction we are going."

Josephine's expression briefly changed from War Face to Science Face. "Go on," she said.

The Morror made sad whistling noises and swayed its tentacles. "There is no . . . *ruhaa-thal*." It seemed to think for a bit, and muttered, "No . . . *cumbakīya kṣetra*."

Something about that sounded really weird— the Morror's accent had changed completely, and I remembered things I'd learned in lessons back at

Beagle. "That didn't sound Morrorish," I said. "That sounded more . . . *Hindi*."

"GOOD JOB, ALICE!" bellowed the Goldfish, thrilled at the least hint of things getting educational again. "That *was* Hindi!"

"I cannot think of the word in English," snapped the Morror.

"*Cumbakīya kṣetra* means *magnetism*," said the Goldfish happily. "And that's true, kids! Unlike Earth, Mars has no magnetic field."

Noel and Josephine looked at each other. "Birds have magnetic senses," said Noel, excited. "And whales and things. You've got something like that too?"

"So Mars isn't suitable for you? Because it hasn't got a magnetic field?"

The Morror rippled its tentacles and lowered its head in what might have been agreement.

"So that's why you chose Earth," said Josephine.

"I chose nothing," said Thsaaa.

"Oh, fine, you're just following orders—*you*, *plural*, then," snarled Josephine, and there was an edge of rage in her voice I'd never heard before. "Why did you come to the solar system at all? And if Mars is so awful for you, what are you doing here?"

"I can tell you nothing more. It is forbidden. And you could not understand."

Josephine looked down at the shining object in her hands. It was still making colors and patterns, but they no longer matched the waves of color flowing over the Morror's skin. She extended an arm, holding it high over the ground and Monica's stamping feet. "Maybe I'll break it," she said.

The Morror let out a whistling cry, tentacles flailing, but then suddenly gathered itself. "No. You won't," it said disdainfully.

"Oh no?" Josephine tensed her arm.

"You told me yourself. You are interested. You like strange things, and that is strange to you. Could you bring yourself to break it, and gain nothing?"

Josephine stared at it for a long moment and then, scowling, lowered her arm. She kept the object well out of the Morror's reach, though.

It started raining.

"Untie me," said Th*saaa*. "I won't escape. Where could I go? Untie me. Untie me."

We picked our way slowly around the lower slope of the great bulge of Tharsis, where the ground was a little smoother under Monica's feet, and the Morror kept chanting, "Untie me," as annoying as a little kid asking "Are we there yet?"

It stopped when the rain got so heavy you could hardly open your mouth without drowning and Monica was splashing through streams of water that would have been thigh deep if we'd been on the ground.

But when a surge knocked Monica sideways and swept us all down the mountainside, it started saying it again, even more urgently.

19

For a few horrible seconds, all we could do was try to hang on and hope Monica didn't overturn completely. The Goldfish reeled through the air above us, in a white haze of water as the rain bounced off its flanks, its eyes flashing as it tried to keep Monica under control. Monica's legs flailed and thrashed, but giant robot spiders do not make good swimmers.

We collided with a spur of rock and stuck there for a bit, though we could feel the current trying to drag us loose.

"*Untie me, please,*" said Th*saaa* urgently. It had the ends of its tentacles coiled around what had been a pipe in the Flying Fox, but with its upper tentacles bound to its torso it couldn't get a good grip.

I was clinging to the same thing, and worrying that I could feel it coming loose.

Carl reacted while I was still thinking; he grabbed one of Josephine's Morror blades and hacked through Th*saaa*'s duct-tape bindings. Of course, this left Carl only one hand to hang on with himself, and his immediate reward was a surge of floodwater that coursed over Monica's back and swept him off before he could even yell.

One set of Th*saaa*'s tentacles wrapped tight around the pipe, the other around Carl's arm, both at once.

Carl and everyone else made up for lost time on yelling. The Morror didn't say anything but didn't let him go.

And that was all well and good, but then we came loose from the outcrop of rock and went swerving downhill again. This time, the Goldfish had Monica tuck her legs in so we were riding something more like a sled if still not like a boat, and then we were hurtling toward another mound of rock. I thought, Oh, god, this is it, but then Monica got her legs around it and gripped and we were more or less stable, though the flood was still surging around us and the rain beat down.

Everyone had started trembling except the

Morror. "We've got to get out of this," I shouted into the roar of the rain. "Goldfish. Can't breathe properly. And the cold. Hypothermia. Pneumonia."

"Can you go and look for any kind of shelter?" Josephine gasped.

"I'll do my best," it replied, and vanished into the rain. I missed it immediately; with the air and the ground brown and churning around us, it was all too easy to imagine it wouldn't make it back.

I started checking to see what we might have lost to the floodwater, but once I'd gotten oxygen masks on everyone, I was too cold and wet to go on. With some hesitation I handed an oxygen mask to Th*saaa*, who then proved that we still had Josephine's bag of strange things, because it whipped its tentacles like a lasso across the platform and snatched its shiny object out of it.

Josephine looked indignant but didn't demand it back, because you can't expect prisoners to actually *hand* you the means for interrogating them.

"I saved your life," it reminded Carl.

"Yeah, I guess you did," Carl said. "Uh. Thanks."

"I hope you will bear that in mind if you should succeed in taking me to your superiors. I suppose you do not have the concept of *ushaal-thol-faa*, but you do at least have crude approximations like *dhan'yavād* and gratitude in your languages, which I believe should have some influence on your behavior."

"Yeah, all *right*. At least you're honest about why you did it," said Carl, shivering, clearly beginning to feel rather *less* grateful.

But Noel wasn't. "THANK YOU SO MUCH, TH*SAAA*," he exclaimed, even though his teeth were chattering. "He's my brother. I know he's kind of an idiot, but I'm still really, really glad you didn't let him drown."

The Morror peered down at him and looked a little startled, or at least I thought it did.

"I was only in trouble because I went and untied you," grumbled Carl. "Where's *your usha*-what-ever?"

Th*saaa* ignored him. It ran the very tips of its tentacles over the surface of its object in an intricate, swirling pattern and then placed it in the center of the platform. Josephine could've grabbed it again, but she didn't, just looked at it warily.

"So come on, what *is* that?" I asked.

"It is a *Paralashath*," said Th*saaa*, which of course told us nothing at all. But then the *Paralashath* came to life again and started glowing, and this time it was giving off not only colored light but heat.

"Oh! Is that what it's for?" I cried, eagerly shifting closer to it.

"No," said Th*saaa*, rather snottily, like it would have rolled its eyes if it had been human. It might not be a fan of our words for gratitude, but *no* was one human word it seemed quite happy with.

"Isn't that too hot for you?" asked Carl. "I thought you guys were all about the cold."

"This is pleasant for short periods. In these conditions, I am not at risk of overheating."

"Is this about engendering more *ushaal-tholfaa*?" asked Josephine sourly. Of course she had memorized the word on one hearing.

"In part," said the Morror. "If you die of cold, I doubt your robot companion would help me reach safety. Or refrain from . . . hurting me."

I noticed for the first time a couple of blackened streaks on its chest and head, where the Goldfish had zapped it.

After that we just focused on breathing oxygen and trying to keep our hands warm. Monica's back was still a horrible place to be in that storm, but it felt a bit less likely to be *fatally* bad.

Gradually the rain started to subside, and then I saw something glowing through the curtains of water around us. The Goldfish was back.

"Okay, kids, the good news is I think I found someplace," it said. "Bad news is I don't think it's safe to move Monica yet."

It seemed particularly unfair that we couldn't get to shelter until the thing we needed shelter *from* calmed down, but there it was. Everyone who wasn't Th*saaa* huddled closer together around the *Para-lashath* and Th*saaa* sat there on its own and watched. Once Noel asked curiously, "*Can* Morrors drown?"

"Yes!" it replied crossly, and that was about the extent of conversation.

At last the torrent gushing round our outcrop dwindled to something that Monica could possibly wade through, and the Goldfish led us slowly down the slope of Tharsis and into a *hole* between two columns of rock. We had to climb off Monica's back and let her scuttle in separately, which meant we had to wade through the small cascade splashing into the cave.

The cavern didn't look, at first, like a good place to get dry, seeing as how water was streaming down the walls and dripping from the ceiling, and the bottom was practically a river. But there was a rocky shelf toward the back under a dry overhang, and with Monica crouching beside that, we had a reasonable amount of space to recuperate in.

Our new floor space wasn't the only thing illuminated by the combined light of the Goldfish and the *Paralashath*; stalactites hung from the ceiling, some long and pointed like icicles, some heavy and swagged like velvet theater curtains. Stalagmites rose from the floor, all crinkly and twisted like melting candles. As the Goldfish moved between the pillars, the rock glowed rosy amber and translucent in places, and strange lacy shadows played across everything.

"Guess we'll be here for a while," said the Goldfish, deceptively casually. "You'll need something to do. . . . How about a math lesson?"

"Let us eat something first, for god's sake," said Carl.

We started sorting through our remaining supplies to see what was still usable. We'd lost one of the Morror blades when Carl nearly got swept away. We still had the shock-ray staff, but right now we weren't as interested in mysterious alien weapons as we were in things we could eat. Some of our food had been washed away too, of course, and almost everything that wasn't in sealed packs or tubs was ruined. Still, the damage could've been worse, though of course we were that much closer to running out, and if we didn't get to Zond *soon* . . . or if we didn't find help when we got there . . .

"Give the alien some lunch," said Carl.

"I cannot eat your . . . Smeat," Th*saaa* said haughtily.

"We don't *only* eat Smeat," I said. "Okay, this isn't exactly dinner at the Ivy, but it's not *that* bad, in the circumstances. We've still got cheese."

"Let it have its blue meat stuff," said Carl. "It's defrosted, anyway."

"We can't keep calling it 'it,'" said Noel, who I thought was coming on a bit strong with this Rights of the Morror business. "It's a person."

"We call the Goldfish 'it,'" Carl pointed out. "It *is* an it."

The Goldfish surely *was* a person, I thought; it was programmed to want to do certain things and behave in a certain way, but it still had feelings and it could come up with its own ways of doing things—it had proved that when it zapped us into doing school-work. I felt guilty this wasn't something I'd thought about before.

"Do you mind us calling you 'it,' Goldfish?" I asked.

"Oh, I'm definitely an 'it,' kids!" said the Gold-fish sunnily.

"Er . . . and you, Th*saaa*?"

"I am not in the same category as a *robot*," replied the alien.

"Okay, fine. Are you a boy or a girl?" Carl asked.

"No," said Th*saaa*.

"Oh." There was a small silence. Carl considered. "Are you more . . . both, or more neither?"

"No," said Th*saaa*.

"Would you care to elaborate, would you like Carl to keep guessing indefinitely, or do you want us to understand you're not going to tell us?" Josephine asked frostily.

"I'm quth-*laaa*," said Th*saaa* wearily. "There is suth-*laaa*, quth-*laaa*, *ruul*, *thuul*, and ma-*lashnath*."

We all thought this through.

"Five sexes? How can you have five sexes?" I asked. "I mean, what would they all *do*?"

There was a slight pause as we all realized what I had asked, and my face got hot and later Carl called me a pervert. But at the time, no one said anything, because everyone totally wanted to know.

Th*saaa* didn't seem to have an emotional reaction that I could make out, except possibly mild boredom. "As you like," it began.

So that's how we ended up being the first humans ever to hear about Morror sex, and at first we were pretty interested. It turned out that though there were five sexes, it was actually really rare to have five parents—it was good if you did, because you'd probably be extra healthy and live a long time, but it was only really possible when there was peace and plenty for all Morrorkind, which hadn't happened in a while. But no one had fewer than three, and though Th*saaa* didn't actually say, "And that's another reason why we think you humans are so primitive," it was pretty clear.

But then it just went on and on, and Th*saaa* kept stopping and explaining that though *usually*, *most* Morrors did it this way, there were like twenty percent or something of them who did it *that* way. And after a while, without meaning to, I sort of stopped listening, and when I started again I'd completely lost track of who was supposed to Harvest the Genetic Material from whom, and who else would then Absorb It through Their Sensory Tendrils, and what climatic conditions were required for a *thuul* to give birth alone, and when they wouldn't be able to without a ma-*lashnath*. And we started nodding and saying, "Oh, yes, I see," in a polite sort of way. And at the end we still didn't know what pronouns to use because Morrors don't *have* pronouns. Well, no, they *do* in some Morror languages, but not in the one Th*saaa* spoke.

So I'm going to say "they" when I'm talking about Th*saaa*, even if it gets a bit confusing. I can't guarantee I mightn't slip up and say "it" or "he" or "she," but that's the plan. Th*saaa* was as happy with this as they seemed to get about anything.

So anyway, eventually Carl created a distraction by eating some of the Morror's food; I guess it was inevitable we couldn't keep him from trying it indefinitely.

"It's actually okay," he said, chewing thoughtfully. "Kind of like crab . . . but more meaty . . . and sort of raspberry."

"Crab and *raspberry*?"

"Yeah, but it works. Come on, Th*saaa*. Have an apricot."

Th*saaa* rippled green and black. "I will soon have no choice. Your army will not have Morror food for me," they said. They warily extended a tentacle to accept a dried apricot, put it in their mouth, and instantly shuddered. "The *texture* . . ."

"Never mind, try something else. Jo! Have you got any of those ginger snaps left?"

Carl and Noel were now equally enthused about interspecies food sharing and were busily sorting through our scant resources in hope of finding something the Morror liked. Th*saaa* listlessly accepted energy bar after cold noodle, and though I suppose you couldn't expect actual enthusiasm, I found its limp disgust a bit irritating. Carl and Noel only saw it as a challenge.

Th*saaa* cautiously tried a lump of cheese and twitched and shuddered, but I thought maybe they weren't totally unpleasant twitches and shudders. Th*saaa* ate a little more and said, "That's so strong."

"That's made of milk," explained Noel.

"Which is a fluid cows secrete to feed their young," muttered Josephine darkly. "Laced with bacteria and then fermented."

That put Th*saaa* off the cheese for the time being. But then they picked up something that quite randomly had survived everything: a bottle of tomato ketchup. Th*saaa* cautiously squirted a dab onto another tentacle and touched it to their mouth.

Th*saaa* went blue, orange, and fuchsia, made a high-pitched *eeeeeeee!* noise, and reached for more.

"You like it!" cried Noel, delighted.

"This would go very well with baked *fal-thra*," said Th*saaa*, busily sucking ketchup off their tentacles. "I wish my *ruul-ama* could have tried this."

"What's a *ruul-ama*?" I asked, but Th*saaa* was either too engrossed with the ketchup to answer or pretended to be because it was a convenient way of not answering questions.

"Are you going to feed it *all* our food?" asked Josephine sharply.

"We don't really need the ketchup," argued Noel, who was just delighted to see the Morror more or less happy.

"Try to keep in mind why we're *on* this messed-up planet instead of at home living our lives," said Josephine. "Also, the small matter of the hundreds of thousands of people who aren't living their lives at all." She drew up her knees and glowered into the black depths of the cave.

After eating, we focused on properly warming up and drying things over the *Paralashath*. You've got to remember that we weren't *quite* as badly off as we could have been in this situation, because our uniforms were made of up-to-date, temperature-controlled, highly waterproof nano-weave. On the other hand, what with all the crashing into things and being attacked by Space Locusts, our uniforms also had *holes* in them, and the flash flood hadn't been particularly kind to the duct-tape patches.

So in the end we mostly stripped down to our underwear and set up a sort of clothesline between stalactites, and then just crouched as close to the

Paralashath as we could and breathed some more oxygen. I was way past the point of worrying about the other kids seeing me in my pants and crop top, and frankly didn't care if our friendly neighborhood alien saw me either. Josephine evidently felt rather different, as she didn't take anything off and ordered Th*saaa*, "Stop looking at us."

Th*saaa* obeyed at once. "I apologize. I only . . . I never thought to see humans so close."

"*That's* the first thing you think to apologize for?" said Josephine.

"We've all been looking at it . . . them . . . Th*saaa*," Noel countered.

"Of course we have! But they *know* what we look like. They've been watching us for years; they've had time to learn our languages, they know a *lot* about how to kill us. We know what? That they like tomato ketchup!"

"You know well enough how to kiiill uuus," murmured Th*saaa*, their speech again getting soft and long and slow.

"But you were the ones with the head start," said Josephine.

"You could not understand."

"You keep saying that. I keep suggesting you explain. Why did you come to Earth? Why are you on Mars? What's the plan?"

Th*saaa* sighed again. "We are forbidden to speak to humans."

"Well, then you've already broken the rules. Are you worrying about being in trouble with your people? Shouldn't you be worrying about the trouble you're in with *us*?"

"We *neeeeeed* the Earth," whispered the Morror, breathing faster and sucking in oxygen from the mask I'd given them.

"And we don't?"

"No, you do not *feel* it as we do—you are so blaaaaank," said the Morror, flashing all kinds of colors.

"Blank," repeated Josephine. And for a moment, she *was* blank, expression just dropped off her face.

Then she leaped at Th*saaa* and grabbed the oxygen mask away. "Is *this* blank?" she shouted, pushing them against the rock wall. And then she was struggling with them while they gasped and she yelled, "*Why?* Just explain all of it! Tell me *why* any of this had to happen!"

"Go, Josephine!" cheered the Goldfish.

"No! *Don't*, Josephine!" protested Noel in distress.

Th*saaa* might have been too surprised to fight back at first, but they weren't tied up anymore, so they wriggled and lashed out with their tentacles. Carl and Noel and me were trying to separate the two of them anyway, so Th*saaa* shortly got free and then hopped off the rocky shelf into the shallow river coursing through the cave and splashed away into the dark, making a wailing noise.

"Oh, well, now we've lost them," said Carl in disgust.

Josephine just stood there gasping and staring, and then she took off as well. I thought for a moment she was going after Th*saaa*, possibly in order to drown them, but then she splashed off in the opposite direction.

"Stay here," I cried at Carl, dragging my boots back on.

"Oh, this one's all yours," he said, sitting down and putting his head in his hands in sheer exasperation.

I put on my uniform jacket and climbed gingerly down from the ledge. "Come on, Goldfish. I need a light," I said. "But when we find her, don't *talk*, okay?"

I waded into the dark, feeling very cold and damp as soon as I was away from the *Paralashath*.

"Josephine?"

The dark water glittered, reflecting the Goldfish's

glow. Josephine's silhouette separated from a twisted column of rock. "What do you want?"

"Well, I don't know, I usually *do* come after you when you charge off somewhere. And it generally works out okay."

"That's why you've ended up out here," growled Josephine. "And nothing about this has worked out okay."

"Well, we're alive. You found us Monica. We're semiclose to Zond. We've got a Morror, even if it is really annoying and *rude*. Look, I *would* say I'll leave you alone if you want me to, but what with this whole situation . . ."

Josephine made a sad, impatient little noise. I decided to try a different tack. "What's going on with you? You're the one who never even wanted to fight them."

Josephine kicked up a spray of water. "I don't want to be a *soldier*. I'm a useless pilot and I hate being told what to do. If I don't get blown up on my first day, I'll end up going crazy and shooting myself."

"Don't say that," I said, but Josephine ignored me.

"But that doesn't mean I'm not *angry*. I want to be an *archaeologist* and a *composer* and I *should be allowed to be*, if it wasn't for *them*—and they were shock-raying London on the day I left, remember? And that *thing*—all I want from them is an *answer*. I'm not punishing them, I haven't said, 'Let's kill them with rocks.' And after everything they've taken away, a lot of people, grown-up people, would think I was more than justified."

"Who did they take away?" I said, very quietly, because I was sure we were talking about a person.

"Guess," said Josephine bitterly.

I had already. I was almost certain who it was, given the people she'd mentioned from home and the person she rather significantly hadn't.

(I hate thinking about dead mums.)

"I'm so sorry," I said.

Josephine swerved round. "Oh, *don't* be," she snarled in a weird, strangled, horrible voice. "She was a musician on the *Queen Guinevere* when they sank it. I was one year old. I don't remember her. So it doesn't matter."

After quite a long time standing there, praying I wasn't going to say the wrong thing, I said, "Of course it does."

Josephine made a noise that was a bit like a laugh, although not very much, and did actually look at me. "Yes, it really does," she agreed. "Of course, Lena and Dad *do* remember her. I know it must be worse for them in lots of ways. But I hate that I can't. I can tell when they're thinking about her, and sometimes they don't talk about her because I'm *there* and I—"

She smacked her hand hard against the stalactite pillar. "I want to know why she's dead. Is that so unreasonable?"

"No," I said. "Of course it isn't. But not like this, okay? This isn't like you."

There was a soft splashing nearby, and a murmur of long, mournful Morror syllables. The Goldfish spun round, but Th*saaa* was still hidden in the shadows and might as well have been invisible again.

"You are speaking of your . . . mother?" Th*saaa* said quietly from the darkness. "I wish she could return to you. I wish my people had not harmed you. I . . . do not believe it should be forbidden to say that."

Josephine didn't answer straightaway. "Why do you think we're blank?" she asked at last, pacing toward the voice until the Goldfish revealed Th*saaa*, flickering orange and green, and somehow I got an impression of confusion. Josephine tilted her head. "It's because we don't change color, isn't it?"

"No," said the Morror, and went yellow.

"Yellow!" I said, suddenly getting it. "Yellow is *embarrassment*."

"No, it isn't," insisted Th*saaa*, but not at all persuasively, and more yellowy than ever.

Josephine's lips parted with fascination, and she breathed, "Oh, Dr. Muldoon would *love* this."

"Noel would too," I said. "Let's go back and show him. Come on—it's not as if anyone has anywhere better to go, and I'm *freezing*."

So we splashed back to the ledge where Carl and Noel were, and everyone had some more oxygen, and Noel was duly thrilled by Th*saaa* the Alien Mood Ring. Th*saaa* might not have particularly enjoyed the attention, but Noel tried to give them a quick rundown on what all the various human expressions meant, so at least it was reciprocal.

"Look, this—GRRR!—is ANGRY! Like when you go . . . ?"

". . . black, purple," supplied Th*saaa*.

"Oh, are you angry now?" asked Noel in concern, because Th*saaa* was mostly lilac and gray now. "I didn't mean to annoy you."

"No. Not angry. Not *this* purple. This is . . . this is something else. I cannot . . . I do not know all the words," and whatever those exact colors meant, Th*saaa* sounded so weary that we left them alone for a bit.

"*Can* you lie?" asked Josephine guardedly, from

across the *Paralashath*.

You'd think it might have been in Th*saaa*'s interest to say that they couldn't, but they said, "Yes. One may force colors to some extent. It is not easy to maintain, unless you are very skilled or very talented. An actor, for instance."

"Is that why you wear invisible suits? So you can lie if you want to?"

"No," said Th*saaa*, and clammed up again.

Josephine looked at the *Paralashath*. It wasn't producing any colors at the moment, just heat, but Th*saaa* had said that wasn't what it was for, and we'd seen the patterns it could make.

"Is this . . . art?" she asked.

Th*saaa* went soft rose and amber and blue, reached out, and swirled the tips of their tentacles across the *Paralashath*'s surface again, and it changed, whorls of turquoise and peach quivering over it. "Yes," Th*saaa* said. "My *ruul-ama* composed it. They were a musician too."

Josephine frowned, and either Noel's human expressions lesson had done Th*saaa* some good or the Morror had realized on their own that this didn't quite make sense. "Ah. I suppose . . . this is silent, so not music? But art, yes."

The *Paralashath* gave off little ripples of heat and

cold in time with the rhythm of its colors, so you could feel the patterns of temperature play across your skin like feathers. Th*saaa*'s colors gradually flowed in sync with it.

Th*saaa* said into the depths of the *Paralashath*: "My *ruul-ama* died over *Karaaaa*, and my *suth-laaa-hum*, working on the northern light shield." There was a pause, and then it explained: 'My parents."

Kara, I thought. The battle that made my mum famous. Maybe she'd even been the one who killed them.

"Yeah, but how old are you?" asked Carl briskly.

"Thirteen," said Th*saaa*.

"Thirteen of our Earth years?" asked Carl, after a grinding silence.

"Of *course* thirteen of your Earth years," said Th*saaa* witheringly. "Why would I give you an answer you couldn't understand?"

We all wondered if maybe Morrors were like dogs and cats, who didn't live that long but were middle-aged at five or whatever.

"And . . . er . . . ," said Carl, "does that roughly correspond to . . . I mean, as a proportion of . . . I mean, are Morrors grown up when they're thirteen?"

"*No*," said Th*saaa*.

"Oh."

"I'm eight," volunteered Noel, but no one else felt like saying anything much for a while.

"We didn't know you were a kid," Josephine said softly.

And all of us stranded war kids sat there quietly in the Martian cavern, waiting for the rain to stop. . . .

"Math, anybody?" suggested the Goldfish.

20

Oh, Christ, that math lesson, you don't even want to know. To cut a long story short, it became obvious that Th*saaa*'s new position was that while humans might have a bit of emotional depth after all, we were still probably drooling idiots compared to the lofty grandeur of the Morror brain. That got Josephine's back up—well, everyone's. So, Josephine was the one who challenged the alien to a math duel for the honor of our respective species.

"Is this really necessary?" I groaned.

"Yes!" cried Th*saaa* and Josephine as one.

Noel lent Th*saaa* his tablet to work on, which Th*saaa* got the hang of pretty fast—we'd already seen that their tentacle tips were at least as dexterous as human fingers. So the Goldfish sent a math quiz over to both of them, and Th*saaa* and Josephine were soon furiously hacking away at the questions.

"Look on the bright side—as long as they're doing that, we get out of algebra," Carl whispered to me as we settled down to watch.

Now, I assumed that invisible aliens who've besieged the planet my entire life couldn't be completely dense. So much as I respected Josephine's brain, I was pretty surprised when she proceeded to wipe the floor with the Morror, who became yellower and yellower. Josephine finished her quiz in about a third of the time and, according to the Goldfish, got ninety-six percent right while Th*saaa* got nothing.

"That is a lie!" Th*saaa* exploded. "You are cheating! You have no *thol-vashla-sleeth*!"

"Aww, no one likes a sore loser, Th*saaa*," chirped the Goldfish with undisguised satisfaction.

But the triumph had gone out of Josephine's face. "It's because it's in base ten," she mumbled, almost inaudibly.

"What?"

"Base ten!" Josephine yelled. "Ordinary math! *Human math!* We work everything by tens because people started off counting on their fingers! But look at it . . . them!"

"Yes!" Th*saaa* proudly waved the three tentacles that grew at each shoulder. "I knew there must be an explanation! You are using the wrong kind of mathematics!"

"There is nothing wrong with our mathematics," snarled Josephine.

So Th*saaa* wanted to do the whole quiz again in base six. And Josephine might have been an intellectual prodigy, but this wasn't something she had a lot of practice with.

"Have you got any logic tests, Goldfish?" she asked.

"You are trying to avoid a fair challenge!"

"I am *trying* to find something with a universal frame of reference!" Josephine retorted.

"Maybe there isn't one," said Carl.

"All right, so we're not going to find out who's cleverest today, and everyone'll just have to learn to live with that," I said in exasperation, while the contestants glared at each other.

"You souuuuuuund like my *suth-laaa-hun-ruul*," grumbled Th*saaa*.

"Your what?"

"I'm pretty sure you just got called an alien granny, Alice," said Carl.

"If you were *that* intelligent, you'd have realized the problem straightaway," muttered Josephine to the Morror. "*I* was the one who did that."

Noel decided to smooth things over by shuffling over to Th*saaa* to show them the various things his tablet could do. "See, it's a bit like a *Paralashath*," he said.

"No, this is a much simpler construction than a *Paralashath*," said Th*saaa* immediately.

Noel shrugged and just played some songs and videos, and then various funny things he'd gotten off the internet at home.

Th*saaa* tolerated this loftily for some time. Then Noel hit play on a particular video, and there was a much more noticeable effect: tendrils swayed and flashed red and pink and Th*saaa* wheezed, "The . . . creature . . . pushed the human . . . into the *pond*."

"Are you . . . laughing?" I asked uneasily. "Or are you *ill*?"

"Please, show it *agaaaaaain*," begged our Morror.

I suppose some things are universal after all. It *was* a particularly funny video of a goat butting a man into a pond.

Noel leaned over to show something else on the

tablet and, as he did so, brushed Th*saaa*'s tentacle with his hand.

"You're a lot warmer than I'd have expected," he said thoughtfully. Tentatively, he held his hand out so Th*saaa* could touch it. "I thought Morrors liked everything really cold."

Hesitantly, Th*saaa* coiled a tentacle tip around Noel's finger. "And I knew you would be cold. And yet . . . I thought it would be like touching something dead. . . ."

"Oh." Noel frowned. "No, I expect it's a bit like what touching a reptile feels like, to a human."

"Yes," agreed Th*saaa*. "You generate less heat and lose it more quickly. We would overheat in warmer climates. Our world was cooler—we were made to keep warm easily." Th*saaa* sighed and flickered sage green and gray. "Humans . . . humans do not need such particular conditions."

After that, the Goldfish said the storm outside had stopped, and we figured we were as dry and ready for travel as we were going to get.

Which frankly wasn't *that* ready. A big part of me really didn't want to move. It was difficult to do it without starting to promise myself things like baths and warm beds and hot pasta and Mum and Dad, and I'd been pretty good at not focusing too much on that sort of thing up until now. I was scared of getting let down and not being able to take it.

We waded out of the cave and piled onto Monica.

Everything outside was still extremely wet, to the point of there being exciting new torrents of flood-water thundering across the landscape, but it was now more possible to skirt around them. Monica was surefooted enough not to slip in the mud.

The umber clouds parted and the little sun came out as we skittered round the flank of Mount Peacock. A misty rainbow hovered over the peach-colored ridges of the land beyond.

Th*saaa* was entranced. Their tentacles spread wistfully toward it, and their colors flickered into sympathetic bands of red, orange, yellow, green. "A *vamala-raaa*! It has been so looooooong," they said.

"Yeah, it has been," I agreed. I hadn't seen one in *years*, even on Earth, and it made me feel a little better.

"There are so few colors on this planet," sighed Th*saaa*.

"That's not really true," Josephine said. "Have you seen the little flowers that are growing now? The purple sea and the grasslands? And even without the terraforming, the sky at night . . ."

Th*saaa* considered. "Yes," they conceded. "Yes.

But you cannot imagine what it is like without *ruhaa-thal*. It is so strange, that you come from a planet that has mag . . . mag . . ."

"A magnetic field, Th*saaa*," supplied the Goldfish. I thought, Wow, Th*saaa* is now in the category of Kids the Goldfish Needs to Teach Stuff. That really *is* progress.

"A magnetic field," Th*saaa* repeated. "It is so strange that you *have* it and you did not evolve to *use* it. This place, it . . . it *hurts*. But yes, I can see it must be beautiful for humans."

"So, tell us about *your* planet, Th*saaa*," said Noel.

Th*saaa* went quiet.

"Or planets, plural?" suggested Josephine.

"I am not allowed. You already know, I am not allowed."

"Yeah, but c'mon, that horse bolted hours ago," Carl said.

"That . . . horse?" echoed Th*saaa*, confused.

"There must be *something* you know is okay," said Carl. "Something that's just about the stuff you do at home. Like, here's an example. We come from a city called Sydney, our parents run a cinema, and I've seen *Hawkflight* so many times I can recite the entire screenplay. It's about a Flarehawk pilot who chases a Morror ship through a wormhole to the Morror home world, and he defeats all the . . . uh, never mind. I mean, in Sydney there are many beaches—people like swimming."

There was a slight pause. "We are aware of *Hawkflight*," said Th*saaa*. "It is inaccurate on almost every possible level."

"There's a fountain in Darling Harbour where the water goes in a spiral and you can play in it," offered Noel encouragingly before Carl could say anything else tactless.

"Darling Harbour stinks of fish," said Carl.

"It does not. And there's an aquarium. There's a pool where you're allowed to feed the rays. And sometimes we used to walk back from the aquarium through Chinatown and eat emperor's puffs . . . they're little batter cakes with custard inside . . ." Noel began to look slightly mournful.

"I have spent most of my life on ships and civilian stations," said Th*saaa*.

"Yeah, but still," Carl said.

Th*saaa* considered. "I have always wished to see the city of Swaleeshashalafay Athmaral-*haaa*-Thay. . . ." (I've given up here, but the name actually went on for much longer than that.) "I have only ever seen pictures, and there are many *Paralashath* artworks by Morrors who lived there. The glowing towers and galleries and stairs, built of ice blocks of every color—and on the horizon, always the steam rising from the sea, from the—the . . . hot, burning things under the water—"

"Underwater volcanoes?" guessed Josephine.

"Yes! Volcanoes. The steam was like—like pillars holding up the sky. And red spirals of *fraaraval* hanging between the buildings, and amber gardens of *lathmalee* . . ."

"Is Swarlyshash . . . thing—is that, like, the capital city?" Carl asked.

"The capital city of what?" asked Th*saaa* witheringly. "The planet? How could a whole planet have a capital city?"

"Can you tell us a Morror story, Th*saaa*?" asked Noel, changing the subject. "It doesn't have to be a modern one."

Irritable bands of orange were winking across Th*saaa*, and I was sure they were going to refuse. But then, unexpectedly, the orange gave way to soft greens, and they actually patted Noel gently on the head with a tentacle.

"I will tell you the story of the Bridge of Thamthol-Tharaa. In the land of Ee-*ee*-Lathwama, there was a beautiful suth-*laaa* who loved a beautiful *ruul*.

The suth-*laaa* had a mane of tendrils as delicate as patterns of frost on a window, and their arms flowed as elegantly in the air as weed in the water, and the *ruul*'s colors changed as gracefully as *theela-va* in the sky. But they were alone, for the thirty turns before there had been many warm winters, and so very few ma-*lashnath* had been born. The *ruul* and the suth-*laaa* met quth-*laaa* and *thuul* sometimes, but without a ma-*lashnath*, the *ruul* and the suth-*laaa* could not have children. So they set out for the land of Safwalaa-*aa*. . . ."

The storytelling didn't go totally smoothly; Th*saaa* soon got annoyed with us because we didn't always know which bits were normal Morror society and which were magic (apparently Safwalaa-*aa* was not a real place—even baby Morrors know that—but the thing about warm winters was totally true). But basically the beautiful suth-*laaa* and the beautiful *ruul* didn't find any beautiful ma-*lashnath* in Safwalaa-*aa*, but they didn't realize it was because all the ma-*lashnath* had headed for Ee-*ee*-Lathwama, looking for *ruul* and suth-*laaa*. Then there was a series of misunderstandings that were probably more hilarious if you were a Morror, but before we could get to the happy ending, Noel interrupted. "What's that?" he said suddenly, and we all tensed up. In our recent experience that question had not been a sign that nice, relaxing things were about to happen.

We were picking our way through the Pavonis Sulci—sharp ridges and flat, narrow-bottomed valleys that streaked the land at the base of Mount Peacock—and Noel was pointing at five specks in the sky. *Space Locusts!* I thought at once—but before I could even say it, I realized they couldn't be. The specks were holding a rotating circular formation even as they hurtled through the air toward us, and the light glittered silvery off their sides.

"Those are human work," said Th*saaa*.

"Drones—or could they be . . . ?" began Carl, squinting. "We're nearly at Zond, aren't we—they could be goads, right? It could be Colonel Cleaver?" He stood up on Monica's back and started waving his arms. "HEY! HEY, COLONEL CLEAVER!"

The little robots dived down toward us from on high.

And, of course, they started shooting at us.

We bounded off Monica in all directions. I crammed myself under an overhanging rock; Josephine was crouching between two boulders on the other side of the little canyon. Carl and Noel had headed *up* rather than down, and were both on a ledge a couple of meters above Josephine's head, flattened against the rock wall. That left Th*saaa*, trying to hide under Monica, but Monica's body was too high off the ground. The drones swept up above us and then swooped back to the attack, surrounding us completely. The air blazed with energy bolts.

"GOLDFISH!" Noel howled from the ledge. Carl had shoved in front of him, but they looked horribly exposed up there.

The Goldfish was already doing its best, dancing in the air, shooting and darting, but it was one fish-shaped classroom robot against five military killing machines. It was really only because the drones seemed so intent on scouring the canyon floor that the Goldfish managed not to be blown to bits itself.

"What are they doing?" I yelled. "Why are they shooting at us? They're supposed to be on our side!"

To my horror, Josephine half rose from her crouch, making herself an even easier target. "They're not shooting at us! They couldn't have missed us all—they're avoiding us!"

An energy bolt scorched the rock beside my head. "They're not avoiding us very *well*," I complained, shrinking back against the rock.

"Sorry, Alice!" called the Goldfish from above, who presumably had been the intended target.

"They're firing at *me*," shouted Th*saaa*,

catapulting away from a volley of blasts. They landed close to the valley wall and dived under an overhang like mine, picked up six stones at once, and hurled them with rather impressive precision: they knocked two of the flying drones off course—but only by a foot or two, and the drones soon recovered and swept back into formation.

"Your temperature signature," Josephine called as Ths*aaa* dived out of the line of fire again. "It has to be. They can see we're human and you're not!"

But there wasn't much Ths*aaa* could do about that.

"Goldfish!" wailed Noel again. "They're going to *kill* Ths*aaa*!"

The Goldfish had actually managed to zap one of the drones so repeatedly, it fell to the canyon floor with a thud. But the four remaining drones looked more than equal to one teenage alien with nothing but stones to throw.

"My *amlaa-vel-esh*! My invisibility gown!" Ths*aaa* wailed. "I need it!"

"It won't help!" shouted Josephine. "You'll show up even colder—it'll just make it more obvious!"

"The shock-ray staff!" I yelled, suddenly remembering it. "Grab it!"

But the staff was still strapped to Monica, and

Th*saaa* wasn't anywhere near grabbing distance of her now. Th*saaa* was pinned against the rock wall with nothing left to hide behind.

Carl burst into motion; he took a huge leap down from the ledge, lurched for a moment atop Monica's back, snatched up the staff, and then hurled himself up forward again. He threw himself on top of Th*saaa*, knocking the alien flat, and the four drones stopped in midair and hovered there, confused. Carl brandished the shock-ray staff—which did precisely nothing until Th*saaa* reached from underneath Carl and looped a tentacle around it. . . .

There was a flash of nasty violet light, and the drones all dropped with a clatter onto the rocks. The valley was suddenly silent, and there was a faint burned, metallic taste in the thin air.

Th*saaa* scrambled free of Carl, their tendrils quivering in all directions and their colors flashing so fast and messily, they were difficult to look at.

"What if they had not stopped?" they cried in an unusually high-pitched voice as the rest of us ran over. "What if they hadn't seen you in time? What if your temperature had not masked mine?"

Carl blinked. "Well, that would have been bad," he agreed.

"You could have *died*, Kuya!" cried Noel, torn

between admiration and horror.

"You have my *ushaal-thol-faa*," said Th*saaa* formally, making an obvious effort to get their colors under control. They extended three tentacles, and Carl, who hadn't hesitated before diving between Th*saaa* and four killer robots, did hesitate now. But then he took hold of Th*saaa*'s arms and let Th*saaa* hoist him to his feet.

"No big deal," he said. But, though I really don't think he'd thought about what he was doing while he was doing it, he couldn't help thinking about it *now*. "That really was pretty cool of me, actually," he confessed, reaching for his oxygen cylinder and taking a deep breath. "Take that, Captain Mendez. I am not *just* about doing things for the spotlight."

"That point would be a lot stronger if you hadn't actually *said it out loud*," said Josephine in exasperation, though she was smiling.

But it was hard to stay cheerful. Mars seemed so cold and unwelcoming and full of things that wanted to hurt us. Finally we caught up to Monica, climbed back onto her, and scuttled onward as fast as we could.

Carl cleared his throat. "I thought—" he began, and broke off. "I really did think it might be Colonel Cleaver. But we'll find him soon, I guess."

"Where did those things come from?" wondered Noel.

"Some of the Auroras have them," said Carl, his expression tight.

"So there has to be a ship somewhere . . . ?"

I could see what was upsetting Carl. "Yes. But it has to be . . . crashed, or malfunctioning," I said. "Or they'd be here. Those things would have transmitted back that they were dealing with something."

"Yeah. I just . . . I really hope the pilot of the Aurora was all right," Carl said.

I thought about Th*saaa*'s wrecked ship and the bodies Th*saaa* had had to drag out of it. The Aurora could have shot down the Morror ship, perhaps, and the Morrors could have shock-rayed the Aurora as it fell. The Aurora could have limped as far toward Zond as it could before dropping onto the rocks. Or, on the other hand, it could have been Space Locusts. But I didn't feel like saying any of it aloud, or asking Th*saaa* about it. I was so tired, and none of it would change the fact that we had to keep going.

"And so those drones were left roaming the sky, hunting for Morrors," said Th*saaa* softly.

"Yeah, but look," said Carl. "Don't worry. They were just robots. *People* won't do that to you. We'll make sure they know you're a kid. They won't hurt you. They'll work something out with your guys, and you'll be back home in no time."

Th*saaa* rippled black and indigo. "They have never had a Morror prisoner before. They cannot waste the chance. They will want to find out . . . everything they can."

No one had a very good answer to that.

I hadn't really been thinking of Th*saaa* as our prisoner anymore, because we weren't getting on so badly now. And, technically, they could have run off whenever they liked. Except that would have almost certainly meant they suffocated or starved, so as choices go, that one didn't really count.

Our last afternoon of travel was as uneventful as an afternoon can be when you are riding a robot spider along with your alien of uncertain status toward a questionable destination. And the oxygen was running out and, by the end, there was no more food. We were crossing another great bare plain as a blazing blue sunset spilled into the pink sky. Fine dust rose under Monica's feet in little spiraling puffs like flares of gas (it also got you very dirty). And there at last was Mount Olympus, the biggest mountain in the solar system, rising above the atmosphere, so huge it was as if part of the sky had been walled off. We rode through the first hours of the night, with its two knobbly little moons, and endless snowdrifts of stars. Then we draped the remains of the tent under Monica's legs, and Th*saaa* lent us the *Paralashath* to keep us warm.

"Can you play something, Josephine?" I asked, because the silence was getting to me again.

Josephine nodded and played something I'd never heard before; more bluesy than those heartbroken songs she'd played in the Labyrinth of Night, but more delicate and glittery than the actual jazz she'd played back at Beagle. It kept floating up high and sounded a bit like what being in a tiny, isolated group of people sitting under all those incredible stars is like.

"What was that?" I asked when she was finished.

"I'm going to call it 'Martian Sunset,'" said Josephine.

"Oh, you made it up? It was lovely."

"*Yoooooou* made it up?" Th*saaa* flickered turquoise and orange and seemed astonished.

Josephine raised an eyebrow at them, though I'm sure they wouldn't have gotten what that meant. "What? You know we *have* music, right? Did you think we just dug it out of the ground like potatoes?" She hesitated. "What does it sound like to you?"

"To me it sounds . . . very . . . bare. With no color

or movement or *shalvulu*—temperature changes . . ." Th*saaa* said.

"We'll introduce you to musical theater when we get home," said Josephine, a little crossly.

". . . but I think I *understand*. You are too *quick* with everything," said Th*saaa*, and reached for the *Paralashath*. "Come here," they added, and curled a tentacle around Josephine's wrist and guided her hand to the glowing surface, steering her fingertip in a pattern that might have been like the symbols we'd seen in the Morror ship.

"Now, play again."

Josephine's dislike of doing what she was told briefly warred with her desire to see what would happen. Curiosity won and she put the harmonica back to her lips and started playing "Martian Sunset" again.

The *Paralashath* answered the music. Colors and patterns streamed out of it, rippling over the sand, and faint drifts of *shalvulu* quivered on our skin. Josephine's playing hitched and her eyes went wide with amazement, and the colors faltered for a second, turned white and gray. She got back in control again, and they steadied and strengthened with arcs of deep blue rising with the high notes and quivers of crimson pulsing with the rhythm over the ground.

Th*saaa* said, "Ah, *yes* . . . I *do* see," and their colors started to sync up with the *Paralashath*'s colors, as they always did, but this time the colors were from the music.

Josephine actually looked a little teary-eyed by the time she finished playing. "That was . . . ," she said rather hoarsely. ". . . Thank you."

"I wasn't sure it would work," Th*saaa* said modestly.

✪

We made an early start the next day, seeing as how there wasn't any food left.

"Was your planet destroyed, Th*saaa*?" asked Josephine quietly as the sun came up. "You said it *was* colder. And all of this . . . it isn't just because you ran out of space for everyone at home, is it?"

Th*saaa* hesitated for so long, I wasn't sure they were going to answer, but then they said, "Yes. There is nothing left of it."

"I'm sorry."

"It was before I was born," whispered Th*saaa*. "Whole nations annihilated, so many *yeeeeeeears* of searching, so many died from the hardship of travel, before they found somewhere we could live."

"And Earth had the magnetic core . . . and it was too warm, but not by so much you couldn't work with it," said Josephine.

"Yes."

Josephine sighed and looked at her bag in her lap. I think one or two of the strange things in there might have been from her mum: maybe the little cushion or the Christmas tree star?

"Does it make you feel better, now that you know why?"

I could see Josephine thinking about it, warily testing herself the way you might press on a bruise to see how much it still hurts. "No," she said in the end, very calmly. "But thank you for asking."

I knew something then, or maybe realized I'd known it for ages, and it made me feel even more tired than I already was. If winning the war meant getting the Morrors off Earth, we were never going to do it. And whether it was fair, or how much of a right we had to be angry about it, wouldn't make a speck of difference. It was just how it was. Morrors weren't going to be a weird little blip in Earth's history after which everything went back to normal, any more than Victorians turned into Tudors or Tudors into Romans. The Morrors were going to stick around forever. It was just a question of how many people got killed before we found some way of handling it.

It was just as well that I'd never really been able to imagine a way of life without Morrors anyway.

"What happened to your planet?" asked Carl. "Why's there nothing left of it?"

Again there was a long hesitation, presumably because Th*saaa* wasn't supposed to talk about any of this to humans, or maybe not at all. "The Vshomu."

We would have asked what the Vshomu was, except that was when we first got a glimpse of Zond Station.

And there was nothing left of that either.

21

Okay, technically that's not true. There was plenty left in the way of rubble and ash and mangled Flare-hawks, and there were even some buildings that were more or less in one piece. But that there'd been a battle at Zond pretty recently, and that it hadn't gone very well for the home team, was not something you could miss.

It was also pretty noticeable that there didn't seem to be anyone around, either to pick up the pieces or to welcome in battered and bedraggled refugee children.

"Oh, god," whispered Josephine, looking at it through a pair of binoculars scavenged from the

Flying Fox. Then, through gritted teeth: "*Faster. Make her go faster, Goldfish.*"

The Goldfish's eyes flashed, and Monica lumbered on quickly enough that the wind ripped at our hair or tendrils and we were too busy clinging on to really talk to each other. Which was perhaps for the best.

Zond Station sat on a plateau amid the foothills of Olympus. The empty plains of Mars stretched away below, and above it the gentle, bare slope of the mountain went on and on until its peak disappeared above the atmosphere.

We climbed off Monica. "Oh, kids . . . ," said the Goldfish helplessly, sagging in the air.

I found that even though I had this heavy, empty feeling, like Earth gravity had suddenly slammed back on inside me, I wasn't actually surprised. Of course I'd hoped there'd be people at Zond to help us, and I hadn't wanted to think about the possibility there might not be. But it'd been there with us all along, the chance that maybe we weren't running *to* anything so much as running away from something that was always bound to catch up. It had nearly caught us once in the Labyrinth of Night, and now it was really here.

Josephine was beginning to shake beside me.

"We're not finished yet," I said to her. Somehow it came out sounding quite calm and sincere, even though it didn't seem to have a lot to do with what I'd been thinking.

"HELLO!" Carl boomed, in that enormous voice of his. "HELLO, IS THERE ANYBODY HERE?"

But no one answered.

Zond Station was much smaller than Beagle Base, and clearly a lot less science had been going on here, though there were a few algae pools and things doing their bit for the terraforming effort. Otherwise, there were a couple of barracks buildings with roofs on, and the blackened remains of a couple more. There was a single farm dome with a wheat field, but it was broken open and nearly everything inside was black and dead.

"The comm tower," breathed Josephine, pointing. It was snapped in two like a breadstick. No wonder the Goldfish hadn't been able to contact Zond at all.

Th*saaa* was changing color rapidly, gray-black-blue-purple, tendrils rippling and swaying.

"Did you know it was going to be like this?" I blurted out.

"You know I did not," Th*saaa* hissed. "I am no better off than you."

"But Morrors did this. You know what's happening. You know why they *came* here, don't you? You'd never tell us."

"Do you think they tell me everything? I am only thirteen. What do your adults tell you?" cried Th*saaa*. "My parents had been reassigned; I was being transported to a training center nearer the Earth. But something happened, and we were called to this awful place."

"That's really it? That's all you know."

Th*saaa* said nothing.

"We need to know when this happened," said Josephine in a thin, breathy voice.

"What difference does it make *when*?" asked Carl.

Josephine ignored him. "Everything's dry. But nothing's smoking anymore. It was recent, but not *that* recent. . . . Some of the lights are still on. . . . Goldfish—can you get any information off the life-support system? When did the main doors last open?"

The Goldfish obediently darted off into the command center. It came back and told us the date.

"A week ago. When the grown-ups vanished," whispered Josephine. "So that's it. Something started here, and everyone at Beagle went to help."

"But they couldn't," I said, and it felt like the silent thing that had chased us here from Beagle was roaring so loud, I could hardly hear myself.

"*Guys,*" said Carl urgently, grabbing Noel and turning him against his chest. "Don't look."

There was the wreck of an Aurora lying in the ruins of the comm tower. Maybe a shock ray had sent it smashing into the tower—I'm not sure. The cockpit was ripped open, and you could see there were *people* still in there.

There was a moment where we all stood there frozen in a huddle. Then Josephine set her jaw and started walking toward them.

"*Don't,*" I said.

"I have to see who they are," she said, in a voice like stone. "Dr. Muldoon came here." And I went stumbling along too, though I wasn't sure I could make it all the way.

We didn't go that close in the end. Just close enough to see that neither of them was Dr. Muldoon or Colonel Cleaver.

But they were still somebody. And I thought, Oh, god, are we going to have to look at every body to see if it's someone we know? Because I assumed there would be lots.

But there weren't, as it turned out. We picked our way through the ruins; into the farm dome, across the space pad, past the ranks of unmanned guns. There were places where it was hard to be sure; some of the buildings were so badly collapsed or burned that we couldn't really tell if there were people under the rubble. But we didn't see anyone else dead. Josephine was moving like a sleepwalker, stumbling and staring. I only noticed that in a dazed, distant kind of way, so maybe that was how I was moving too.

And then, in one of the launching bays, we found a big splash of blood on the ground, and some empty bandage wrappings scattered about. Someone had been hurt, and someone had tried to help them, but *neither* of them was here now.

". . . That's good, though?" Noel said. "I mean, maybe they're still alive."

"When did your ship crash, Th*saaa*? You'd been there a few days when we found you—long enough to lay the bodies out and cover them. Was it the same day this happened?" Josephine sounded almost like someone in a trance now.

"Perhaps. I cannot be sure," said Th*saaa*.

"You said something happened and your ship was called here. This is what happened. Your ship was called to help. Wasn't it?"

"I don't know," said Th*saaa*.

Josephine took in a long, long breath and let it out in a sigh. She said, in a strange, faraway little voice: "I do." She closed her eyes and then opened them, and when she spoke again all the haze and shock had gone and she sounded cold and sure: "The people here got into a fight with so many Morror ships they couldn't handle it themselves; they had to call in reinforcements from Beagle Base, and even then it wasn't enough. Of course, your side was calling for backup too. Maybe the humans had no idea there were Morrors on Mars until they were under attack, or maybe they found Morrors here and struck first.

"Either way, you're here. They lost. Humans don't have control of Mars anymore. The Morrors do."

She was looking at Th*saaa* hard enough to bore a hole in them.

"But the Morrors don't want Mars. It's no good to you because it hasn't got a magnetic field. And there's nothing here that's much of a target. Okay, a few hundred kids being trained to fight you, but you've never gone for kids like that before, and you didn't attack Beagle Base. So it wasn't that.

"So why would Morrors come to Mars when the humans here weren't threatening you, when they were getting *out of your way*. Unless . . . Your planet is gone. You need the Earth and its magnetic field. But humans don't *need such particular conditions*, and after all, we're so *blank*, aren't we? You saw a place humans were going voluntarily, where we can live and you can't, where we were millions of miles away from the thing you want most. The only thing wrong was that it wasn't *all* of us.

"You're going to resettle humans here. So you can have Earth to yourselves."

The wind rasped across the wreckage of Zond Station, and there was no other sound. Then Th*saaa* whispered, "It seemed the kindest way."

"*Kind!*" Carl exploded.

"We did not want to wipe out an intelligent species entirely! We could not allow you to stop us from building the *Vuhalimath-laa* for another fifteen years!" said Th*saaa*. "What else could we do?"

"What *else*? Oh, rack off," said Carl.

Josephine cocked her head. "You were building what?"

Th*saaa*'s tendrils trembled and fluttered, and they didn't say anything.

I felt an almost overpowering urge to curl up in a ball until someone else came along to sort everything out, but I tried to make myself focus. "This isn't helping us," I said. "We need a new plan. There's got to be something here we can use. Food. Oxygen. Goldfish, do you have the plans for this base?"

"Forget that—what we need is a *ship*," said Carl.

No arguing with that. So we went looking for one.

The hangar doors were wide open. And right at the back, looking small and lonely, there was a single untouched Flying Fox.

Carl let out a sigh when he saw it, which was probably mostly relief but maybe exhaustion too.

"There was a science post at Schiaparelli Crater, wasn't there?" I said. "Or back to Beagle?"

"Want to just lift it straight out of the atmo? Maybe we'll find a nice space cruiser wandering past," Carl said, managing almost to smile.

"Let's find supplies first," I said.

Then Th*saaa* moved.

They were completely without color now. Just dark gray dappled with black and frost white. They turned, and those six tentacles whipped out—four of them hooking round our ankles and yanking, or simply knocking us off balance, so within a split second we were all on the ground. And at the same time, two tentacles stabbed straight into the Goldfish, knocking in one plastic eye. The light went out inside the Goldfish, and it crashed to the ground. Th*saaa* dragged out the invisible suit from inside it and ran for the Flying Fox, throwing on the suit as they did so.

"Th*saaa*!" wailed Noel, sounding more heartbroken over this than anything else we'd seen on Mars, and that made me furious. I scrambled up and chased after them, and Carl and Josephine were soon charging along with me.

But we couldn't *see* Th*saaa*. Even though we knew they were heading for the hatch of the Flying Fox, we couldn't see how close they were or what they were doing. I tried to grab for the hatch myself, and something knocked me away. And then it was too late: the hatch opened and closed before we could do anything.

I had a glimpse of controls moving inside, as if by themselves. I jumped up and banged on the door and screamed, but the ship began to move, with me still clinging to the outside.

Th*saaa* must have had some trouble working out how to actually *fly* a human craft; they just taxied out of the hangar and wove around awkwardly in the launch bay for a while, which must have looked ridiculous with me helplessly spread-eagled across the side of the ship. But then it began to move faster and faster until I dropped off. The others came running up as the ship finally lumbered into the air and swooped away.

"They just left us!" cried Noel. "They left us to *die*."

"It's not that bad," I said, sort of mechanically. "Maybe it's not that bad. There's stuff here. Shelter. At least enough oxygen for a couple of weeks. Not all the plants are dead. We can just kind of . . . live here for a while."

"But how could Th*saaa do* that?" Noel cried.

"We're the enemy," Josephine said flatly.

"But we aren't! Not *us*!"

I wondered if maybe you couldn't really blame Th*saaa*. If I was taken prisoner by some Morror kids and saw a chance to get away, it would probably seem moronic not to take it.

But that didn't make me feel any better.

I'm going to give up, I thought. I'm just going to give up completely.

But only for a few minutes.

So I stayed on the ground, hugging my knees. Carl kept yelling and swearing at the horizon where Th*saaa* had vanished. Josephine sat down heavily next to me, and I turned my forehead against her shoulder and shut my eyes.

"We'll work something out. We will," I said.

Then Carl stopped shouting. He backed up, a few paces closer to us. "Oh, Christ," he whispered. "Look."

I lifted my head and looked along the line of his pointing arm. A dark cloud had risen on the horizon. Whirling pillars of dust scoured the land ahead of it.

The Space Locusts were coming.

22

Thousands, millions of Space Locusts now, the dark mass of them seething and heaving high into the purple sky. Already we could hear their buzzing on the wind.

"We need to get under cover," I said. "Goldfish! Oh."

I'd forgotten for a second. I'd been going to ask again if the Goldfish had plans of the base so we knew where to look for basements or bunkers. But the Goldfish was lying lifeless on the floor of the hangar. I got a burning feeling in the back of my eyes and throat.

"How long do you think before they get here?" I asked.

"The horizon's only a mile and a half away," Josephine whispered. "All that's slowing them down is what they're eating. . . . Maybe ten minutes, if we're lucky."

"Right," I said. And for what seemed like far too long under the circumstances, we all stayed put in a heap on the ground.

"We need weapons," said Carl. "At least this is a good place to look for them."

"Okay," I said, getting up. "Three minutes. We'll look for anything that might hurt them or anywhere we can hide. Meet back at the dome."

And we ran.

There had to be an armory around somewhere, but after the first panicky minute I didn't think I was going to find it. I decided I'd focus on looking for shelter, so I ran from the barracks toward the back of the base, because maybe there'd be fortifications built into the mountainside itself. Sure enough, I found a trench leading to a heavy door set into a huge slab of gray concrete amid the red Martian stone. On the other side of the door, there was a tunnel, and stairs leading up into the mountain. For a wild moment I thought maybe I'd find a whole underground base, with all the soldiers missing from the surface, who would know exactly what to do about the Space Locusts. But I only found a little control room looking out over Tharsis and empty rooms behind, with a poured-concrete floor extending into natural caves.

I glanced at the bank of controls beneath a band of windows of thick glass. It did not strike me as a time to be sensible about not pressing strange buttons, so I did some brief experiments and found I'd fired some sort of energy cannon. The blast went off westward in the general direction of the Space Locust swarm, though I'd be surprised if I'd hit any part of it. Still, it was a satisfying thing to have found.

I must already be out of time. I ran back down to the heart of the base, yelling, "I've found somewhere to hide!"

"I assume you were responsible for the fireworks," Josephine's voice rang back at me.

"Yes, but I hope someone's got something more portable."

Carl, thankfully, had come back with armfuls of energy guns. Noel, on the other hand, was just pitifully dragging the Goldfish along the ground by its tail, and Josephine didn't seem to have found anything except a couple of canisters of some kind of liquid. She was crouched over her oxygen tank, doing something to it.

"What are you up to?" I asked.

Josephine looked up. "Making some adjustments," she said. She'd taken the mask off the oxygen hose, which she now pointed into the air. She released a glorious spray of red fire, arcing a good twenty feet, and laughed. And as laughs go, it sounded pretty crazy, but it was so good to hear it anyway.

"Nice," I said.

"Maybe it'll keep them off." She shouldered the improvised flamethrower.

Around us, the first few Space Locusts smashed into the Zond Station ahead of the swarm, plowing through the soil, into the farm dome; churning up the algae pools.

"Run!" shouted Carl, tossing me an energy gun.

"We can't just leave the Goldfish," whimpered Noel.

I looked down at it. Maybe it wasn't exactly rational—taking it with us would have to slow us down a little—but I thought it deserved more than being left to be eaten by Space Locusts too. "No," I agreed. "We can't."

We could hardly hear each other by now; the sky was growing darker, and the buzzing was a booming roar that seemed to come from everywhere. Streams of dust coursed across Zond, and we could feel a strange wind on our skin.

Carl and I carried the Goldfish—it wasn't heavy, just bulky and awkward, with no good handholds. Behind us, Josephine ignited pretty much everything even vaguely flammable, leaving walls of fire between us and the oncoming Space Locusts. It did make me feel a little less defenseless, but it also made me think, Even if they don't get us, even if they pass on and we're not eaten—what's going to be left of Zond Station? Where will we look for food and oxygen and shelter?

There really wasn't any more hope. Even though everyone was being so brave and brilliant, there just wasn't.

But I couldn't stop what I was doing, for everyone else's sake, and they couldn't either. And I thought stupidly, Well, you never know, maybe *something* good will still happen.

So we kept on trying to do the impossible.

We slammed the door to the tunnels behind us and ran gasping up the steps. We weren't doing that well with the oxygen now—we shared a few puffs from Carl's tank and left both Noel and the Goldfish toward the back of the cave. You could barely see out of the cave because of the clouds of dust and the boiling mass of the swarm itself. Carl called dibs on the big gun immediately and fired off an energy blast into the oncoming wall of darkness, and made a sizable hole in it.

We cheered. But the gap closed up again, and then the Space Locusts truly fell upon Zond Station and were devouring it within seconds.

Had they seen us? Could they smell us? Had those first few at the Jeromiana Waterlands somehow passed on a curiosity for the taste of humans? I don't know. But it felt as if the Space Locusts were as desperate to get to us as we were to get away from them. Even with all that Carl could throw at them, there were just so many coming in from everywhere that there wasn't any barrier thick enough to keep them out.

A little hole opened at the edge of the window, glass dust spilling down the bank of controls. A single Space Locust's head squeezed through, then more, gnawing and worrying at the gap so that it spread and spread. "Get away from there, Carl," Josephine screamed. He scrambled back, and Josephine jumped *forward* and swept flame across the opening. The effect wasn't instantaneous; a few of the Space Locusts simply swooped through the fire into the chamber, but some of the ones behind weren't so fast or lucky, and they blackened and dropped to the ground like lumps of coal.

But there were a handful of the creatures inside with us now. I had a vague memory of promising Miss Clatworthy, "I'll try to kill lots of aliens," so I aimed and fired and aimed and fired again, while Josephine kept hosing fire onto the widening hole in the wall like a firefighter in reverse. But step by step, the Space Locusts forced her back as more of them wormed through. One of them took a slice out of my scalp before Carl shot it. I met Josephine's eyes for a fraction of a second and felt sure we were thinking the same thing: We're not going to last much longer.

Then there was the sound of an explosion.

"What *is* that?" I said, to no one in particular.

A torpedo burst against the control center. Dead Space Locusts and debris showered inward. We were all knocked off our feet. If the Space Locusts hadn't already forced us so far back from the window, we'd probably have been killed.

"*Huuuuumans!*" wailed an unearthly voice.

"It's TH*SAAA*!" screamed Noel, jumping to his feet.

The windows had been blasted in completely, leaving a ragged hole behind. Outside, a shape bobbed against the daylight, in a cloud of dust.

"Are you all *aliiiiive*?" keened Th*saaa* into the ruins.

We rushed for the gap in the wall. The Flying Fox was hovering outside, the hatch open, Th*saaa*'s tentacles waving from within and changing color madly.

The silhouette of the Flying Fox abruptly lurched away. "I cannot fly this ship very well!" Th*saaa*'s voice called from somewhere below. Indeed, the Flying Fox was wobbling about so badly, Colonel Cleaver would have given Th*saaa* a detention on the spot.

"Th*saaa*, you bastard!" Carl bawled. He scrambled over the rubble up to the hole and, without ceremony, jumped out. It would have been terrifying if I hadn't already burned through my entire capacity for feeling normally scared; I was now getting by on some wild fiery feeling instead. But Carl landed with a *clunk* on the Flying Fox's roof, and the Flying Fox wobbled even more worryingly as he climbed around the hatch to slide inside.

Almost at once the ship steadied as Carl took over the controls. Then it was hovering beside the gap with Th*saaa* standing in the doorway, long tentacles reaching out for us.

"I am sorry," they said immediately.

We didn't have time for apologies. "Alice! Down!" Josephine yelled, and loosed a burst of fire over my head as I ducked. A cooked Space Locust dropped to the ground beside me.

"Get in the ship!" cried Th*saaa*, though it was easier said than done. Space Locusts that were stunned by the explosion were waking up and wriggling into the air.

"The Goldfish!" Noel insisted.

"Grab it! Throw it to Th*saaa*!" I ordered. Noel dragged the Goldfish up to the hole and dropped rather than threw it, but Th*saaa*'s tentacles were strong, and the Goldfish was flipped inside. "Now you," I panted to Noel, and he jumped while Josephine and I stood back to back, me trying to zap the Space Locusts that came in from outside, and Josephine toasting anything that moved in the shadows.

"Go on. Get out!" Josephine screamed, painting fire around the room. I hesitated. "Go *on*, I've got to be last, I can't jump carrying this, and we need the cover."

I gritted my teeth and jumped for the ship. I felt Th*saaa*'s tentacles lock around my arm and waist in midair. Then I was inside the Flying Fox, yelling for Josephine, who stood right on the edge and set off one last massive torrent of fire. Then she let the flamethrower fall from her shoulder, and leaped.

Th*saaa* caught her, flung her back into the ship beside me, and slammed the door shut.

"Kuya, go!" Noel cried, and Carl yanked viciously on the controls, climbing so steeply that the g-force got in the way of my efforts to sit up. We hurtled north around the curve of Olympus, out of the grip of the swarm. I thought about trying to get up onto one of the seats, but decided it was too much of a bother when I could curl up on the nice comfortable floor and cry. Josephine, sprawled beside me, had chosen the blank staring approach for the time being.

Th*saaa* was standing over us, in various somber shades of navy and teal.

"I am sorry," they said again, softly and formally. They patted us awkwardly with their tentacles. "Are you badly hurt?"

"Still conscious," croaked Josephine beside me. "That's a good sign."

I couldn't even answer at first, as I needed to think about it. I hadn't noticed it in all the excitement, but now my left arm wanted me to know that it hurt. I thought I might have broken it when the explosion knocked me over. Still, I did *have* a left arm, and a right arm, so I knew I should count myself lucky. Staggeringly lucky, in fact.

"Th*saaa*! You killed our Goldfish!" Noel howled.

"I *deactivated* your Goldfish. Surely it can be fixed," said Th*saaa*.

"But you just ran *off*," said Noel, who had taken it all very hard.

"I wanted to get back to my *people*!" cried Th*saaa*. "I did not want to be a prisoner or an experiment!"

"Noel, Th*saaa* came back," said Carl shakily from the helm.

"And I would have sent my people to find you—I did not mean to leave you there forever. I would never have left you to *them*. When I saw their swarm in the sky . . . I had to return for you." Th*saaa*'s tentacles waved fretfully in the air and then covered their face. "*Ohhhhhhh*, if you had not fired that cannon, I might never have found you."

I managed to get up and into a seat, hugging my arm against my chest. "Thank you," I said.

"Th*saaa*," said Josephine, lifting her head from the floor, "you recognized the Space Locusts."

"Space Locusts?" echoed Th*saaa* curiously, like

they didn't understand the word *locust*. But it didn't matter. "I have never seen them, only heard the stories. But yes, I know them. No Morror could mistake them.

"They are the Vshomu."

23

"**T**he Vshomu drift through space," said Th*saaa*. "They feed on whatever they find—the organic compounds in the rocks and dust, the ice of comets. But when they come to a world full of life, they *feast*, and their numbers . . ." They made an expressive movement with their tentacles.

"Explode," supplied Josephine.

"Yes. Explode. They never stop feeding until there is nothing left. Then many of them starve, their numbers decline again, very fast, and the survivors drift on. Their sight is very keen. They are the reason we learned to make ourselves invisible. But all we learned of them . . . all we know . . . came too late to save our world. They stripped it to the core, which cooled and died. For so many years, all we could do was run from them."

"Yeah, and you *led* them to us!" said Carl.

"It's not their fault," said Noel, who was mollified by now.

"I don't know. The Vshomu have devoured so many worlds across the galaxies," said Th*saaa*.

"They'll eat Mars," I said.

"At that rate, they'll eat the *solar system*," said Josephine.

"We must tell my people," said Th*saaa*.

"We have to tell *everyone*," I said.

"Okay," said Carl. "So everyone's had a chance to freak out back there except me. Does anyone know where the hell we're even going?"

"The Morror base," said Jósephine. "They must have one on this planet. Don't they, Th*saaa*?"

There was a pause while we all tried to get used to the idea of running into a horde of hostile Morrors on purpose.

"Is there a map on this ship?" asked Th*saaa*.

"Sure," said Carl, calling one up in the corner of the viewport. Th*saaa* gazed at it thoughtfully, then reached out with one tentacle and pointed to a place on the screen.

"I think," they whispered, "we should be searching there."

I'd stopped crying by now, so I lurched over to the helm and said, "I'll fly if you want," so that Carl could have a fair turn at freaking out.

"Oh, for god's sake," said Josephine, scrambling off the floor. "You can't pilot with *one hand*. I'll do it."

"Er," Carl and I said simultaneously, remembering Josephine's turn at the simulator and the wreckage of the obstacle course back at Beagle.

Josephine seemed unworried, though. "I've at least had more relevant training than Th*saaa* has. It's not really *that* hard."

It was true, actually; seeing as we weren't currently taking off or landing or shooting invading ships or dodging Vshomu, piloting wouldn't be much more complicated than just telling the computer where to take us. She nudged me out of the way and took over at the controls, and we kept on flying and did not blow up. Josephine gave a very small smile.

Carl flopped into one of the seats at the back of the ship and Noel gave him a hug, and I flopped alongside them. I couldn't help but wish the Goldfish was keeping an eye on the piloting, just in case.

But the Goldfish was still just a broken piece of luggage in the back of the ship.

"Do you think they're alive?" asked Josephine as we sped through a sky stained orange with Martian dust. "The people from Zond and Beagle . . . Dr. Muldoon?"

Dr. Muldoon's name couldn't have meant anything to Th*saaa*, but they rippled pink and orange at her in what might have been encouragement. "I hope we will find everyone."

☆

The thing about someone pointing to a place on a map of an entire *planet* and saying, "I think it's somewhere over there," is that at *best* that means flying over an approximately Massachusetts-sized bit of ground without any idea what the thing you're searching for looks like.

So basically we had to zigzag back and forth and round and round for ages, getting more and more cranky, and Th*saaa* said more and more things in their language that I'm sure were incredibly rude. And none of us had had anything to eat that day, and it was *weeks* since anyone had had a cup of tea.

Then, after hours of this, Th*saaa* yelped, "There! There!" and leaped toward the viewport in order to point at . . . nothing.

"What? Where?"

"We've gone past it now," said Th*saaa* in grumpy purples and ambers.

Josephine doubled back, and we flew around for what seemed like another million years.

"That is the exact place you were pointing out," said Carl.

"Clearly that cannot be true, because it is not there," said Th*saaa*.

We flew on.

"There! There!" cried Th*saaa* again.

"Yeah, that's a very nice rock face," said Carl.

"The entrance is invisible," said Th*saaa*. "What else would you expect?"

"I'm . . . really not that enthusiastic about flying straight into a rock face," said Josephine.

"I can see it," I whispered. I could make out that sort of vague shimmer in the corner of my eye that I was getting used to where Morrors were concerned. "You can fly into it. It's a big square hole in the rock, like a gate. . . ."

"I *hate* how you are not even looking at the screen when you say that," Carl moaned.

"It's *there*," I said. "That is . . . at least, I think so."

"Well, that's just lovely," Josephine said.

"*I* can see it perfectly well," announced Th*saaa*. Th*saaa* wasn't actually looking straight at the screen either, but doing the same corner-of-the-eye thing I was.

"*Obviously* I can't see it if I *look* at it," Th*saaa* said scathingly when this was pointed out. "It is *invisible*."

"Oh, bloody hell," moaned Carl.

"Go on," I said. "Down . . . *no, Jesus, right a bit*! And a bit more down . . . *not that far down*! And there. There. Straight ahead."

At this point I had to look at the viewport properly and couldn't help but wince, because we were, on the face of it, about to splatter ourselves against a massive rock wall like a bug on a windshield. It was hard to hold on to the belief that this was a good idea.

Josephine let out a shriek as she navigated the last few yards. . . .

And then the wall was gone, and it was dim all around us.

We were in a huge chamber inside the mountain. It was very obviously not a natural space; it was square cut and terraced into different levels, and though it was much starker and emptier than the inside of the Morror ship, there were colored lights set into the ceiling and the floor, far below us.

And there didn't seem to be anybody there.

"Aaargh," said Josephine, panicking after flying through a wall and now having to pilot a Flying Fox in a sudden confined space.

"Give it to me," said Carl, swiftly taking over the controls.

"I'd have been all right," said Josephine, aggrieved, as he lowered the ship toward the rock floor.

"Is there some way to cast one's voice outside the ship?" cried Th*saaa* sharply, in very urgent colors.

"Uh, a PA system? Yeah, I think this thing—"

"Give it to me. *Now.*"

Josephine handed them a microphone, and Th*saaa* started to talk into it, just as my eyes adjusted to the light inside the chamber and I started to pick up that faint shimmer of *something.* . . .

Not just in one corner of my field of vision, either. *Everywhere.*

"Morthruu Mo-*raaa* uha-*raaa* porshwur*aaa* va, ha'thraa vel Th*saaa* athla-*haaa* quurulu nas hur*uuu*-mua . . ."

There was an instant of silence. Then another voice spoke, loud but in soft, long, rippling syllables. "*Shuwathaaaahal-vaaa-raha, ath-shal vel lamnawath vramla-shaaa ath amna-clath.*"

"We should go outside," said Th*saaa*. "But stay behind me."

Josephine flicked a button to open the hatch, and we stepped out. Th*saaa* spread their tentacles in front of us like a shield.

All around us, Morrors started uncloaking.

✧

I hope we had decent excuses for being overwhelmed even before we found ourselves surrounded by aliens. Anyway, I became slightly dizzy. It wasn't just that there were so many Morrors, and they were all changing color and rippling their tendrils, but they were so different from *each other* as well as from us. I don't know if I'd have figured out about the five sexes if I hadn't known it already, but as I looked, I could see that there were Morrors with lacy manes, and narrow-built Morrors whose manes covered nearly their whole faces, and very tall Morrors who didn't have tendrils at all. But it wasn't *just* that—it was that they had different-shaped mouths and eyes and no two color palettes were really the same. I mean *of course* they weren't all the same, but in our recent circumstances, it had been hard not to think of Th*saaa* as the standard representative of the typical Morror.

For one thing, these Morrors were all *grown-ups*, and thus *bigger*.

For another, other than invisible suits I guess Morrors didn't really do military uniforms, or else their clothes had some sort of meaning I couldn't get. Many of them wore long A-line kilts like Th*saaa*'s, but in all different colors, and some of them had fin-shaped trains, and others wore layers of transparent fabric, or cream-colored robes with holes cut away here and there so you could still see the color racing across their skin.

Anyway, all of that was very interesting, but you also had to take account of how several of them were holding things that were plainly weapons. Colorful, pretty weapons. But weapons. Pointed at us.

"Hello," I said, giving the Morrors a silly little wave.

The Morrors talked among themselves. The sound of their voices rose and fell: sometimes they'd get very vociferous, but sometimes it seemed that most of what they wanted one another to know was in the color and play of their tendrils, so they didn't actually have to say much.

And tides of color kept sweeping round the group like someone was dragging a paintbrush from one Morror body to the next, though any Morror might be dimmer or brighter. And there were streaks and twists that didn't get passed on with the dominant color, which would sometimes get into a little eddy in a smaller group or meet a splash of a totally different color, which would either sweep around and turn the other way, or bounce to and fro, which I thought maybe meant the Morrors were disagreeing with one another.

Th*saaa* was talking and waving their tentacles too, but their colors didn't seem to be meshing with everyone else's.

"Are they saying 'Get out of the way so we can shoot your little human friends'?" asked Carl.

"That is not a helpful comment," said Th*saaa*.

"Yeah, but *are* they?"

Th*saaa* didn't seem to want to tell us, which I couldn't help feeling was not a very good sign.

Josephine huffed impatiently. "Why are they standing around when the planet's being eaten?"

"I *have* told them," Th*saaa* insisted. "They're discussing sending a party to see if the Vshomu are really there or if it is some human trick. Be *patient*."

Josephine sighed enormously, was patient for two and a half seconds, then muttered, "Oh, to hell with this," and reached into her bag.

The Morrors raised their weapons, and one of

them thundered, "KEEP YOUR HANDS VISIBLE," in startlingly perfect English.

Josephine lifted her arm.

She was holding the dead Vshomu that we'd killed in the first Flying Fox.

Some of the Morrors cried out—short, almost-human yelps or long rustling roars like faraway landslides. Some of them went silent and gray and half transparent. I thought that along with *Paralashath* and *shalvulu*, I might possibly have picked up another word: it was *au-laaa*, and it meant *no*.

Then several Morrors left, some of them possibly crying, and the ring around us broke into smaller, messier groups talking even more animatedly than before. No one seemed to be pointing guns at us now, and Th*saaa* lowered their tentacles and looked at us nervously.

Then a stocky Morror—one of the mane-all-over-face ones—came up and whisked the Vshomu out of Josephine's hands and took it back to the group to talk over.

Josephine said indignantly: "That was *mine*."

"How is a dead Vshomu *yours*?" I asked.

"It was in *my* bag," Josephine grumbled.

A pair of Morrors came over to us. The first was very tall and one of those I found hard not to think of as bald, because they didn't have tendrils, just color patches. The other was dressed in a gold kilt with a triangular fin at the back and had a cloud of curly tendrils standing out like an Elizabethan ruff around their face.

"Hello," said the big one without the mane. "I am Swarasee-*ee*. This is Flath. Come with me, please, humans. Flath will look after Th*saaa* now."

Swarasee-*ee* must have been the one who'd told Josephine to keep her hands visible: they spoke incredibly good English with no Morror accent or long vowels like Th*saaa* had at all. In fact, if you shut your eyes, you'd probably think you were talking to a woman from California.

Flath didn't talk to us, just towed Th*saaa* away. Th*saaa* looked back anxiously. "I hope it will be all right," they called plaintively.

"What are your names?" asked Swarasee-*ee* politely.

"Josephine Jerome."

"Carl Dalisay, and this is Noel."

"I can say my own name. Why do *you* always have to go first?" Noel grumbled.

"Alice Dare," I said.

Swarasee-*ee* paused and looked at me in mild

perplexity. "Alistair?" they repeated.

I sighed at considerable length while Carl chuckled. "Terrific, that's just terrific," I said.

Swarasee-*ee* led us down over the terraces, between what I was pretty sure were some invisible ships, under rows of rainbowy lamps.

"Where are you taking us?" I asked. "This is a waste of time. We need to get back to Earth and warn everyone, or *no one* will get to live on it."

Swarasee-*ee* said nothing, but their spots turned blue and orange by turns.

We were walking toward the rear wall of the chamber. There didn't seem to be anything in particular there, except that it was a long way from all the other Morrors. I reminded myself that the Morrors *hadn't* wanted to wipe out humans and so Swarasee-*ee* probably wouldn't be taking children into a nice quiet corner to kill us without bothering anybody else.

Then, because I happened to look nervously at Josephine to see if she was thinking the same thing, I noticed how shimmery the back of the cavern was.

"Oh!" I said.

Swarasee-*ee* stretched out their tentacles to the wall, which rippled faintly as they peeled aside a panel of invisible fabric.

"In you go!" they said, sounding almost as perky as the Goldfish.

There didn't seem much point in making a fuss about this, as there were enough Morrors around to put us anywhere they pleased. So in we went, though it was hard not to keep worrying about how stupid we'd feel if it turned out we *were* being led to our doom, and Swarasee-*ee* sealed it up from outside.

Wide steps led down into another chamber of bare red stone—a bit warmer than the one outside, which was nice—and wide and almost as empty as a sports field. But not quite, because about fifty human adults were sitting or lying about in groups in the middle of it, looking thoroughly fed up.

"Dr. Muldoon!" Josephine cried. "You *are* alive!"

Dr. Muldoon stood out because of her long red hair. There was a field hospital area over to one side, with about ten people covered in bandages or attached to IV's and so on. Dr. Muldoon was among them, helping out, even though I knew she wasn't that sort of doctor. She was in full military uniform, something we'd never seen her in before, though of course the Morrors had taken all weapons off her. She looked as if she *should* be tired, with her hair all loose and dirty looking around her shoulders, but she still seemed far more awake than anyone else.

"Josephine," she gasped, and came running. "What are you doing here?"

"Kids!" cried Colonel Cleaver as he came rolling up from the back of the group. I say rolling because he didn't have his robot legs. He was sitting on a bit of metal paneling that looked as if it might once have been part of a Flarehawk, with wheels clumsily attached, and he was pushing himself along with his hands.

"They took your legs?" exclaimed Noel, horrified. "That's awful."

"Never mind that. Did they capture Beagle Base? Are you okay? Where are the others?"

"They're still there. We didn't exactly get captured," said Carl, and after that of course we had to explain everything, which got quite complicated. I was not used to either Colonel Cleaver or Dr. Muldoon being apologetic. But they were now—in fact, not just them, but a load of other adults we didn't even *know* bustled up to say how they were very, very sorry about everything that had happened to us, and that they hadn't been there to stop it. And that's before they even *knew* more than ten percent of what had happened to us. While I'm not going to say I was against receiving a bit of adult sympathy, I wasn't sure this was a good use of our time.

So I thought maybe we'd better not tell them everything until later, and I glanced at the others and saw that Carl and Josephine had already had the same idea. But Noel was completely oblivious and went on saying things like "And then when the spaceship crashed for the *second* time . . . ," which made everyone wring their hands and fall all over themselves to say they hadn't meant things to turn out like that. Then Colonel Cleaver hugged us all and most of us said "Ow," and that's how they found out my arm was broken and that Josephine had cuts and Carl was singed and everyone was generally the worse for Space Locusts. The grown-ups were in the process of getting even more upset when Carl bawled, "ANYWAY. The planet's being *eaten* and is there any *food*?"

"James, get them some *food*!" snapped Dr. Muldoon at a poor man with the photosynthetic patches on his arms from Beagle Base, as if he should have known to do it already.

We sat down on the floor of the chamber to eat and go on explaining. There was a mix of human and Morror food ("The light-blue spirally stuff is better than it looks," said James apologetically), some Smeat, some raisins, but no tea. Dr. Muldoon put my arm in a sling and cleaned us up a bit.

"Of course, our actual *medical* doctor was hit by a shock-ray rebound," she said, sighing, dabbing on disinfectant.

A woman waved feebly from one of the beds. "You're doing fine, Valerie."

"Why did they take your legs, Colonel Cleaver?" asked Noel timidly.

"Ah, it's no big deal. I can get around without them," said the Colonel.

"He kept climbing the walls," said Dr. Muldoon, looking slightly tired at last. "Literally. Trying to disable that seal." She stared glumly at the curtain we'd come through, which was back to looking like a bare stone wall.

"You say that like I stopped," said Colonel Cleaver, grinning, and I remembered him climbing up the tower at the base using just his arms.

"We've tried pulling it down, and digging under it, and cutting through it," said Dr. Muldoon. "And frankly, we've been doing it more for entertainment value than anything else, because even if we got through, there'd still be the small matter of the Morrors on the other side."

"Weirdo invisible no-good clowns that they are,"

said Colonel Cleaver. "Forget my legs—it's her you should be worried about."

"The one who speaks such good English knows who I am," Dr. Muldoon said. "It keeps asking me about accelerated terraforming."

"They haven't hurt you?" I asked.

"They're not stupid. You can't get a scientist to do anything useful by torturing her. But they started hinting they might separate me from the others or take me off the planet altogether. And I can't understand why they're so interested; they're already altering Earth to suit them—they don't need my help with that. But I don't imagine they're asking out of sheer curiosity."

"We know why they're interested in terraforming," said Josephine.

Dr. Muldoon looked at us keenly. "Do you? And what did you mean, the planet's being eaten?"

And finally we managed to get them to listen to a decent account of why the Morrors had come to Earth, and what the Vshomu were. Josephine didn't have the dead one anymore, but she did have some pictures she'd taken of it on her tablet.

". . . and they eat planets," said Dr. Muldoon flatly, in the end.

"Yes."

"They're eating Mars."

"Yes."

"Mars."

"With us on it, yes."

"*My life's work,*" thundered Dr. Muldoon, springing to her feet with fire in her eyes. "My *home.* I create *scientific miracles* out of *rock and dust*, and *vermin* come along and *eat it.*"

"We're actually pretty worried about Earth as well," I said, but I'm not sure Dr. Muldoon really heard me, seeing as she was racing up the steps toward the seal.

"Morrors!" she shouted. "Let me out! I need specimens! I need my lab! I need to *kill them all.*"

"There are millions of them, you know; you probably can't kill them all yourself," said Noel.

"We've gotta evacuate, Muldoon," said Cleaver. "I've got to get those kids out of Beagle right now. HEY, MORRORS!" he bellowed at the wall. "Are you going to let us out of here? Or are you leaving kids and prisoners of war to be eaten alive?"

"Oh, I don't think it's a good idea to *annoy* them," Noel moaned anxiously.

"Yeah, Morrors!" boomed Carl at the wall.

"What are you *doing* out there? We have places to be!"

Dr. Muldoon raised her fists and would probably have pounded them against the wall if it had actually *been* a wall, but as it was more of a kind of holographic curtain thing, she ended up just grabbing handfuls of it and yanking them around as best she could.

"Morrors!" she yelled. "Are you listening? Are you still even there?"

"Morrors!" Josephine joined in. "We've got to get back to Earth! We have to warn the government! We have to start cooperating!"

"Morrors!" I shouted, pulling at the seal. "You can't fight the Vshomu and us at the same time! And if you couldn't get rid of the Vshomu on your own before, what chance have you got this time? You *need* humans now. You have to talk to us so we can *help* each other!"

"Morrors!"

"Morrors!"

Then, quite suddenly, the wall fell. It detached from its fastenings high above with a hissing sound and crumpled, shimmering as it dropped, until it lay in a weird half-invisible pile at our feet. All the Morrors were there on the other side, looking at us. And all the other humans gasped at the sight of them—all that time shut up inside the mountain and they'd never seen the Morrors uncloaked.

"Yes," said Swarasee-*ee*. "We agree."

24

Being stuck in the middle of an alien evacuation procedure might have been less bewildering if we could at least have *seen* the ships that teams of Morrors kept vanishing into. But we couldn't, and we couldn't understand what the Morrors were saying either, except when Swarasee-*ee* or one of the others said something to us in English, which was mostly "Wait." So we just stood around feeling rather awkward and vulnerable, and wondering if Th*saaa* had already gone, except for Colonel Cleaver, who'd gotten his legs back and was striding around amid the Morrors, looking ready trample Vshomu beneath his robotic feet.

"This is it, cadets," he said at last. "A couple of

our Day-Glo pals here are taking me out to Beagle to get the rest of the kids."

"Oh, aren't we going with you?" asked Noel, dismayed.

"Their biggest carrier will only take fifty," said Cleaver. "They say they're calling more ships in for the rest. Don't know how far we can trust them, but doesn't seem we've got a choice. This way you'll get home sooner, and you all need decent medical attention."

I nodded. I was sorry he was leaving so soon, but I found I didn't want to go back to Beagle anyway; I wanted to see Kayleigh and Chinenye and Mei, but too much had happened, both when we were there and afterward. And just hearing the words *you'll get home* made me feel slightly dizzy.

"We're really glad you're all right," I said. "We were worried."

"Seems like these vo-sho-whatevers would have eaten the lot of us if it weren't for you kids," said the Colonel cheerfully. "And I've had enough of things eating me to last a lifetime. So. Good work, cadets."

He threw us a salute. We all saluted back, except for Josephine, who, being a genius, had been looking at something else, and then got confused as to which arm to use. Cleaver scrutinized her thoughtfully until she started squirming, then said gruffly, "Good soldiering, Jerome—knew you had it in you," and dropped a big hand onto her shoulder.

"Thank you," said Josephine as the Colonel walked away. When he'd gone, she muttered to me, "None of this changes anything. I'd still be an absolutely awful soldier."

"Well," I said, "if this works out, perhaps you won't have to be."

A tall quth-*laaa* Morror—at least, that's what I assumed they must be because they had the same kind of tendrils as Th*saaa*—came along and sighed, "I am Warth-*raaa*. *Come thiiiiiiis waaaaaaaay,*" at us, being not as good at English as either Th*saaa* or Swarasee-*ee*.

"Do you have to—to run off anywhere else, Dr. Muldoon?" asked Josephine, trying to sound casual.

Dr. Muldoon smiled. "No. Swarasee-*ee* and I need to be on the first ship to reach Earth; someone has to be the one to brief the EEC. And I need you to make sure I have all the facts."

"Hey, kids!" called an unmistakable perky voice.

"Goldfish!" Noel cried in delight before we could even see it.

The Goldfish came swimming over the heads of

the remaining Morrors, with Th*saaa* hurrying along behind it.

"You're okay!" it said. It showered us with sparkles. "I'm so proud of you guys! Doesn't that just show you what teamwork can do?"

"Well, teamwork, flamethrowers, and energy torpedoes, yes," Josephine said.

"They fixed you!" Noel said, reaching up to hug it.

"Oh, I wouldn't say that, Noel!" said the Goldfish, with that faint edge to its perkiness that meant it was in fact profoundly cross. "These pesky Morrors! You can't expect them to *fix* anything. Not properly, anyway!"

"Why? What's wrong with you?"

It still looked a mess, of course. There was no light behind its right eye, which had been stuck clumsily back into place with glue, and it still had all its scrapes and dents. But it was flying and talking.

"They took out your zapper, didn't they?" said Josephine.

Carl burst into tactless laughter. The Goldfish's left eye flashed red, but indeed, nothing happened.

"We could hardly let it fly around armed," said Th*saaa*. "It started trying to attack us the moment it was reactivated."

"Look, I know it must be very confusing for you, but a lot of things happened while you were . . . deactivated, and now we and the Morrors are kind of on the same side," I said.

"It's more of an informal truce," said Josephine.

"And now you can't make us do history," said Carl, who hadn't stopped laughing.

The Goldfish went into a massive sulk and stopped talking to everybody.

"I'm sorry it's being so rude," said Noel to Th*saaa*. "Thanks so much for fixing it."

Th*saaa* flared their tentacles dismissively. "It is really quite a primitive device," they said. "It was simple to repair."

Josephine cocked her head skeptically. "Did you actually do it yourself?"

Th*saaa* shuffled and went slightly yellow. "Well . . . no. I got a grown-up to do it."

"Th*saaa*!" called Flath, rippling green and peach and gesturing. "*Athwara sel lamarath-te!*" And Warth-*raaa* beckoned to us again, with the same colors.

"Just a minute," I called.

"I have to go," said Th*saaa* hurriedly. "But first, I want to . . . Josephine. Please take this."

Th*saaa* was holding out the *Paralashath.*

Josephine went very still and wide-eyed. In fact, we all did.

"Because it may be a while before we see each other again, but when we do, I hope neither of us will be prisoners of war," said Th*saaa*. "And because of the music."

Josephine stared at the *Paralashath*, which was pulsing softly with the same colors streaming across Th*saaa*'s skin. Then she reached into her bag and fished out her harmonica. "Then you take this," she said. "For the same reasons."

Th*saaa* took the harmonica, and Josephine hugged the *Paralashath* to her chest.

"Thank you," said Th*saaa*, turning solemnest blue as Flath led them away.

"You *gave* them your *harmonica*?" I hissed at Josephine incredulously as Warth-*raaa* herded us off toward an invisible ship.

Josephine threw me one of her withering looks. "Yes. I gave them my harmonica. I didn't give away my ability to buy a new one."

✧

The Morror ship swooped out of the cavern and into the lavender sky. Sunlight streamed in through the windows and glittered in the bands of color around us on the walls. The wild, empty ground plunged away as if we'd dropped it. We could see the dust left by the Vshomu, huge clouds of it now, clogging the sky. But they hadn't ruined Mars yet. We rose higher, until we could see the green-and-red patterns of the tundra, then the shape of the new continents in the bright new sea. And somehow, despite the fact that we'd been clamoring to get off Mars for hours, it felt shocking to be actually doing it. I suppose it should feel shocking. Jumping on and off planets is a shocking thing to ever be able to do.

Mars shone and shrank until we tore free of the purple sky and it hung in the dark like a pendant made of copper and amethyst and jade and gold.

"Beautiful," whispered Josephine, pressed against the window.

Her breath frosted in the air. The spaceship was just as colorful as the one we'd found on Tharsis, but even colder. The Morrors had seen this problem coming. You might have hoped this meant they would have some advanced, alieny way of dealing with the problem of transporting easily chilled humans, but in fact they just piled a few wardrobes' worth of spare clothes onto us and left us to huddle in a corner.

We did a lot of huddling on that voyage. Occasionally we'd try to warm up by jumping up and down as the ship was too small and the situation too urgent for a decent round of the Getting Around as Much of the Spaceship as Possible without Touching the Floor game. The ship was faster than the *Mélisande* had been, but not *that* much faster—as in we were going to get back to Earth in about three days rather than a week, but we weren't going to flit back magically in twenty seconds, which is of course what we wanted to do. And there weren't proper beds for us; the Morrors roosted in alcoves, so we had to stay huddled in the pile of clothes on the floor to sleep. Camping on an alien spaceship is weird and going to the bathroom is even weirder, and that's all I'm going to say about that.

I missed Th*saaa*. The grown-up Morrors were just like grown-up humans in that they talked almost exclusively to other grown-ups (Dr. Muldoon, in this case) and didn't tell us what was going on. Swarasee-*ee* did at least show us how to make the *Paralashath* work as a heater (though we couldn't have it on all the time because the Morrors got too hot), and Josephine tried to ask them about the people who made it and what it meant.

"I'm sorry, I have never been very interested in *Paralashath* as an art form," said Swarasee-*ee* politely.

Unfortunately, once we'd been in space a few hours, the Goldfish stopped sulking.

"Hmm, looks like we've got a lot of time on our hands," it said. "What *shall* we do?"

"Oh, no," I said.

"How about . . . biology? Alice *loves* biology, don't you, Alice?"

"No," I said.

"Well, too bad," said the Goldfish. "Let's talk about *biomass*."

We cast despairing looks at Dr. Muldoon, who was sitting cross-legged on the ground, wrapped in five layers of Morror kilts and jabbing important things into Josephine's tablet. "As an EDF officer, I'm ordering you to stop this," Dr. Muldoon told the Goldfish.

The Goldfish didn't care. It started projecting the carbon cycle all over the place.

"Look at them," said Dr. Muldoon. "They're frozen and traumatized and they should all be in the hospital."

"And they're *very behind with the syllabus*!" The Goldfish panicked.

"This time you really can't make us do it," said Carl. "You can't zap us."

For a few seconds, the Goldfish seethed silently

in the air, eye flashing red.

Then it started buzzing.

"*Bzzzzzzzzzzzzzzzzzzzzzzzzzzzzzzt*," it went, at the volume of a decent-sized road drill. "*Bzzzzzzzzzz Bzzzzzzzzzzzzzzzzzt.*"

"Are you malfunctioning?"

"Nope," said the Goldfish airily, and carried on buzzing.

"Aha. I see what you're doing," said Carl. "It won't work."

"*Bzzzzzzzzzzzzzzzzzzzzzzzzzzzzzzt*," said the Goldfish.

"Aaaaargh!" said Warth-*raaa*, waving their tentacles in frustration. "Maaaaaake it stoooop, or we will *breeeeeaak* it!"

The Goldfish stubbornly kept buzzing.

"Oh, FINE!" cried Josephine. "But I'm not borrowing my tablet back from Dr. Muldoon—she's doing important work!"

The Goldfish practically evaporated in the force of its own smugness. Until Carl decided to liven things up by pretending to pass out.

✫

And then we saw a pale bluish star that was brighter than the others, and it grew in the dark, like a flower.

"*Oh,*" I said, feeling tears come into my eyes. I

wonder if maybe I'd been afraid it wouldn't still be there.

"Yes," said Swarasee-*ee*. "Home."

We watched Earth in silence. From this distance, it didn't look as if it could possibly have any problems at all.

"Swarasee-*ee*," said Josephine. "Th*saaa* said something about humans stopping you from building the *Vuhalimath-laa*. What is that?"

Swarasee-*ee* went yellow, purple, and black, and said something to Warth-*raaa*, whose tendrils swished crossly. "Th*saaa* should not have spoken about that."

"They shouldn't have spoken about lots of things," said Josephine, "and if they hadn't, you'd still be in the cave with the Vshomu on the way. Come on, it can't make that much difference now."

Swarasee-*ee* made a grumbling noise and hesitated. Then they pointed. "*That* is the *Vuhalimath-laa*.*"

For a moment I thought they were pointing at the planet itself. It made sense: maybe they just meant the humans were stopping them from building a *home*. But then I made out the first faint glitter of the web of reflector disks that enveloped the world.

"Oh, is that all?" I said. "Just the light shield. The big fridge you've shoved Earth into."

"Big fridge . . . ? Ah, I understand. That is not all it is for," said Swarasee-*ee*. "If it were complete, it would be the same as our gowns, or our ships."

"An *invisibility* shield for a whole *planet*," said Dr. Muldoon, making frantic notes on her tablet. "It could hide us from the Vshomu?"

"That was always our hope," said Swarasee-*ee* sadly. "Of course, we prayed it would never be needed. We thought we had run far enough."

We fell silent again. You could have stared at the approaching Earth, hypnotized, for hours.

Except that just then a squadron of Flarehawks charged out from inside the *Vuhalimath-laa* and started trying to blow us up.

✧

A torpedo skimmed past our port bow. The ship shuddered ominously.

"Uncloak!" screamed Dr. Muldoon. "Go visible! We have to show them we're not a threat!"

"It is impossible," said Swarasee-*ee*, frantically working the controls. "The invisibility of our ships is inherent; it does not *turn off.*"

"Open a channel! Let me talk to them!"

Swarasee-*ee* pulled at some leaflike controls, and an unpleasantly goopy, weblike device descended from the ceiling. Swarasee-*ee* spared two tentacles to put this over Dr. Muldoon's head, while still steering the ship with the other four. "Speak."

Warth-*raaa* said something urgent and went indigo and neon orange.

"This is Dr. Valerie Muldoon, I'm a— For god's sake, don't fire at them!"

But Warth-*raaa did* fire at them. In fairness, the humans had just fired at us. And it wasn't *just* us, of course; there was a whole fleet of invisible Morror vessels behind us bristling with shock rays, and that was all you needed to put together a perfectly respectable space battle.

The ship dived. What with the artificial gravity, we couldn't really *feel* the motion, but we could see it on the viewport, and that was an excellent way to make yourself space sick, as if we hadn't already got enough problems.

"Can anyone hear me? I'm an EDF officer aboard a Morror vessel—" shouted Dr. Muldoon as something in the ship blared a warning.

The Flarehawks plunged after us, graceful as

homicidal ballet dancers, flinging torpedoes like ribbons of light.

"Oh, come on, we *can't* get killed by our own side!" groaned Carl, wrapping his arms round Noel.

Then there was a thud, and all the lights went out.

We went flying.

It took me a second—in which time some cold-blue backup lights had come up, and I bounced from wall to wall to ceiling and into the Goldfish—to work out that the torpedo must have damaged whatever made the artificial gravity work. I'd been flung into the air, and at first my brain couldn't catch up with why I was *staying* there.

I grabbed the edge of one of the Morrors' sleeping niches to anchor myself and looked around.

"Dr. Muldoon!" shouted Josephine, launching off the floor to reach for her.

Dr. Muldoon was floating limply just below the ceiling. Spherical drops of blood hung in the air like tiny planets.

The Morrors, having more limbs to hang on to things with, were doing rather better than we were. Warth-*raaa* had scrambled their way back to the helm and was doing their best to steer us out of danger; Swarasee-*ee* had opened a panel in the floor and was wrangling with the workings of the ship.

I heard Dr. Muldoon groan softly. I kicked off the wall and swam through the air, bounced into the ceiling, and crawled my way along it toward the helm. I dragged the goopy web thing over my head.

"Hello? Hello!" I said, floating there above the control panel, watching the Flarehawk squadron leader lunge straight toward us, the blue glow of the Earth framing it like a halo. "We're human passengers on the Morror ship. Please stop torpedoing us! We've got very important news, and we swear we're not trying to shoot anyone. We need safe passage to Earth."

I found I'd screwed up my eyes toward the end of this, in anticipation of being exploded. Nothing happened. I opened them a crack.

The Flarehawk had stopped moving. It didn't fire. It seemed so close that, if we hadn't been invisible, the pilot could almost have looked inside and seen me.

"Oh, god," whispered a voice over the channel. "Alice?"

Swarasee-*ee* fixed the gravity. I might have

dropped to the ground even if they hadn't. Everyone except the Goldfish landed in a series of thuds and groans.

I pulled myself up to my knees and steadied the communicator on my head. I breathed, "Mum?"

25

"**A**lice . . . Alice. This is impossible—how can you be . . . have they hurt you? Are you all right?"

"It's really me, Mum," I said, "and I'm fine." That might not have been completely true, but it would do for now. "I'm not a prisoner or anything. There's a lot to explain. But the main thing is that there are these horrible things called Vshomu that ate the Morrors' planet, and they're *in our solar system* now, Mum, and they're absolutely awful; they ate bits of Mars and tried to eat us and we have to stop the war with the Morrors or they'll eat Earth as well—"

I was, I suddenly realized, getting slightly hysterical.

"Alice," said Mum, sounding completely in control again. "Slow down. Now, these Vshomu. Would they have anything to do with the swarm of small flying objects coming up behind you?"

"What? YES!" I screamed, absurdly looking over my shoulder as if I'd be able to see them.

Mum's ship pounced straight over ours like a cat, and I saw the flash of her torpedoes light up the windows. "Squadron!" I heard her saying over the channel. "Concentrate all firepower on the small incoming creatures! Do not attack the Morror vessels. Repeat, *do not attack the Morror vessels.*"

She always did understand things quickly. It had been so long; I'd forgotten that about her.

"Mum, don't let them touch you! They'll eat right through your ship!"

I turned anxiously. Dr. Muldoon was propping herself up on her elbows and groaning, and Josephine was dabbing at a cut on her head with a Morror skirt. Carl and Noel were already pressed to the windows; I ran and joined them.

I could only see bits and pieces of the battle, but there was one ship that moved just *beautifully*—that was the only word for it—like a bird of prey sweeping through a flock of sparrows, and I was sure that was Mum's.

I suddenly really wished I had a Flarehawk of my own, sure I could have picked off a reasonable number of Vshomu given the chance; I was *trained* for this, and it would have felt better than just sitting there waiting to see if Mum won or not. But I couldn't have done a thing with the Morror ship, which seemed to be fairly broken anyway. And so was my arm, come to that.

Her ship was out of sight now. Some debris that might have been fragments of exploded Space Locusts floated past the window. I ran back to the communicator. "Mum, Mum—are you all right?"

"Well," said Mum's voice, sounding slightly out of breath. "That was exciting."

Swarasee-*ee* plucked the communicator from my head. "Good afternoon," they said, sounding for all the world like the kind of automated helpline my parents used to complain about back on Earth. "Am I right in thinking this is Captain Stephanie Dare?"

"Who is this?" asked my mum.

"My name is Swarasee-*ee*."

"What . . . ? A Morror. You don't . . . sound like a Morror."

"I have a special knack for languages."

"You know who I am."

"Oh, yes," said Swarasee-*ee* rather grimly. "We

know who you are." And there was a pause in which the atmosphere of the ship seemed even more icy than it had before, with both of them just listening to each other's silence and to the memory of fifteen years of war. "Our ship is damaged," said Swarasee-*ee* finally. "I doubt we can reach Earth without help."

"We can tow you in," said Mum. "But I can see there's a whole fleet behind you; I can't be responsible for escorting that many down to Earth."

"What do you *mean*, you can *see* them . . . ?" began Swarasee-*ee*, sounding faintly scandalized, but then they shook it off. "It is of no importance. I agree the other ships can wait in orbit until terms are agreed."

"Off we go, then," said Mum briskly. And there was an odd feeling as if something was squeezing the ship, and then we were moving again, faster and faster.

Earth came rushing to meet us.

☆

I was warm. I'd more or less forgotten what that was like.

I also felt as if someone had placed a large piece of furniture, possibly a chest of drawers or a big desk, on top of my chest. I groaned.

"Alice. How do you feel?"

"Urgh." I lifted one arm and watched it drop back onto the blankets in disgust. "*Heavy.*"

Mum laughed. "Yes, shifting gravity that suddenly is a pain, isn't it?"

"Where are we?"

"Earth."

"I know *that*—I mean which country?"

"Oh. America. New York."

"Oh, that's nice," I said. "Can we see the Statue of Liberty? It is still there, isn't it?"

The main thing I remembered from landing was being knocked flat by the gravity, and a lot of people gasping at their first sight of visible Morrors. Then we'd been scooped into ambulances and whizzed off to the hospital. Someone had put a cast on my arm, although by that time I'd had trouble keeping my eyes open, and after that I couldn't remember a thing, except it had clearly involved going to bed.

"It's still there."

I looked at Mum properly. She looked smaller and more ordinary than I remembered. I'd been finding it harder and harder to picture anything when I thought of her except that bloody poster.

"Alice, you've had such a terrible time, and I nearly *killed* you."

"I've been being nearly killed all week," I said grandly. "Doesn't bother me that much now."

"That is not a reassuring thing to say to your *mother*," Mum said, and crawled half onto the bed to hug me.

A very tiny, spiteful part of me thought it was only fair if she had to do some worrying now; I'd been doing it long enough. But mainly it was just wonderful to curl up against her and not have to pretend I wasn't bothered about where she was or what she might be doing. She was *there* and alive and not going anywhere for a bit, hopefully. And her arms were warm and her hair smelled of the coconut shampoo she always used, which I'd completely forgotten about, but now I remembered.

"It wasn't all terrible," I said. "And I'm not dead. And I'm glad I got the chance to watch you fight. I mean, I can't say I enjoyed it *at the time*, but still, you really are amazing at it."

Mum sniffed a little. "You've done these incredible things."

"Oh, those," I said, trying to sit up. "What's going on? Is the war over?"

"Not quite, but—"

"Why *not*?" I burst out, indignant.

"It takes a long time to finish a war."

"I don't see *why*. Everyone just has to stop fighting each other and start fighting the Vshomu. It's not complicated."

"It *is* complicated," said Mum. "There's the status of the territory the Morrors have occupied, the climate, the invisibility shield . . . a lot of loose ends. But there's a cease-fire. The EEC President's flown in, and there's a Morror delegation in the UN now."

"So . . ." I felt better for hearing the word *cease-fire*. "Do you think it will be okay?"

"Yes, I do," said Mum. "At least, as okay as it can be when the solar system's infested with planet-eating bugs. It'll have to be okay. There's no real choice, for humans or Morrors."

"No, that's exactly it," I said. And I flopped back onto the pillows, but the wave of tiredness eased off sooner than I expected.

"I don't need to be in the hospital," I said. "There's nothing particularly wrong with me."

"You've got burns, cuts, a broken arm, hypothermia, gravitational readjustment syndrome, and dehydration."

"Like I say," I said, waving a hand and feeling I could milk this grizzled-old-veteran act for a while yet: "*Nothing.*" And this time I did succeed in making Mum laugh.

"So, what about everyone else? The kids from Beagle . . ."

"They've only just landed. Some of them will probably be turning up here later. Things got pretty bad out there, from what I hear."

"But . . . ?"

"But no fatalities, no."

"Oh." I'd known the news wouldn't be any better than that, really, but it still wasn't *good*. I thought about Kayleigh and Chinenye and everyone else, and how I had no real idea what they'd been through. And even though I knew I couldn't have done anything useful, I started to feel bad about leaving them. I never even said good-bye.

"They're alive. And you saved their lives."

"I didn't really. That was all Josephine; I'd never even have *thought* to go off on my own and . . . Mum, my friends, are they here? I want to go and see them."

Mum didn't try to stop me from climbing out of the bed, and she propped me up when I put my feet on the ground and got wobbly.

"Why do we need so much gravity?" I complained. "Completely over the top."

We shuffled out of the room and into a corridor. I thought of something. "Can I," I said, "have tea and beans on toast?"

Mum laughed. "Well—in principle, of course you can. But finding the right kind of baked beans and tea in America . . ."

" . . . has got to be easier than on *Mars*," I said.

"True. Yes, then."

"Spaghetti carbonara would do in the meantime."

A hovering hospital robot came around the turn of the corridor. Someone was hanging on to it with both hands, letting himself be pulled along, bare feet skidding on the ground. The robot did not seem happy about having a passenger; it twitched as we saw it, and the person fell off. But he jumped up for another turn, letting out a cry of "WOOHOO!"

It was Carl, obviously.

"Leave the robot alone," said Mum. "You'll break it."

Carl saluted my mum, which was a weird thing to witness, but Carl seemed to get a strange kick out of saluting people. "A man from the EDF came into my room and told me I was a hero," he said. "In which case, a ride on a hospital robot is not that much to ask, is it?"

I couldn't help but think that whoever had said that to Carl had been very, very unwise, but my mother only said, "You've got a point," and let him latch onto the robot for one more swoop along the corridor.

"So hey," he said to me breathlessly, coming back. "You took forever to wake up."

I suppose, compared to the kid I'd seen jumping into the ocean months ago, he looked terrible; too thin and too pale, and covered in bruises where he wasn't covered in bandages. Compared to *me*, though, he looked in unreasonably good shape. "How come *you're* so lively?" I said.

"Because I am a *hero*," said Carl, grinning. "Eh, I was as limp as a rag a few hours ago, but you get over it. I've just been really bored. And my parents aren't here yet. And the Goldfish's been nosing about, and I don't trust it not to give me a physics quiz. No respect for heroes, that fish."

"Where's Noel?"

"I'll show you. He was tired out, though." Carl led us through a set of double doors to a room halfway down another stretch of corridor. "Oh, no, the Goldfish's got him."

I peered round the door. Noel was still curled up in bed. The Goldfish was hovering over him, but it wasn't teaching him anything. It was singing gently, the Mandarin song it had sung to me back on Beagle Base.

We tiptoed past so that we wouldn't disturb Noel and the Goldfish wouldn't notice we were there.

A soft play of colored lights was marbling the white paint of a wall outside another room.

A crisp voice from inside said, "Interesting. But what is it *for*?"

"It's *art*, Lena—I already told you. Ow."

"It would be worth examining the internal workings."

"You will *not* take it to bits. It's mine. Ow."

Josephine's fingers were clasped protectively over the *Paralashath* lying on her chest. She looked smaller in the bed, and even more battered and fragile than I'd remembered. It might have been partly that her hair was combed and styled and so took up less space. A somber young woman was just finishing the last braid, Josephine wincing all the time.

"This is Lena," she greeted us. "She has no soul and she tortures young girls."

"Nice to meet you," said Lena gravely, rising from her chair. She seemed to keep *on* rising for some time; she must have been six feet two at least.

She wore little glasses, and a dark suit, and her hair in a chignon, even though I knew she was only eighteen. She did look a bit like Josephine around the eyes and forehead, but I couldn't imagine Josephine ever growing up to be that big, or that tidy, or so composed and still and unfidgety. Lena shook everyone's hands.

"Lena, this is Carl," said Josephine. "He can fly a spaceship through a cloud of Vshomu and come out the other side."

"And I am the first person to pee on the *Acidalia Planitia*," said Carl happily.

"Oh, for god's sake. He is also disgusting, but we have to put up with that. Noel is a lot less gross, but sadly he isn't here right now to balance Carl out; he was the first one to spot a Vshomu."

"And he stopped the Goldfish from hurting Th*saaa*," I said.

Josephine smiled up at me. "This is Alice," she said more quietly. "She's handy with duct tape when you've been partially eaten or exploded. But mainly she stops people from going crazy or giving up."

For a moment I had the weirdest feeling I was going to cry, and I didn't know why.

"Duct tape is always good," said Lena.

"This is Josephine, Mum," I said. "She figured

out why the Morrors were on Mars, and she finds giant robot spiders and builds flamethrowers, and she's my best friend."

Lena frowned. "Josephine, you didn't mention anything about a flamethrower."

"If you didn't want me to build flamethrowers, you shouldn't have taught me the basic principles when I was six," said Josephine. "It worked well."

"*Everything* seems to have worked out well," I said.

"Of course it did," said Josephine serenely. "I was never in any doubt it would."

And we laughed, because that was hysterically funny, and Josephine added, "Alice. Let's go outside."

So we did. There was some talk of wheelchairs for both Josephine and me, which neither of us wanted. But I managed to shuffle along on my own feet, leaning on Mum, and Lena simply hoisted Josephine over one shoulder and walked off with her. Josephine protested heartily and Lena ignored her until she gave up.

The hospital grounds weren't particularly beautiful. There were a lot of military vehicles and tarmac. But there were some flower beds, and roses growing in them. And the sky was bright blue.

"Isn't it sunnier than it used to be?" I said as Lena plonked Josephine down on a low wall.

"The Morrors," said Mum, tilting her face up to the sunlight. "They said they'd let more light through. They're doing it. And it's summer."

EPILOGUE

Later there was this whole business where we got medals for Conspicuous Gallantry, and of course that was nice, but it's not really the point of the story, so I'm going to skip it. It only happened because this one newspaper ran a campaign of headlines saying things like REWARD THE PLUCKY KIDS OF MARS! and people got a bit hysterical. And Dad always particularly hated that newspaper, and since then some human and a suth-*laaa* Morror fell in love and now it's doing a campaign about OUTLAW MORROR-HUMAN MARRIAGE SHAM.

So the medal thing was nice, and *gallantry* is a really enjoyable word to say, but it's all also slightly embarrassing.

They've just finished building the *Vuhalimath-laa*. They *can* adjust it to let sunlight through, somehow, even though from the outside, Earth is invisible now. If you're flying in from Mars or Saturn, you just see the moon orbiting an empty space. So Earth is colder than it was before the Morrors came, but not as cold as it was when we left for Mars.

Of course, that doesn't mean everything's sorted out and everyone's happy. Mum wasn't kidding about it being complicated. A lot of countries left the Emergency Earth Coalition, because they wouldn't accept Morrors living on Earth permanently, even though the Morrors are plainly staying here whether anyone likes it or not. A lot of them live in Antarctica, which they're calling Uhalarath-Moraa, and it hasn't officially been recognized as a country yet, but Dad says it probably will be soon. And not all the Morrors are happy either—some of them don't think there's enough room on Earth and still want a planet to themselves, and recently they did find a chilly little uninhabited moon out there that might be okay for them with a bit of terraforming. Dr. Muldoon, who recovered fine from her injuries, is helping with that when she isn't doing ungodly experiments on people, or flying out to Mars, or mentoring Josephine.

She had a lot of work to do to get the EEC to put

much effort into defending Mars as well as Earth from the Vshomu, but at last they understood that leaving Mars as a place for Vshomu to feed on and *breed* is a really terrible idea. It's not going to get its own *Vuhalimath-laa* any time soon, but the EDF do go out there regularly and clean up any Vshomu infestations that they find.

It got scary about six months ago, when a big cloud of them turned up and started chewing on the moon. But at least we've had a lot of warning about them, whereas the Morrors hadn't got a clue until their actual planet started being eaten, and by the time they began to get organized, it was too late.

Mum still spends a lot of her time out there, doing what she's best at: defending Earth in her spaceship. Now she *protects* the light shield instead of trying to destroy it. She doesn't come home every night, but she does *come home*. And we live together with Dad and Gran in Warwickshire, and that's all I wanted.

✿

Not all Earth's Morrors live in Uhalarath-Moraa. Some of them live anywhere on Earth that's cold and will have them.

Th*saaa*'s two surviving parents run a ski resort in the Swiss Alps. A year after we returned to Earth, we all got together to go and see them.

Josephine and I rode up on the ski lift with our families. Carl and Noel had gotten there already. It was summer again, but the mountains were still gleaming with snow. On a crag above the ordinary chalets, between banks of fir trees, there was a large domed building painted in whorls of color, and outside it stood Thsaaa with their parents, waving their tentacles.

"Hi, Thsaaa," I said. "Erm, *Vel-haraa*, Thsaaa, *alvaray sath lon te faaa*? How was that? I've been practicing."

Thsaaa went pitying colors. "It's nice that you tried," they said. "I think we should stick to English."

"Thsaaa!" Thsaaa's *thuul*-lan gave them a light cuff with a tentacle.

"Don't mind them," Thsaaa's quth-*laaa*-mi said to us placidly. "They're aaaaaaaalways like that."

"Hi, team!" crowed the Goldfish, bustling up to us over Noel and Carl's heads. Someone had fixed its eye and given it a new coat of paint, but it was never going to look quite as good as new again. Not that it seemed to care. "Hi, Alice, hi, Josephine! Long time no see! Have you learned anything exciting about the history of Switzerland today?"

"Can you believe Noel and I got stuck with this as a *reward*?" Carl groaned.

"I *asked*," protested Noel. "It's my friend."

"That fish is a good fish," said Carl's dad. "It's gotten your grades up across the board. I won't hear a word against it."

Th*saaa*'s parents showed us their house, though it was too cold to stay in there for long. But we saw that there were *Paralashath*s of different sizes and shapes on pedestals. And there were two empty sleeping niches, lined with multicolored pebbles, for the two parents who wouldn't come back.

Th*saaa*'s *thuul*-lan and quth-*laaa*-mi had put a big table outside in the snow. It was warm enough if you kept your coat on. We ate baked *fal-thra* and tomato ketchup, and Th*saaa* was right, they do go really well together. And we watched the last few skiers shooting down the slopes as the sun went down.

"*Do* Morrors ski?" asked Carl dubiously.

"No," said Th*saaa*. "We toboggan."

"Are you going to help your parents run the ski resort when you grow up, Th*saaa*?" asked Noel.

Th*saaa* turned soft, thoughtful shades of blue and aquamarine. "I want to study the history of our people," they said. "Our art. The *Paralashath*. So much has been lost."

We were all quiet for a bit after that.

"I asked what you were going to do when you

grew up the first time I met you," said Josephine to me. "And you wouldn't even think about being anything except a soldier."

"There was no point, then," I said.

"What about now?"

I hesitated. I had been thinking about it, of course, but I hadn't talked about it yet. "I think I want to be a doctor," I said.

I was a little worried Mum might be sad I didn't want to be a fighter pilot like her, but she said, "You'd be a wonderful doctor."

"And are you still going to be an archaeologist and a composer and . . . all the other things?" I asked Josephine.

"Oh, yes," she said confidently. "And I'm doing a lot of biochemistry with Dr. Muldoon. But I've been thinking lately . . ." Josephine looked up at the sky. The stars were beginning to come out. "Do they have *space* archaeologists? Because I think they should."

I laughed. "So, a multidisciplinary scholar, artist, and explorer, in space."

"Yes. Shut up."

"What about you, Carl?" asked Mum.

"Fly spaceships," he said, shrugging.

"I have this awful haunting fear you will end up

a politician," said Josephine.

"Nah. Just spaceships. Maybe I can be your pilot, Jo; you'll need someone to get you there."

"And we might need a doctor," said Josephine.

"And Noel can be a space zoologist and categorize any animals we find," I said.

"Are there other people like us out there, Th*saaa*?" Josephine asked. "I know Morrors searched a long time before they found a place *you* could live, but did you find anyone else along the way? Places where there are people?"

The stars above the Alps were huge and wild and clear. Th*saaa*'s long tentacles rested loosely around our shoulders.

"There are millions of worlds," Th*saaa* said.

ACKNOWLEDGMENTS

Thank you so much to my wonderful editors Sarah Hughes and Alyson Day, and to Lynne Missen for the warm welcome (and all the books!). Thank you to Jo Hardacre, too, for bringing such imagination and energy to *Mars Evacuees*. Thanks to Goro Fujita for the beautiful cover—I never thought I could end up with *two* lovely covers, one for each side of the Atlantic!

Thank you, Catherine Clarke at Felicity Bryan, for your laser-guided agenting, for a life-saving suggestion about the sequel, and for exploding, "They just don't *get* it!" in the back of a taxi when a different publisher rejected *Mars Evacuees* on the grounds of featuring too many girls in space.

Thank you, Zoë Pagnamenta, for flying the Martian flag high on distant shores.

Thank you, Rochita Loenen-Ruiz and Ivy Alvarez, both of whom generously talked to me about Filipino and Filipino-Australian childhoods. I hope I didn't mess up too badly. And Rochita, additional thanks for being so enthusiastic about the idea and being such a warm reader of my work. Readers, you should check out both of these writers: www.rcloenenruiz.com and www.ivyalvarez.com.

Thank you, John Rickards and others, for calculating how far a twelve-year-old could jump on Mars.

Thank you, Samira Ahmed, for letting me chat about Mars on your radio program, for pushing me toward public stages and people toward the things I write.

Thanks to my family for their unwavering support.

Thank you, Mrs. Cooke, for reading us *Good Night, Mr. Tom* and for believing I could be a writer in a school where encouragement was in short supply.

And thanks again, Freya, for telling me—at a crucial moment—that you wanted to read this book. Even though you thought Alice was an old-fashioned name and that I'd started too many sentences with "And." I needed to hear it. All of it.

Read an excerpt from the exciting sequel,
Space Hostages!

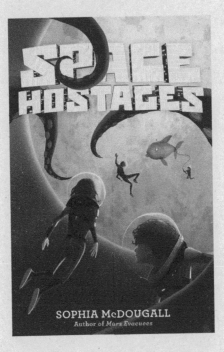

You can't cry in space.

You can give it a good try, though.

Tears won't *fall*, without gravity. They collect on the surface of your eyes and you can't wipe them away, so on top of being thrown out of a spaceship, you can't see.

I mean, I hope this doesn't happen to people generally, but it was happening to me.

I kept struggling. It was stupid, because there was nothing to fight, nothing to grab hold of. *Nothing.* Nothing so huge and total I was going to drown in it. But I still kicked and flailed. All that did was spin me over in helpless cartwheels. I saw the planet swing around as I tumbled, a blur of green and gold through my tears.

I tried to stop moving, to stop breathing so hard. Need to save oxygen, I thought.

But save it for *what*?

I screwed my eyes shut and tried to shake the tears free. It didn't really work, but when I opened them, I could make out a frantic scribble of movement against the dark sky. One other human out here with me, no more than the length of a room away, but unreachable; we could flail all we wanted, but we'd never be able to touch.

And then I somersaulted over again, and there was too much water in my eyes; I couldn't see him anymore.

The planet rolled past again, slower this time, a bright disc of light carving through the black. I saw the dim outlines of continents. I wondered if they had names. I wondered if anyone down there would ever know I was there, drifting past above their heads, forever.

☆

We weren't supposed to be here.

No one was supposed to be here.

1

I still have moments when the fact that I'm friends with an alien strikes me as kind of weird. I'll be chatting away to Th*saaa* and suddenly I'll be thinking, Tentacles. My friend has tentacles. Or, But seriously, *five* sexes? Or, It is just not *normal* for a person's skin to change from stripy blue to spotty green while they talk about what they watched on TV last night.

It is normal, though. It's been a year, so I ought to be over it by now. It's just that we don't have many Morrors living in Warwickshire; it's not snowy enough anymore, and there aren't many job opportunities for them. Th*saaa* lives in the Swiss Alps, so I don't get to see them as much as I'd like.

It was another rainy day. I'd come home, groaned

hello to my dad and Gran, staggered upstairs, and flopped onto my bed, where I was now trying to gather the energy to peel off my work overalls for a shower. Even though the war with the Morrors is over, I'm still an Exo-Defense Force cadet, and I still have duties, though these days we weren't so much defending Earth from aliens as defending Kenilworth from wet rubbish and the Leicester-to-Birmingham train line from long-fallen rotting trees. The ice didn't get as bad around here as it did farther north, during the war when the Morrors were freezing the planet over, but it was still *pretty* bad, and it turns out fifteen years of snow and then floods of meltwater can do quite a lot of damage. There are always supposed to be more robots coming to help, but they never seem to actually arrive. There are some things I like about National Service, like the fact that I get to have some medical training even though I'm only thirteen, but clearing rubble in the rain is not as fun and character building as the government broadcasts try to make it out to be.

But it was only two afternoons a week, and I always got to come home and eat a hot meal with my family, so it definitely beat plodding across Mars in the freezing cold wondering if you were going to starve, suffocate, or be eaten by Space Locusts first, which was how I'd spent the previous spring.

Though sometimes I found myself . . . missing all that. Messed up, I know.

The ChatPort light flashed yellow on the ceiling. I managed to lurch into a sitting position and clap my hands, and there was Th*saaa*, standing in my bedroom. Not really, of course, though I could see a flickery slice of their sleeping niche behind them and a couple of different *Paralashath*s, which Th*saaa* composed with, softly changing color at the edge of the projection.

"*Vel-haraaa*, Th*saaa*," I said happily. My school doesn't teach *any* Morror languages, which I think is stupid. Ten million aliens live on Earth now, so we're probably going to want to know what they are saying. So I'm trying to learn online when I can. There are twenty-three surviving Morror languages, but I'm mostly sticking to Thly*waaa*-lay, which is what Th*saaa* speaks.

"Your accent, it does not improve, Alice," said Th*saaa*, pronouncing it more like Al*eece*, which is not a Thly*waaa*-lay thing.

"Well, neither does yours. You sound more and more French," I said.

Th*saaa* spread their tentacles in what I considered a very French kind of way, if French people had tentacles, and said, "*Non*, I do not sound French. I sound *Swiss*."

"How's the Kshetlak-laya going?" Th*saaa* likes studying the dead Morror languages that didn't make it when their planet got eaten by the Space Locusts—or Vshomu, which is the proper word for them. Th*saaa* had been working on this long poem in the only Morror language I've heard that doesn't sound like sighing or wind in the trees. At least it's closer to a poem than anything else, but it's supposed to be performed along with a specially composed *Paralashath*.

Th*saaa* went melancholy colors. "I have hit a difficult passage. I cannot get the text to harmonize with the *Paralashath at all*."

"Maybe it's deliberate," I said. "You know. Experimental." Th*saaa* flicked their tendrils impatiently. "Okay, I know! It's all too subtle and complicated for me to understand. We did this poem in English today. It goes:

> "*I must go down to the seas again, to the lonely sea and the sky*
> *And all I ask is a tall ship, and a star to steer her by . . .*"

Th*saaa* normally likes nothing more than discussing poetry, especially if there's an opportunity to explain why Morror poetry is better, but this time they said abruptly: "What are you *weeeearing?*"

"What? *Work clothes,*" I said. "Not all of us get to do our National Service just showing *Paralashath*s to little kids in schools."

"I am aiding the reconciliation process," Th*saaa* protested. "Can you please put on something more formal?"

"Do I have to wear a ball gown to talk to you now?" I said. "Wait, what are *you* wearing?"

Th*saaa* normally wears a long, plain kilt and nothing else, but today they were wearing an ivory robe with a pattern of oblong holes cut into the fabric over the chest, to show the colors changing with their moods in the spots and tendrils on their skin.

"Fancy," I observed.

"I am speaking to you as an *official Morror envoy,*" they said. (Don't call Morrors he, she, or it. They aren't, so it's rude.) "I have been entrusted with a message by the Council of Lonthaa-Ra-Mor*aaa*! This is not a casual occasion."

"Well, you didn't tell me!"

"I'm telling you now!"

"All right!" I sat up straight and tried to behave. "Do I really have to change my clothes?"

I got a little worried they might be going to say they were leaving. The Morrors have their own country on Earth—Uhalarath-Mor*aaa*, which used to be Antarctica—and there are Morrors dotted about in cold pockets of the world like the Alps, but with the entire Morror species to accommodate, it's still pretty crowded. So they'd just finished terraforming a little moon orbiting a gas giant in the Alpha Centauri system, and seven million Morrors who'd been living in spaceships and space stations around Earth had moved there.

Th*saaa* can be a bit of pain in the neck, but they are my friend. And Alpha Centauri is a lot farther away than Switzerland.

"No," conceded Th*saaa*. "I apologize. I am a little nervous." They gave their tendrils a brisk little shake and stood up straighter.

"You have heard, perhaps, that the work to make Aushalawa-Mor*aaa* habitable to my people is complete."

"Yes," I said, feeling an extra tinge of anxiety.

"Dr. Muldoo-*oooon* has helped my people very much."

(Th*saaa* rather likes Dr. Muldoon's name.)

"Yes."

"I will read the message to you now."

Th*saaa* spread out a long, narrow scroll, illuminated in many colors, across all six tentacles.

"Dear Plucky Kid of Mars—don't *laaaaaugh*," said Th*saaa* crossly. "This is an important document."

"Sorry. It's just . . . they do know that's not our official title, don't they?"

Th*saaa* sagged a bit. "They do seem convinced it is," they admitted. "I tried to explain. You know how it is."

"Grown-ups don't listen to you," I agreed.

"Dear Plucky . . . ," Th*saaa* began again, and gave a very human sigh. "Dear Alice Dare. All the nations of Ra-Mo*raaa* owe you a debt for your part in bringing an end to the long war on Earth. Today, humans and Mo-*raaa* uha-*raaa* live in peace, and a new world welcomes the first Mo-*raaa* uha-*raaa* settlers. To celebrate the peace between our peoples, we invite you and your fellow Plucky Kids of Mars to join us on May the thirty-first of this year, for a ceremony to inaugurate the Mo-*raaa* uha-*raaa*'s new home."

"Oh, *yes*," I said at once, bouncing a bit on the bed. I didn't hesitate, or think of getting chased by space locusts or crashing spaceships on Mars or anything else bad that had happened the last time I'd left the planet I was born on. "This is amazing, Th*saaa*. You're coming? You're a Plucky Kid of Mars too."

"Yes, I will come. It will be an opportunity to learn more about the culture of our people."

"And also *fun*, maybe," I said.

"La*hee*la wath-eyaa, Th*saaa*," complained the voice of one of Th*saaa*'s parents, in what I was pretty sure was agreement. An additional set of multicolored tentacles waved through the ChatPort, and Th*saaa*'s quth-*laaa*-mi called cheerfully: "*Hiiiiiiiiii*, Alice!"

Th*saaa*'s parents are a bit worried Th*saaa* is kind of a stick-in-the-mud.

"And the others?" I said.

"Carl and Noel are coming."

I hesitated. "What about Josephine?" I asked.

"Josephine seems difficult to reach," said Th*saaa*.

"Yeah," I said, relieved it wasn't just me. I used to talk to Josephine on ChatPort all the time; she'd stayed with us in Wolthrop-Fossey twice, and we'd all gone to Switzerland to visit Th*saaa* together. But I hadn't heard from her in a month. I knew she was working hard. She was doing her World Baccalaureate, even though she's my age. Most people do it at eighteen.

She'd said I was her best friend. But I'd been starting to feel a little as if perhaps that was only because we'd nearly died together several times on Mars. And now that we were back on Earth, perhaps she wasn't so interested in someone reasonably clever but nowhere near ready to take her exams five years early.

I shook the thought away. Josephine wasn't like that, she *wasn't*, and if I knew her at all, there was no way she'd turn down a chance to visit an alien planet. We were all going to be together again in space!

"How will we get there?" I asked. "Morror ships are freezing."

"It is a human ship, with chilled chambers for Morror passengers."

"Oh. So, an Archangel Planetary ship," I said. I knew a bit about Archangel Planetary. Rasmus Trommler, the man who owns the company, had been in the news a lot, partly because he invented Häxeri, which is a programming system that makes computers work so much better it's in practically everything now—even the ChatPort—and partly because of scandals and court cases. Also, I'd been on Mars with his daughter, Christa, and putting it nicely, we hadn't gotten along very well.

Anyway, the only human-made ships that could go as far as Alpha Centauri were Archangel Planetary ships.

"I am honored by the Council of Lonthaa-Ra-Mor*aaa*'s kind offer," I said solemnly, feeling perhaps it was time I started living up to Th*saaa*'s fancy outfit and their request for formality. "I accept with gratitude."

"I hope your parents will let you come," said Th*saaa*.

Until then it hadn't occurred to me that I had to ask anyone's permission.

"They will," I said. "I'm sure they will."

Th*saaa* rippled farewell colors at me, and the ChatPort faded out.

Then it flashed on again. "Oh, and Alice," said Th*saaa*. "Congratulations on the book."

I ran downstairs into the living room, where Dad and Gran were watching TV, and said, "We're going back to *space*!"

"What?" said Dad and Gran at the same time. Mum was off on a mission so it was just the three of us.

"The Morrors want us to go to Aushala-wa-Mor*aaa*," I explained. "Carl and Noel and Josephine and me and Th*saaa*, because we helped stop the war."

"Ausha . . . wah?" Dad seems to have trouble

hearing the differences between a lot of Morror words.

"I thought that was what they're calling Antarctica now," said Gran with an edge of a grumble in her voice.

"No," said Dad, understanding in his face now. "You know. Morrorworld."

"Alice! The Morrors want to take you to their *planet*?" said Gran, horrified.

Fair enough. A year ago, that would have been a really scary sentence. But things change.

"They want us there for this ceremony, to sort of declare the planet open." I wondered if you could cut a ribbon on a whole world. "And we've declared peace with them now. They're nice."

"Alice," Dad said, looking a bit gaunt, "I'm glad the war's over. But I think it's a bit of a stretch to say they're *nice*."

I got slightly upset. "I thought you liked Th*saaa*."

"Th*saaa*'s a kid. It's one thing for you to be friends with a Morror *kid* . . ."

"And what about Th*saaa*'s parents? They were nice to you. They gave you baked fal-thra in Switzerland."

"I'm not saying they're all bad people, Alice."

Gran grunted. "Then they gave us a good

imitation of it for fifteen years."

"Gran!" I said.

"Of course, you can't remember the world the way it was before."

"I have to live in the world the way it is *now*," I said. "And it has Morrors in it. That's partly why I wrote that stupid thing. How're we ever going to have *proper* peace if we don't get to know each other?"

"Your book is not stupid," said Dad with automatic loyalty.

He shifted to make an inviting space on the couch that somehow I couldn't help but flop into. He put his arm around my shoulders.

"Alice, I know you care about humans and Morrors getting along," he said softly. "And I know you want to see your friends. But I nearly lost you on Mars, and I didn't even know how close it had been until it was all over. And Mars is, what, fifty million miles away? How far is the Morrors' planet?"

"I think it's about . . . forty trillion miles," I admitted. "But this is different. We're not in a war. And you and Mum could come.